SUBURBAN JUNGLE

Chronicles of the Undead: Book 2

JAIME HERNANDEZ

Suburban Jungle
Chronicles of the Undead: Book 2

This is a work of fiction by
Jaime Hernandez

Cover Art by AJ Powers of Indie Book Covers and
Trailers © 2021

For Val, Caralise, and Jessie

You are my world.

Acknowledgements

First and foremost, thank you to my fans.
Without you, none of this would be possible.

Thank you to Charlene, Chrys, Johanna, Karina, and
Nancy for your invaluable insight.

Thanks to my editor Casey Skelton of Wasteland
Editing Services for helping to bring my story to life.

Thank you to AJ Powers of Indie Book Covers and
Trailers for another incredible cover design.

Chapter One

Day 3

As Max slowly drove east following the path of the horde, he silently berated himself for not getting home sooner. If only he'd made it there before the mass of thousands had trudged down his street. His wife and daughter might have been safely at home when he arrived, instead of out there somewhere by themselves. A chill ran down his spine as he thought of his fourteen-year-old daughter Camille surrounded by zombies and running off on her own to lead them off and protect her family. Feeling tremendous guilt, he knew that if he had been there, he would have found another way to keep everyone safe. Deep down, he felt that he had let his family down. He had wanted nothing more than to hold Anna in his arms when he walked into the house, but he wasn't surprised when he found out that his wife had gone off in search of their daughter. She was as smart and stubborn as she was beautiful, and he knew that she would do anything to protect their children.

His face a dark mask of regret, he pushed forward with his search. He sighed as he ran his hand through his thick black beard, feeling the sore spot on his chin from when a zombie had pulled out a small chunk of it. His black curly hair was slicked back with a rubber band, and his eyes were so dark they were almost black, but they seemed even darker in his worry and grief. His years of working construction gave him a muscular build, and he stood a few inches shy of six feet.

He nearly forgot that Vince was in the SUV with him until he lit a cigarette and offered one to Max.

"Thanks man," Max said as he accepted the smoke.

They had been driving slowly for nearly an hour while closely watching for anything out of place at the houses they passed. Anything that might signal Camille may be hiding in one of them. Following the path of the horde was like driving through zombie slush. Blood, guts, oily piles of fat, entrails, occasional limbs, and discarded shoes and clothing littered the road.

"How far east do you think we should go?" Vince asked.

"I think it's about time to turn south and drive up and down as many of these streets as we can," Max replied. "I don't think she'd have gone more than a mile or so this way. Probably not even that far."

They were nearly two miles out, so Max turned right to start a block-by-block search, slowly driving up and down as many side streets as he could. It was impossible to hit every single street no matter how hard he tried. Too many little roads ran off little streets and crisscrossed into so many different developments. There were a few zombies scattered about, but nothing he couldn't easily avoid. Occasionally one or two shuffled around in the middle of a street, but Max had no problem going around them. He wanted nothing more than to run them down but knew better than to let his anger and worry get the best of him and make him jeopardize their vehicle.

Hours passed as they drove street by street with no sign of another living person. It was a creepy feeling to drive through entire neighborhoods that seemed to be completely void of people. Many houses looked perfectly normal, while others showed signs of a struggle or were completely overrun with zombies. Bloody handprints on doors that were often hanging off their hinges, broken windows, dead bodies on the ground, and occasionally small groups of zombies were all that remained of most of the areas they drove through. Wrecked or abandoned cars were strewn about on every street they encountered.

Before he knew it, they were near the big red barn that Michelle and the kids had hidden in on the first night.

"Camille knows this place. I'm going to drive down to the barn to check it," Max said.

"There's only a handful of the dead here. I doubt she's in there," Vince said.

"Well, she's gotta be exhausted and may have found a place to rest. She isn't necessarily going to be trapped and surrounded," Max responded as he pulled into the long drive, not stopping until he reached the rear of the barn.

One of the doors stood wide open. Before getting out of the SUV, he could see pieces of the blown tire that Joey had changed on the ground. He walked inside the quiet barn anyway just to be sure it was empty. There were a few strewn about empty water bottles and wrappers from protein bars, most likely leftover from Jesse's family, but no sign of his daughter. Just thinking of Jesse's name reminded him of how quickly his whole world had been turned upside down. Throughout their search, they hadn't seen or heard another vehicle driving around. The potential search area covered miles, though, so for all he knew, Anna could be safely driving around on the other side of town.

He got back in the car, looked at Vince, and shook his head. He looked out the windshield at the setting sun and wondered how he was going to find them. Traveling in the dark was much more dangerous with the limited streetlights, and if he used his headlights, he'd be drawing zombies straight to them. Without the lights, he might drive right up to a horde without realizing it. Camille was somewhere out there on foot with nothing but her knife. He was determined to keep looking until he found her.

"I wish the cellphones had lasted another day or two," Max said. "I'd know where Anna is, and Damon would be able to let us know if Camille made it home."

"Damn, I just thought of something. I don't know why I didn't think about it before," Vince started. "With all that camping gear I have out in my garage, I have a set of handheld radios. The range is only good for about two and a half miles, but it's something. We could hold onto one and drop the other off at your house. It doesn't help with your wife right now, but you could keep in touch with Damon."

"Well hell, you up for a trip back to your house?" Max asked with a grin. Finally, a little bit of good news. It wasn't much, but it could end up being huge later on.

"You remember how to get there?" Vince asked, knowing full well that Max knew exactly how to get there.

Max made a turn to head back toward Vince's place. Stray zombies were stumbling about, but nothing he couldn't avoid. He had to zigzag a bit and make a couple of detours, adding more time to the trip, but twenty minutes later, they were on Vince's street. He cut the headlights and slowly drove down the street, watching for any of the dead that might be lingering nearby. There were three shuffling along a sidewalk, two houses past Vince's, so Max stopped in front of Vince's house, and they both pulled their knives.

A frail, incredibly thin fifty-something woman with a huge bite torn from her neck stumbled about barefoot and half-naked. A lumbering thirtyish man in jeans and a t-shirt with bite marks up and down both of his arms stood just behind her. An elderly woman in a floral nightgown and one fluffy slipper stood in front, barely keeping her balance to stay upright. Max went straight for the muscular man while Vince took out the two easier threats. Within seconds, all three zombies lay dead on the ground. They both looked around to make sure there weren't any more nearby. With the coast clear, they ran to Vince's garage. He pulled out his keys and opened the side door, and they both hurried inside.

"I've got two gas cans over by the lawn mower that should be full or close to it. We're almost on fumes in that SUV, so why don't we take my truck instead?" Vince suggested. "I just filled it up, so we'll have a full tank and at least six or so gallons in the cans."

"Good call," Max said. "I'll grab our packs from the SUV while you look for the radios." Max walked to the street while keeping an eye on his surroundings. The nearest zombie was standing by itself down at the far end, so he carefully grabbed all three heavy bags and brought them back to the garage. When he walked in, Vince held up the radios with a grin on his face.

"I've got extra batteries, too," Vince said as Max put all three backpacks in the back seat of the extended cab of the truck. He handed the keys to Max so he could drive. They quickly got situated, not opening the garage door until Max was ready to back out. The noise and light of the garage door opening drew two zombies from the neighbor's backyard, but before they could step onto the driveway, Max had the truck in the street and hit the gas.

By the time they got back on the road, it was pitch black outside with almost no moon. Max drove home, making good time, dodging zombies here and there, and making a few extra turns to avoid larger groups. At the last turn before his street, there were at least fifty zombies stumbling around the intersection.

"Holy shit," Max said as he hit the brakes. If he'd been driving without the headlights on, he would have plowed right into them. He reversed and turned around so fast that Vince grabbed the handle near his head to keep himself steady in the passenger seat.

"Whoa man, take it easy!" Vince said.

"We're way too close to my house man," Max said. "I've gotta be careful here, or else we'll lead them straight to it."

"Yeah, okay. I'll watch our backs and make sure we don't gain any followers," Vince said. He turned in his seat to keep an eye out behind the truck as Max made a few extra turns to throw off any nearby zombies.

"We clear?" Max asked.

"Looks like we're good, brother. There was a handful, but you lost them when you circled around," Vince said.

Once on his street Max made a slow pass and didn't see any of the dead nearby, so he turned back toward his house. He pulled up the driveway to the wall near the front of his property that was invisible from the street because of the heavily wooded lot. He took another quick look around before he jumped out to open the gate then pulled up to the garage. Everything looked the same as when he'd left. He opened the screen door and climbed through the metal bars his son had installed, with Vince following behind him. He knocked softly on the front door. Within seconds, Damon had the door open so they could climb through the second set of bars. The hopeful look in his son's eyes was quickly dashed when he saw that only Vince came in after him.

"Anything?" Max asked Damon.

"Nothing. Michelle, Joey, and Lucia are sleeping. The guys are in the family room. We haven't seen Mom or Camille," Damon answered. It was what Max had expected to hear, but he still let out a heavy sigh. They went to the kitchen to grab a couple of flashlights from the stack of supplies on the counter.

"I've got a set of handheld radios," Max said. "I'll keep one on me, and you keep the other one on you at all times, okay? Keep it on channel ten. They're good for about two and a half miles. Call me on the radio if your mom or Camille come home."

"That's awesome," Damon said as he looked over the radio. "I hate sitting around here, Dad. You're all out there, and I'm stuck in here doing nothing but waiting."

"I need you here so that I can focus when I'm out there. And when Joey wakes up, he's going to need his best friend," Max said.

"I know. It just sucks," Damon said. "I'll take care of everything here until you get back."

Max paused to hug Damon as they walked to the front door. "I love you, and I'll be back as soon as I can. Call me on the radio if you need me," Max told him. Damon walked them outside to the truck in the driveway for one last goodbye before he went back inside and secured the front door.

"I hate leaving him like that," Max said with a heavy sigh, then added, "Let's go find my girls."

Max turned right out of the driveway to head west, the opposite direction the horde had gone. He wanted to circle back to the street behind his to see if there was any sign of Camille. He could be searching for miles all around only to find her around the block. It was at least worth the time to check. He made the first right and saw about a dozen zombies in the street, much more than he had expected. He sped up to try to get past them before they could try to surround them in Vince's truck. He missed all but one. A middle-aged man in torn pajamas hit one of the headlights before falling to the side. Max made the next right onto the street that ran parallel behind his. A few dozen zombies were shuffling around together in the middle of the street. They didn't seem to be focused on any one area, and he didn't want to try to drive through so many, so he turned around.

"I'm going to go around and come back from the other end of the street just to make sure she's not here. It didn't look like they were interested in anything in particular, but I'm not going to feel right about leaving the area until I'm sure," Max said.

"They looked like they were just grouped in the street. I didn't see any approaching any of the houses. That was a good call to go around, I think," Vince said.

They backtracked and went around to the other end of the street. It was more of the same. It looked like some of the group had started to follow the truck when they had turned around a few minutes prior, but none of them seemed to be interested in any of the houses.

"Well, I guess some of them will probably turn again to follow us out this way," Max said as he turned around again. He watched his rearview mirror to see some of their heads slowly turn to follow the sound of the vehicle.

"Maybe we should zigzag a few streets north and to the east. We haven't checked this area yet," Vince suggested. "I doubt she got more than a few streets in any direction, definitely not more than a mile. She's probably hiding in a house or a garage around here."

"I'm keeping the headlights on. If she's watching, she'll see us. She won't recognize the truck, but hopefully, she'll come out," Max said, although he wasn't sure if she would make herself known to what would appear to be strangers in a strange vehicle. He wished he knew where his wife was. Sound traveled well, now that there wasn't much to be heard other than the dead, but they hadn't caught sight of any headlights or heard the noise of another vehicle.

They drove around for a few hours, canvassing as many streets as they could. Everything was such a mess that it was hard to tell if anyone living had been in the area. Abandoned cars sat everywhere, sometimes blocking streets or intersections entirely. There were innumerous car accidents with zombies trapped inside most of the vehicles. The dead walked about here and there. Dead bodies lay on porches, sidewalks, driveways, yards, and even in the middle of streets. With the moonless night, it was even harder to discern if there were any signs of life. They hadn't run across a single living person in all of the hours they'd been driving. There could have been families alive in many of the houses they passed, but they had no way of knowing.

"We can't be the only people alive around here," Vince said.

"I don't disagree," Max replied. "But unless people make themselves known, we've got no way of finding out. I'm sure some of these houses must have living people inside. At least I damn sure hope so."

"I think there's safety in numbers. Once we find your wife and daughter and get back to the house, we'll have a decent-sized group. Hopefully, we'll find more to add to it," Vince said.

Max nodded his agreement but didn't have room in his mind to worry about finding other people until he had Anna and Camille back home safe and sound.

Chapter Two

Night 3

As the heavy darkness of the moonless night descended upon them, Anna's voice grew hoarse from yelling Camille's name over and over again. They drove with the headlights on, knowing that they were lighting themselves up like a Christmas tree buffet for all of the zombies in the area. Suburban streetlights were few and far between, not allowing them safe visibility to avoid the dead on the road. Emily had swerved to avoid more zombies than Anna could count, but without the headlights, they would have hit the dead and lost the SUV in the process. Going on foot at night with innumerous zombies, surprising them at every turn, was a prospect they both dreaded, and all Anna could think about was her fourteen-year-old daughter out there somewhere on foot all by herself.

They had been driving around for hours. When they didn't find Camille right away and saw the path of destruction from the horde, Anna had insisted on following it further. She feared that her daughter hadn't been able to get away or hide. If she were hidden in a nearby house, she would have heard Anna calling her name. The reality was that Camille could have been anywhere.

"We're driving on fumes, Anna," Emily said. "What do you want to do here?"

"I can't go home without my daughter," Anna said adamantly. "Let's try to get gas at the next big intersection."

"Do you think the pumps are still on? That they're going to work with a credit card?" Emily asked doubtfully. "We need to have a plan in case we can't get gas."

"We find another car, or we go on foot. I'm not giving up," Anna said as she pulled her card from her backpack. "You try my card while I keep watch."

Abundant street lights were leading into the intersection where the cross street briefly widened to four lanes. On the road ahead of them was nothing but blood, guts, bones, random body parts, and crawling zombies that were paralyzed or unable to walk on broken bones. The same zombie slush they'd been driving through since leaving Anna's house. The smell permeated everything so thoroughly that all they could smell was death.

As they approached the intersection, they looked carefully at two brightly lit gas stations. At least a dozen zombies shuffled around aimlessly in the street, and several dozen more staggered around both gas stations, likely drawn by the lights.

"There's too many here for us to stop," Emily said. "They're already turning toward us." The nearly silent SUV wasn't so silent when there were no other competing noises in the darkness.

"We're lit up and moving, so we're practically ringing the damn dinner bell," Anna replied in aggravation. She didn't want to deviate from the path the horde had taken but knew they were going to have no choice but to take a detour to find gas. They could loop back when they were done.

"Do you think Camille could have gotten this far on foot? Maybe we should gas up and head back, check some of these side streets," Emily said.

"I don't know. I just don't know. We could be going the wrong way, just getting further and further from wherever she is," Anna dropped her face in her hands.

"I think we should find a place to get gas, then start backtracking," Emily said. "We may be pushing too far to the east, and we haven't gone south yet."

"All right, let's head south to the next gas station and work our way back from there," Anna said, then starting yelling Camille's name again.

"Maybe stop yelling for a minute so you don't draw more zombies to us before we can get gas," Emily suggested gently. Anna glared at her for a moment, then conceded that Emily was probably right.

They drove about ten blocks to the next main intersection. There were only a handful of zombies nearby, and they weren't clustered together. Emily pulled up to the gas pump, swiped Anna's card, and hoped for the best. She was stunned when the transaction was approved and immediately started filling the tank while Anna kept watch.

A dead man in a mechanic's uniform was slowly shuffling toward Anna. He held a wrench in his hand but didn't realize it and certainly didn't know what to do with it. The front of his overalls was stained a dark red from his previous meals, and dried blood was caked around his mouth. Anna sighed then kicked the zombie in the knee to knock it down. As soon as it fell to the ground, she thrust her knife into its ear. She hopped back up quickly to make sure none of the others were getting too close. There were only about half a dozen more nearby, and they were all making their way toward them and their SUV, but they all moved slowly. Anna looked over at Emily to see if she was almost done pumping the gas.

"I'm going to run inside and get some gas cans. We might not be able to fill up again, so I want to get as much as we can," Emily said. "Are you good here?"

"Yeah, I've got them. Be careful going inside. It could be full of zombies for all we know," Anna replied. Emily nodded then headed for the door.

The inside of the gas station looked like the set of a horror movie. Dead bodies lay scattered on the floor, and a headless zombie lay on the counter next to the register. Blood was splattered freely on the walls, shelves, counter, and floor. Someone had put up a pretty good fight in the store. Emily slipped and nearly fell after walking through an unseen puddle of blood. She gasped at the amount of blood on the floor and the eight bodies within sight. She stood quietly for a moment to make sure she was alone. She didn't hear any rasping or moaning, but she didn't have a clear view of the whole store.

She silently made her way to the side aisle where car supplies were sold, and carefully stepped around two bloodied bodies. The gas cans were only a few feet away and were nearly within reach when an ambulatory zombie took her by surprise as it rounded the corner in front of her. As it caught sight of her, it lurched forward, raised its arms, and reached for her, its hands grasping her long blonde hair and taking hold. Emily let out a startled yelp as her hair was violently pulled, forcing her head forward, and the zombie's face came within inches of hers. She thrust her knife and missed entirely. She tried to kick the zombie away to buy herself time, but its hands had too tight of a grip on her hair. She cried out when she felt her hair being ripped from her head, blood running down into her eyes. She took a breath, focused, and plunged her knife into one of its eyes. When the zombie didn't drop,

14

she thrust her knife in further and twisted it as hard as she could. The zombie fell, lifeless, but took her down with it as both hands still grasped her hair. Emily struggled to free herself from the fingers intertwined with her hair, sobbing as her head rested against the chest of the dead body. She sliced her knife through the fingers of one hand and pried open the fingers of the other before she was finally free. Handfuls of her blood-stained hair stayed with the zombie, and more blood ran down her forehead into her eyes. She got to her knees, but before she could stand up, she felt a cold hand grip her shoulder from behind. She screamed and tried to swing her knife around at the zombie that managed to sneak up on her. Her knife uselessly tore through its cheek, exposing its broken teeth. She used her whole body to push back against its chest, desperately trying to keep the snapping jaws from reaching her. She turned to her side, grabbed the zombie by its shirt, and pulled it in close to plunge her knife through its ear. Breathless and with tears running down her face, she got to her feet and made sure no other surprises were lying in wait for her. She wiped the blood from her eyes, grabbed a few gas cans, and hurried back out the door.

Anna nearly bumped into Emily coming out the door. She'd heard her scream and had feared the worst, so she had her gun out and was ready to start firing.

"I'm fine," Emily said in a shaky voice. "Let's just fill up these gas cans and get out of here."

Anna got a good look at Emily's bloody, matted hair and the blood running down her forehead and had a good idea about what had happened inside.

"I took out the few that were lingering out here. You fill up the gas cans, and I'm going to see what first aid supplies they have inside. Your head is still bleeding," Anna said.

Emily tried to clear her head as she filled each gas can. She shook with revulsion thinking of the zombie holding her by her hair and the other that managed to sneak up behind her. She wasn't used to fighting or using a weapon of any kind. She resolved to be more careful and knew she needed to work on her aim. She ran a hand through her blood-streaked hair and thought about cutting it off or at the very least making sure it was tied up in a bun. She watched the parking lot for more zombies as she continued filling the cans.

Anna stepped inside the little store and immediately saw the two zombies that Emily had fought off. Both were good-sized men; Emily was lucky to have survived that close call. She gingerly sidestepped puddles of blood on the floor as she made her way down another aisle to the very limited first aid supplies on one of the shelves. Peroxide, bandages, cold medicine, and aspirin. That was it. The nurse in her was pretty irritated at finding such limited supplies. Why wouldn't they at least carry some gauze or tape? The band-aids were useless, so she grabbed several bottles of peroxide and a roll of paper towels then checked to make sure the front door was still clear before she went back outside.

Emily had just finished filling the last of the gas cans and was placing them in the back of the SUV. The closest zombie was across the street, so they had a minute. Anna grabbed a wad of paper towels and held them to Emily's forehead.

"Tilt your head back so I can pour some peroxide. Hey, at least you're already blonde," she said with a little laugh.

16

Emily couldn't help but laugh herself. She turned her face to the night sky so Anna could clean her wounds. She went through two full bottles of peroxide before she was satisfied. She took a few seconds to clean the worst of the blood from Emily's face as she kept an eye on the zombie, slowly shuffling their way.

"Okay, we're good," Anna said. "Let's get going before some of his friends join him." She glanced at the lone zombie stumbling persistently in their direction. They both got in the car, Anna behind the wheel this time. Emily had done just fine driving them, but Anna felt the need for a little more control as she searched for her daughter. She wanted to be able to make every single little turn as she felt like it.

They had already gone about ten blocks south to get to the gas station, and they were a few miles east of Anna's home. She decided to start driving in a grid pattern north and south between the street they were on and the street ten blocks north that the horde had gone down. There were countless roads, developments, and little side streets. Nearly an endless number of places Camille could be. And that was if they were even headed in the right direction. Camille could have gone north toward the lake, or she could have looped around and gone west past their house.

With fewer zombies in the immediate area than had been at the first gas station, Anna drove up and down streets yelling Camille's name out the window. Her voice was hoarse, and she didn't sound like herself, but she could still yell her daughter's name.

"Anna, you're going to lose your voice completely," Emily said. "Just focus on driving and not hitting any zombies while I call her name for a while." Anna was stubborn as hell but knew that her throat and voice could use a break. She drank some water as she drove, and Emily called out Camille's name.

Her search grid was hard to follow because there were so many winding streets. She despaired over the many that she missed, worried that her daughter would be hiding somewhere they had skipped. She made another turn, and suddenly there were zombies everywhere. She plowed into a half dozen of them before she could hit the brakes or attempt to steer around them. She looked at the crowd of at least fifty of the dead to see what had their attention. There were a hundred more swarming a house on the right. The zombies in the street were overflow that couldn't get any closer to the house.

"Oh my god," Anna exclaimed. "Someone's in there. Camille could be inside that house!" Before Emily could respond, Anna pulled her gun and started firing at the zombies in the street. She wanted their full attention so she could try to lead them away from the house. The gunfire was effective as nearly every single zombie turned its head to see what new meal might be awaiting them.

"Shit, Anna!" Emily hollered over the raspy moans. "They're going to swarm us. Switch it into reverse now!" There were so many zombies in the street that they were already pushing against the front of the SUV and were quickly surrounding the sides of the vehicle.

Anna put the SUV into reverse and put her foot down on the gas. Much to Emily's surprise and terror, she only went about five miles an hour. Anna wanted the zombies to follow her so she could circle back around and see if Camille was in the house. Several zombies found grips on the hood, and one held onto the passenger side mirror, going for a forced jog as Anna drove backward. She hit the gas just a little bit harder to free them from the

18

clinging zombies. She sped up a little more then turned around so she could drive straight forward. She slowed back down to make sure she still had their attention as she laid on the horn and fired her gun wildly. The zombies followed. Anna slowly led them two blocks down and one block to the side, then sped up and rushed back to the house. A man leading three young children out the front door was hurrying toward his truck in the driveway. No sign of Camille. The man waved his thanks as he got into the truck and drove away with his children safely inside.

Anna choked back a sob. She'd thought that her daughter might be inside that house. While a part of her was happy that she had been able to help the trapped family, another part of her felt devastated. For a few minutes, she had felt such hope that she might have finally found Camille. Now the searching started to seem futile. There were hundreds of streets to search, and so many neighborhoods within neighborhoods. She was beginning to feel hopeless, but there was nothing to do but continue searching.

Chapter Three

Night 3

It was after two in the morning when they heard a series of gunshots. It sounded like someone had emptied their gun. The echo around the silent area somehow made it harder to determine where the sound of gunfire had come from. Max was pretty sure it wasn't coming from his home nearly a mile behind them. It seemed to come from the other direction, but there was just no way to narrow it down. He listened but didn't hear anything else. He was so focused on the gunshots that he didn't see what was coming up on the road in front of him. Just as Vince yelled for him to look out, it felt like the truck was being pummeled with boulders. Max had driven right into a couple of dozen zombies. Some glanced off the bumpers while others flew through the air. Three landed heavily on the hood, with one right on top of the windshield. The safety glass immediately broke apart, and the zombie fell onto the dashboard and rolled into their laps.

"Holy shit," Vince yelled as he batted the head away from his leg. Gnashing teeth nearly tore through his jeans. As he pulled his knife, another zombie fell from the hood into the car. With one hand, he held the thrashing zombie by its long dark hair to keep its teeth away from his leg while he used his other arm to push against the chest of the second zombie reaching right for him. Max stabbed wildly at the second one but missed as he tried to simultaneously drive through the crowd and keep the third one from coming through the window. He hit the gas, braked, swerved back and forth, and hit the gas again to no avail. The third zombie crawled through the broken glass and grasped the steering wheel as it tried to reach for Max.

Max pulled his gun and made the easy headshot with the zombie only inches from his face. The sound of the gunshot inside the truck was deafening, even with the busted-out windshield. Blackish blood sprayed his face, and his ears started ringing. He continued to try to escape the crowd of the dead while Vince struggled to hold off two zombies by himself. Max finally had a clear shot at the second one, so he took it. The body instantly dropped, lifelessly and heavily, landing firmly on top of the first one that Vince was trying to fight off. The dead body pushed the long-haired zombie right into Vince's stomach. Before he could do anything, he felt the immense pain and pressure of the teeth sinking into his body. It tore a large chunk of flesh from his abdomen then dug further for a rope of intestines. Within seconds it was chewing through the slippery strand and pulling out more. Vince screamed in pain, unable to reach the zombie's head with the other body lying on top of it. He reached blindly with one hand as he tried to push the second body off his lap with the other, and the zombie bit down on his fingers, tearing them jaggedly from his hand. Tears running down his face, he cried out loudly at the anguishing pain shooting up his arm. A second later, the pure agony caused him to pass out.

"Fuck," Max yelled. With Vince passed out and the second zombie dead on the floorboard, he shot the feasting zombie in the head. He finally made it past the dead in the road and drove another half a mile before he felt safe enough to stop. He looked at Vince with most of one hand ripped away, and half of his abdomen pulled free and falling out onto the two dead bodies. Whether he had passed out or had died, it didn't even matter at this point.

"I'm sorry buddy," Max said quietly as he thrust his knife through Vince's ear. He was still amazed at how quickly everything could go to shit. One minute they were driving while the next, they were fighting for their lives. He shook his head and looked around at the mess. There was bloody gore all over the inside of the truck along with three dead bodies, four if he counted Vince. He looked around outside and didn't see any zombies nearby, so he got out of the truck and pulled the headshot zombie from the truck. It still had one hand on the steering wheel. After he rolled it to the ground, he went to the passenger side. Full of anger, he grabbed one body at a time and pulled the dead weight to the ground. He took one last look at Vince, then gently pulled him from the car and laid him on the ground. Feeling like an asshole for doing it, he went through Vince's belt for his spare knife and gun. Their backpacks held all of the extra weapons, ammo, and water, so he said a quick goodbye to Vince and got back in the driver's seat. Using his shirtsleeve, he wiped as much blood from his face as he could. A quick look in the glove compartment revealed a pile of napkins from fast-food restaurants. He opened a bottle of water to wet the napkins and wiped the rest of the blood from his face. His hands were covered with gore, so he used an entire bottle to clean them up. They were still bloodstained, but he felt better having gotten himself cleaned up a bit. His head was reeling with what had just transpired. He felt guilty about Vince, but he knew he'd done the best he could. Driving through a crowd of zombies while fighting off the three that had come through the windshield had been a nearly impossible feat. He was lucky to still be alive.

Hearing the telltale shuffle of zombies, he looked up to see that he'd drawn the attention of a handful of the dead, so he put the truck in drive and hit the gas. He was surprised the truck was still running after taking such hard hits. With no windshield and with blood splatter all over everything, he decided to try to find another vehicle.

Max turned down the next side street with his headlights off and let the truck coast along slowly. He was looking for a house with a damaged front door or busted bay window with a car in the driveway. He figured he'd have easy access to a house, car keys, and a vehicle if he went for a house that the dead had already been through. About halfway down the street, he found what he was looking for. A newer oversized black truck was parked in the driveway of a house with an open front door and a broken living room window. He put the truck in park and quietly walked up the driveway. The front door was wide open and was smeared with dark, dried blood. He stood there for a moment listening for any sound coming from inside. Hearing nothing, he slowly stepped inside the house and paused again to make sure there was no noise coming from within. He was about to walk through the little foyer to start the search for keys when he noticed hooks hanging just inside the door. The keys for the truck hung from one of them. He sighed with relief at finally catching such a lucky break. Grabbing the keys, he walked back outside, unlocked the truck, and turned the key in the ignition. He wanted to make sure it ran before he transferred his supplies. It started right up and showed an almost full tank of gas. He walked back over to the mess that remained of Vince's truck. He unloaded the three heavy backpacks and the two spare gas cans. He checked his surroundings then made two trips to load everything into the truck in the driveway. A few zombies were starting to stumble out of nearby houses and backyards, so he put the truck in gear and went on his way.

It was nearing four in the morning, and his eyes were tired. Damon hadn't radioed, which meant that no one had come home. He had to keep going. There was a gas station coming up at the next main intersection. If the place looked clear, he was going to make a quick trip inside for some energy drinks. He turned off his headlights as he approached and saw that the gas station was surrounded by zombies. He immediately perked up and forgot how tired he was. About a hundred of the dead mindlessly circled and pushed against the building, which could only mean one thing. Someone was alive inside. He thought through his options quickly. He had more than enough ammo to kill a hundred of them, but they would reach his truck before he could take them all out. He could fire one of his guns, turn on his headlights and try to lead them off, but he wasn't sure whether or not it would work. He figured he had one go at this. Then he had another idea. He glanced at the two full gas cans behind the passenger seat. He would draw the zombies out then start a fire to keep them occupied. If everything went according to plan, he could sneak back to the door of the gas station to check on whoever was trapped inside. It wasn't a very detailed plan, and there was no guarantee that it would work, but he figured it was his best option.

Max pulled spare guns and ammo from one of the backpacks and laid everything out on the passenger seat within easy reach. He turned his headlights on, turned the CD player on full volume, and hit his horn. He fired a few shots in the general direction of the zombies, not concerning himself with headshots. Right now, he just wanted to get their attention. He pulled around the corner near the back of the gas station and quickly poured most of the contents of one of the gas cans on a couple of the trees that lined the rear of the parking lot. He poured the rest of the gas on the concrete leading away from the trees. He lit a cigarette, watched, and waited as the entire crowd slowly turned and headed toward him. The closest zombies would be on him in less than a minute. He reversed a few feet as more of them came around the sides from the front of the gas station. He killed the music, and the headlights, then tossed his zippo on the ground near the trees. The gasoline on the ground immediately caught fire, and he watched as the fire moved across the ground and through the parking lot in a line, then quickly spread to the trees. The zombies were all so focused on the bright fire dancing in the inky black sky that they forgot about Max as he slowly and quietly reversed into the street.

Max saw the fire spread to some surrounding trees, and although he hadn't intended to set the neighborhood on fire, he watched as a garage just behind the trees went up in flames. Most of the dead were drawn to the fire. He turned the corner and slowly made his way to the front of the gas station, where only a half dozen of the dead remained. He pulled up close to the front door of the building before getting out. With his gun within easy reach in his holster, he held his Gerber knife in his right hand and rushed the first zombie. He thrust his knife through its ear before it even realized he was there. He made quick work of the second and third, but the last three were so close together they were nearly touching. He kicked the middle zombie in the knee to knock it to the ground and shoved the one on his left, causing it to stumble backward a couple of feet and giving him the time he needed to take out the one on the right. He grabbed it by its hair and stabbed his knife through its eye. As he pulled his knife back, the zombie on the left was nearly upon him, so he grabbed one of its reaching arms and jerked it sideways so he could thrust his knife into its ear. The last zombie was still trying to make its way back to its feet, so Max knelt down and quickly took it out.

He stood up and looked at the front door of the gas station. Most of the building was constructed of thick cinderblocks and cement, with the only windows being the doors themselves. Luckily for whoever was hidden inside, the zombies had been spread out around the entire building. If they had been focused on the doors, the sheer weight of so many bodies would have caused the glass to break. The door had to be pulled open from the outside, so the zombies hadn't been able to open it. If it had been a push door, they would have been inside long before Max had ever stumbled upon them. He pulled the door, and it opened easily. Whoever was inside either hadn't thought to lock it or hadn't been able to. He quickly scanned the immediate area and saw a dead cashier on the ground behind the counter. Looking up and down the few center aisles, he didn't see anyone alive or dead but saw smears of dried blood on the floor. He quietly walked along the outer wall to make sure he hadn't missed anything, then turned toward the office, restrooms, and storage room. He cleared the restrooms first, finding two dead bodies in the men's room. Both wore uniform shirts bearing the name of the gas station. One of the bodies was so badly mangled and had so much damage to its head that it hadn't been able to reanimate. The other had a few bite marks on its arm, and a fatal bullet wound had nearly split its skull in half.

Moving on to the small storage room, Max quickly ascertained that it was empty of both the living and the dead. That left the office. Whoever was holed up in the building must still be barricaded inside of the office. He put his ear against the door but heard nothing.

"Camille?" Max said softly. He slowly turned the doorknob and pushed the door open, holding out hope that his daughter might be hidden inside. His eyes were immediately drawn to a body slumped over the desk. One arm hung limply over the side of the chair, and a gun lay on the floor less than a foot away. It was an older man who had probably been in his late fifties before he took his own life. His manner of dress suggested he was the owner of the gas station. A safe next to the desk stood open with easily visible cash, receipts, files of paperwork, and additional ammo meant for the handgun on the floor. Splattered blood on the desk and wall looked fresh. Max touched the man's neck and found it to be slightly warm. Max's shoulders slumped in disappointment. The man had been surrounded and must have given up hope only hours ago. It had all been a waste. The fuel for the fire, the burning distraction for the zombies outside, the risk Max had taken to try to help whoever had been trapped in the building. There was no sign of his daughter. He bent down to pick up the handgun off the floor and pocketed the extra ammo from the safe.

He needed to make a quick escape before the zombies lost interest in the fire he had set, or else he would find himself trapped inside the gas station. Max left the office and went back to the side of the store behind the cashier's counter. He grabbed a few packs of cigarettes and quickly threw a half dozen energy drinks into a plastic bag.

A quick look outside showed a handful of zombies in the parking lot, but none anywhere near his truck. He pushed the door open, went outside, and got back into the truck.

Max turned out of the gas station and saw that the flames behind it had spread from the trees and garage to several houses during the time he'd been inside. Most of the zombies were still enthralled by the flames, allowing him an easy exit as he turned the corner to continue his search for his daughter.

Chapter Four

Night 3

Late into the evening, when it was fully dark outside, Michelle and Lucia had both fallen asleep after they'd sobbed endlessly over the loss of Jesse. Joey had shed a lot of tears with them and had tried his best to comfort them. He was the man of the family now, and he would do everything he could to protect his mom and his sister. He was relieved when they had fallen asleep, hoping that they would find an escape from the pain in their dreams, but he was still wide awake, so he quietly left the room.

Joey walked into the kitchen to find Damon comfortably and quietly talking to two strange men. A tall, muscular black man sat at the counter, and a much shorter and younger Hispanic guy stood near the sink. Both wore fire rescue t-shirts. Joey's eyes met Damon's, and his friend stopped talking, jumped up, and walked over to hug him. "I'm so sorry, Joey," Damon said quietly as he held him in a tight grip. Joey nodded and let go.

"This is Frank and Junior," Damon said as he made introductions. "They were trapped in their firetruck, and our dads saved them."

"We're so sorry about your dad, son," Frank said as he shook Joey's hand. "We wouldn't be alive if it weren't for him."

Joey wasn't sure what to say to that, but he wasn't surprised that his dad and Max saved some people on their way home.

"It's good to meet you, Joey," Junior said. "If there's anything you need, you let me know."

"Thank you," Joey could see that both men were sincere, and he knew that his dad must have trusted them.

"There's another guy, Vince. He's out with my dad right now looking for Camille, my mom, and Emily," Damon told Joey. He could tell that Joey wasn't ready to mingle with new people. "You want to go do a perimeter check?"

"Yeah, let's get going," Joey said. He appreciated that there were more people there, presumably good people since Max had brought them home, and he knew there was safety in numbers. But talking to them was the last thing he felt like doing at that moment.

Frank and Junior could tell that the boys needed some space, so they excused themselves and said they were going to try to get some rest on the couches in the living room.

Damon and Joey kept their knives on them all the time, so they were ready to head out. They moved the duct tape and strip of curtain off the top corner of one of the windows near the front door to make sure the area was clear before they opened the door. Seeing nothing in the darkness, they removed the lift bar, opened the door, and climbed through the three iron bars installed across the doorway. They repeated the process on the screen door of the enclosed front porch then quietly closed it behind them.

Once outside, they stood still and scanned the yard in front of them. Seeing nothing out of the ordinary, they moved to the side fence by the Wright's house. Joey was grateful that Damon knew and understood that he didn't feel like talking. Together, they hopped up onto oversized tree limbs hanging over the fence to see if things looked clear in the neighbor's front yard. With the moonless night, visibility was incredibly limited. Seeing nothing, they moved on.

As they approached the front of the yard, the lingering smell from the horde that had passed by earlier that day was noxious. They climbed the wall near the front of the property to get a better look. Putrid blood covered the street, tree lawns, and sidewalk. Scattered rancid limbs, random shoes, and scraps of clothing were strewn about the street. The darkness was so complete that they couldn't make out any details. They assumed bumps on the road were body parts and splotches were blood. There was a small bit of barely visible movement in the lane closest to them. It was a crawler. The zombie had no legs and was slowly pulling its torso along using only its mangled hands. Not worth bothering with, they left it and quietly moved to the other end of the brick wall.

Two zombies were stumbling around the front yard of a house two doors down across the street. Their moans were quiet but persistent.

"What do you think?" Joey asked Damon.

"I'd say take them out, but I'm betting they're going to join the crawler. Maybe we should just let them pass," Damon said. Normally, he would take out any nearby zombie, but these weren't a threat, and they weren't going to come near the house.

"They could be a problem later for your mom or dad, especially for Camille. If she's making her way back here, you know she's exhausted," Joey said. He knew how to do things safely and normally wouldn't put himself at unnecessary risk, but he wanted to kill them. He wanted to kill as many as he could because they killed his dad.

"You think so?" Damon whispered. The slow-moving crawler had moved a few feet closer up the road. He looked at Joey and knew that he needed a kill. "All right, let's do this."

"You take the crawler. I want the two shamblers," Joey said firmly. Damon raised his eyebrows at that, and Joey nodded.

They hopped over the brick wall, and Damon walked quickly toward the crawler while Joey jogged toward the zombies across the street. The road was slick with blood, guts, and various detritus. Bones and bone fragments lay scattered like stones.

As Damon approached the crawler, he slid through a thick puddle of blood and nearly lost his footing. He righted himself, then bent down, grabbed the atrocity by its long hair, and plunged his knife through its eye. The putrid smell and obnoxious pop of the bloody, milky eyeball was something he would never get used to.

He looked up to see Joey slip and stumble over rotting flesh, blood, and entrails that were covering the sidewalk. He fell on his ass and let out a soft yelp. The two zombies in the front yard were now only a few feet away from the sidewalk. If the crawler hadn't gotten their attention, the boys most definitely had. Their raspy moans grew louder as they closed in. Joey jumped to his feet and viciously thrust his knife through the eye of the closest one while throwing a high kick at the other's chest. It stumbled backward but stayed on its feet. Before Damon could do anything, Joey grabbed the second zombie by its close-cropped hair and plunged his knife through its ear.

Neither worse for wear other than Joey smelling like the dead, they huddled for a moment. "You okay, Joey?" Damon asked. "That fall looked painful."

"I'm good. The fall just surprised me, is all," Joey said. "Let's get back over the wall."

With no more zombies in sight, they carefully made their way back across the street and climbed back over the wall into Damon's yard. They both felt a rush of adrenaline after killing the dead.

"Let's finish the perimeter check," Damon said. "Those neighbors are dead. My sister and my mom took them out." He pointed to the neighbors on the other side of his house. He grew quiet for a moment, full of worry about his sister.

"Come on, let's finish this," Joey said. They hopped up to look over the fence now and then to make sure the neighbor's yard was clear. They passed the side of Damon's house and started to check the rear of the yard. They were nearly at the end of the fence when they heard the telltale sound of zombies. They both quickly ducked down.

"There's more than one, a few at least," Damon said softly. He carefully climbed up to a tree branch so he could see. He held up six fingers to tell Joey what he saw. None of the zombies noticed him, but they were lingering on the backside of the fence.

"Six, we can do that," Joey said, thinking carefully. "All bunched together?"

"Not that close, but close," Damon said. "I think we have to. My parents and Camille think this yard is safe to cut through. If they try to come through here, they could get into trouble."

"All right, we drop at the same time. I'll go left, and you go right," Joey whispered. He looked at Damon and could tell he was nervous, but they were both high on adrenaline. "Get ready."

Damon climbed his tree, and Joey climbed the tree to the left. The zombies still hadn't noticed them. With a quick nod, they jumped down. All six zombies immediately turned toward them. They were in a frenzy seeing two possible meals and stumbled into each other as four went after Damon and two went for Joey.

A shiver of fear went up Damon's spine as he realized that four of the zombies were reaching for him all at once. He thrust his knife wildly as he pushed and kicked at two of them to buy himself some time. The closest zombie was at least a foot taller than him, so he kicked the side of its knee, and the zombie fell to the ground. A chubby thirty-something woman stuffed into a tiny swimsuit grabbed his left arm, and he thrust his knife upward, hitting her chin. The knife stuck in her jawbone for a few precious seconds as he tried to pull it out. He kicked her in the stomach as the knife fell free, and she lost her balance. As she fell backward, he shifted his focus to the two zombies on the right. A teenage girl about his age stood stark naked with thin fingers reaching for him. She had a lump of flesh missing from her neck, which caused her head to flop around freely. He desperately grabbed for her hair and plunged his knife into her ear just as the other zombie tried to grab his arm. He knocked its hand out of the way and tried to reach for its hair, but it brought its other hand up and grasped his shirt. Full-on panic settling in, Damon grabbed the zombie around its neck and stabbed it through the eye. The first two zombies that he had knocked down had both found their feet again. He tried to stab the swimsuit zombie but missed as she slowly reached for him. He grabbed her by her hair and finally drove his knife home.

As Damon fought four zombies on his own, Joey was unexpectedly left with just two for himself. He made quick work of the first, a hunched-over little old lady who could barely stand. The second looked to be a bodybuilder in his previous life. He dwarfed Joey in height and width. Joey shoved and kicked him to buy himself time to figure out how to kill it. It grabbed Joey's shoulder, and Joey went with it. As the zombie brought its mouth closer to his face, Joey stabbed it through its eye. It fell so fast and so heavily that it took Joey's knife with him. He looked to his right and saw Damon struggling with the last of the four zombies. It was freakishly tall with incredibly long limbs. Without thinking, Joey jumped on its back to throw it off balance so Damon could kill it. The risky gamble paid off as Damon finally thrust his knife into the beast's eye.

"Holy mother of shit," Damon said, breathing heavily. He had thought he was a goner for sure.

"Fuck. I didn't expect them to split the way they did. Sorry, man," Joey said. He felt awful that Damon had just gone four on one.

"It's done, at least it's done," Damon said. At the sound of a snapping twig, both boys looked up to see three more zombies headed their way.

"Motherfucker. The yard's been breached somehow. We have to take them out, or else they're going to draw more to your fence," Joey said as he caught his breath. He hurried to pull his knife from the huge zombie lying on the ground.

"Joey, there's more coming behind them," Damon said.

"We've got no choice," Joey said as he rushed the closest zombie. A middle-aged man wearing shorts and a polo shirt was covered in bites. There were so many holes in his body that Joey was amazed that the man had

35

reanimated. He reached for the zombie's arm, and his hand went right through a bloody hole with stringy flesh and tattered muscle. His fingers slipped on the detritus and brushed against bone, so he grabbed the bone in a firm grip and pulled downward to stab the zombie through its eye.

Damon easily took out the second one, a young child half his height. The third zombie was an old man wearing pajamas and worn-down slippers. It moved slower than the others and didn't seem to hear or see very well because it turned in Joey's direction just as Damon was about to kill it. He thrust his knife upward in its neck at the rear of the base of its skull, and it dropped to the ground just as he slid his knife out.

The first three zombies were down, but more appeared throughout the heavily treed yard. The boys started to fear that there were way too many for them to take out by themselves, but they couldn't stop now. There were so many shuffling toward them that they might be able to take down the fence.

"Shit, there's gotta be at least two dozen of them!" Damon said.

"Let's just try to keep them spread out. Kill one, then zigzag around even if you're not going to the next closest one. They'll keep moving around, trying to keep track of both of us. As long as they don't all clump together, we should be able to do it," Joey said as he took out the zombie closest to him.

"Make sure you watch your own back since we're splitting up," Damon said.

They zigzagged through the rear of the yard, taking out zombies as they went. As Joey plunged his knife through the eye of a ragged face covered in dried blood, he felt a hand grasp at his ankle. Before it could lock its grip, Joey kicked the crawler in the head, snapping its neck. He stomped on the head as hard as he could until he finally heard the skull crack, and squishy brain matter started to ooze out.

They continued further into the deep yard about halfway to the house. They couldn't tell if the house or the fence had been breached, but they knew they had to take out all of the dead before they concerned themselves with that. For every zombie they killed, it seemed like one or two more took their place.

Even with their night vision limited, they could see at least three dozen zombies stumbling around the property, which led them to believe that there were probably more that they couldn't see. Damon was struggling with three zombies coming at him from every angle when he heard Joey yell for help. Nearly frantic with worry, he kicked one of them to the ground and managed to kill the other two before looking for Joey. He ran past a few zombies shoving a couple of them to the side as he looked for Joey.

"Fuck no!" Damon yelled when he saw Joey fighting off six zombies at once. One of them had a solid grip on Joey's arm, limiting his ability to maneuver and about to seal his fate.

Out of nowhere, a tall, bearded man dressed in a t-shirt, jeans, and a cowboy hat brought his ax down on the zombie arm that had grabbed Joey. The hand remained affixed to Joey's arm, but the zombie's head was severed from its body with another swift swing of the ax. The man held a knife in his other hand and wore a handgun in his holster. He quickly took out three more while Joey removed the dead hand from his arm.

"Holy shit, thank you," Joey said, nearly breathless.

"Don't thank me yet son, we've got at least three dozen more deadheads to deal with," the man said as he swung his ax down and split a zombie's skull cleanly in half. He was tall, fairly muscular, and he moved fast. "Y'all spread out, or they're going to swarm us," he yelled as several more zombies closed in on them.

Damon and Joey broke away and shoved a few zombies so they could spread out and take them down in smaller groups. For every zombie they killed, the man killed three. Adrenaline alone had kept the boys going, but once the man showed up to help them, they regained their confidence and were determined to clear out every last zombie.

For Joey, it was personal. They had killed his dad, and his grief was fresh and devastating. With every zombie he killed, he felt he was getting a little piece of vengeance. He got louder and moved faster as he tried to kill as many as possible. He pushed, kicked, stabbed, and stomped zombie after zombie, but they kept coming.

"Where the fuck are they coming from?" Damon yelled, although he didn't expect an answer. Killing them didn't feel personal to him. It was simply necessary. He felt no hesitation or remorse whether they were pint-sized or twice his size. He recognized a kid from school and thrust his knife through the boy's eye without a second thought. They were monsters, not people.

The stranger helping them didn't look familiar. Damon briefly wondered how the man had even come across them but didn't dwell on it because the zombies required his full attention. They had finally made a dent in the number of the dead.

They continued moving around the entire yard, keeping some space between them to kill every last zombie. Bodies lay everywhere. Shattered skulls, crushed decapitated heads, occasional limbs, entrails, and guts were strewn throughout the property.

"Boys, I think we got them all," the man said as he, Joey, and Damon gathered together near the rear of the house to catch their breaths. "Keep your eyes open, because it's dark as hell out here."

Joey and Damon were both covered in gore. Bits of flesh, slippery lumps of oily fat, brackish blood, and putrid fluids had sprayed them nearly head to toe. They were both exhausted. The battle to kill the zombies had quickly turned into a fight for their lives that had lasted nearly an hour.

"Thanks. We wouldn't have made it without your help," Joey said. "I'm Joey."

"Damon. How did you find us?" Damon asked.

"My name's Lance, son. I was cutting down the street there when I saw dozens of them deadheads focused on this old place. I figured someone must have been trapped inside until I saw them all pouring through the gate into the backyard. I got a little closer and heard you boys fighting them off," Lance said as he introduced himself. He had a bit of a southern drawl to his voice.

"I wonder what drew them here in the first place," Joey said.

"We'll probably never know son, but all it takes is for one of these deadheads to walk a certain way, and then all of the others follow it. I've seen it time and time again since the shit hit the fan," Lance said.

"We should check the house. Make sure no one's hurt or trapped," Damon said even though he was so tired he felt like he could sleep standing up. "At least make sure the doors are secure."

"Yeah, this place was secure yesterday," Joey said. "We cut through the yard, and nothing was out of place."

"Well, that might just be what did it, son. Just one of these deadheads could have seen you and pushed on the gate. Eventually, there were enough of them to force it open," Lance said. "But I'm good to check the doors and windows on the house with y'all just to be safe."

They quietly climbed the rear deck stairs and walked toward the patio door only to find it intact, locked, and blood-free. A quick look at the rest of the back of the house showed nothing out of the ordinary, so they decided to go check the gate. If everything was clear, they'd repair the gate and call it a night.

"Now y'all be sure to keep it extra quiet up by the gate. More of them deadheads could have followed from the street," Lance said. They found that the gate was wide open but unbroken. He took a quick look at the darkened front yard and didn't see any threats. "Looks like all the deadheads cleared the area and wound up in this yard."

As he turned back to Damon and Joey, a massive zombie stumbled out from behind a tree just a few feet from the gate. It must have weighed four hundred pounds. Dressed in suit pants and a button-down shirt bursting at the seams from the rolls of fat hidden behind it, the zombie stumbled forward as it reached for Lance. Its grossly obese body fell into Lance's back and knocked him to the ground so fast that he didn't know what hit him. Joey and Damon both leaped forward but not before the gargantuan creature sunk its teeth into the back of Lance's neck.

Lance screamed and writhed in pain as the zombie ripped a tennis ball-sized piece of flesh and muscle from the back of his shoulder. It shook its head like a dog with

40

a new chew toy. Joey grabbed it by the shirt collar and plunged his knife through the monstrosity's ear. It went limp, still on Lance's back. Damon helped Joey roll the dead zombie to the side.

"Well, I'll be damned. I can't believe one of those deadheads got a little taste of me," Lance said weakly. With that, his eyes closed.

"Holy shit," Damon said. He'd never seen anyone get bitten before. It was nothing like seeing Mr. Wright nearly dead on his living room floor. This guy was alive, talking and killing zombies five minutes ago.

Just as his eyes started to open again, Joey knelt over Lance and thrust his knife through his ear. He began to weep, wondering if this was how his dad went. He grabbed the man's knife, ax and handgun then darted back through the gate. Damon hurriedly pulled the gate closed and latched it. They quietly made their way back through the yard, climbed the fence, and headed to the house with their arms around each other.

It was nearly three in the morning when they walked in the front door and replaced the lift bar. Lucia was tossing and turning in her sleep, but the noise woke Michelle, so she got up to see what was going on. She wanted nothing more than to see Max and Anna with Camille in tow. As she walked down the hallway, she saw that it was Damon and Joey who had just come in.

"What the hell happened?" She asked. They were both covered head to toe with dried blood, slimy guts, and who knew what else. "Are you okay?" She demanded.

"We're fine, Mom," Joey said tiredly. "Not our blood."

"We were doing a perimeter check, and the yard behind us was full of zombies. We didn't realize how many there were until it was too late. We were stuck and had to take

41

out all of them, or they would have taken down the rear fence," Damon explained.

"Why the hell did you go by yourselves in the first place? We could have all gone together," Michelle admonished them, her voice rising.

"We didn't know, Mom," Joey said. "We thought there were six of them, and there ended up being around seventy of them."

"Seventy? Holy shit. You killed seventy of them?" Michelle asked.

"Yeah," Damon answered. "We had some help, though. This guy came out of nowhere and took them down fast. He probably killed nearly half of them himself." Damon looked down, thinking of Lance's last moments.

"He got bit at the end. We secured the property and latched the gate. No more will be coming through there," Joey said with a finality that made it clear he was done talking. "We need to shower." He turned away and headed for the bathroom.

"I'm going to use my parents' shower, and then I'm going to sleep," Damon said.

Michelle was left standing there feeling a bit startled and speechless. The boys were no longer kids. They'd matured nearly overnight.

Chapter Five

Night 3

Anna and Emily drove through one subdivision after another, dodging occasional zombies and stranded cars. Anna continued to follow the roads and developments north to south as they slowly headed in a western direction that would lead back to her house. They were two blocks off of the main street when Emily spoke up.

"Slow down, Anna," Emily said suddenly. "Listen."

Anna slowed the SUV to a near crawl before realizing what it was that Emily had heard; shuffling, stumbling footsteps. A lot of them. Probably hundreds of them.

"Another horde?" Anna asked in disbelief and desperately hoped it wasn't anything like the first horde they had experienced. She quickly cut the headlights and peered ahead in the darkness to see the zombies passing by on the main street.

"I don't think they saw us, but I was yelling for Camille, and the headlights were on. I think we'd better find another way out of this development and fast," Emily said hurriedly.

As they watched, they saw dozens of the dead break off from the pack and turn down the street they were stopped on.

"Hell, I think enough of them saw us," Anna said. "They're heading straight for us." The zombies were nearly two blocks away, but there were so many that the SUV would be surrounded and overcome if they didn't get out of there quickly. Anna turned around in the nearest driveway and sped down the street in the other direction. She made several turns, one right after the other, and kept her speed up to put some distance between them and their followers. Before she knew it, she'd gone almost two miles. There was plenty of distance between them and the mini-horde, but nearly two miles of streets and homes that she'd passed without searching for Camille.

"I don't know what to do," Anna said in anguish. "Camille could have been back there somewhere. We could have driven right past her and never known it."

"You're no good to your daughter if you're dead," Emily said. "We'll keep searching, and if we don't find her, then later on, we'll go back and check that area. We can't do anything with so many zombies back there."

Anna sighed and started driving a new grid search. She turned down another side street then turned into another small development. They called Camille's name as they drove and started dodging more zombies in the street. Nervous about the number of dead in the area, Anna decided to try to cut sideways through the development and loop around. It wasn't until after she made her turn that she realized her mistake. The dead were everywhere. They were all shuffling aimlessly with nothing to garner their attention until they saw her SUV. A couple of hundred zombies honed in on them from every direction. They were nearly surrounded almost immediately. Anna hit the gas to try to plow her way through the crowd before the dead could find handholds on her vehicle.

She drove straight through at least a dozen of the dead. A man wearing a full suit and tie landed on the windshield, instantly cracking the glass. His face and especially his hands were shredded so terribly that all of his fingers were ripped off. This kept him from finding a grip near the windshield. When Anna jerked the wheel, he slid right off the hood, but another quickly took his place. What had probably once been an attractive twenty-something brunette in a cute jogging outfit was now a bloody mess with bites of flesh missing from her arms. She hit the damaged windshield with enough force that it shattered inward, and she fell into the front seat with it. Most of her body landed on Emily's lap, but her head fell back up against Anna's leg. Before Anna could react, Emily thrust her knife through the jogger's eye. The putrid, milky, bloody fluid that escaped when the eye popped ran across Anna's leg. Emily shoved the body to the floor in front of them, smashing it down with her feet, making sure it was out of Anna's way as she continued to drive.

With a couple of hundred zombies bearing down on them and no windshield to offer a measure of protection, Anna had no choice but to continue driving straight through them. They were everywhere. There was nowhere to swerve, nowhere to turn, so Anna kept driving forward. She winced as the SUV drove over several bodies, the bouncing vehicle throwing both women around inside. They simultaneously heard a loud crunch as a skull was flattened by a rear tire and a loud pop as the tire blew out. The SUV instantly became more difficult to control but she pushed forward on just three tires because she had no other options. The only thing that was working in their favor was that the zombies moved so damned slow. She continued to hit those right in front of her with some glancing off the front of the SUV, some falling to the sides and others sliding beneath it. They were almost through the crowd and had to keep going.

"Look! Up ahead to the right," Emily hollered to be heard over all of the noise. "There's a bar on the corner. If we can just get a little bit ahead of the dead, we can hide in there."

Anna looked and saw a small bar she had driven by many times. It was in an odd location at the end of a residential street where it intersected with the main road. She took a deep breath and pushed down harder on the gas pedal. There were more zombies behind them than there were in front of them. They had made it past the worst of them. If she could just get past the small group still ahead of her, they might have a chance to get to the bar. The main road up ahead was full of zombies, but they weren't gathered near the bar. The small group still in front of her had been whittled down to less than a dozen. As she dodged several of them, she was unable to avoid the last one. Its body fell under the SUV, and the front passenger side tire blew out with a bang. The vehicle was still moving forward slowly while heavily damaged as the entire passenger side hung low and metal scraped asphalt with flying sparks. They made it to the edge of the parking lot before the SUV came to its final stop. They had a buffer of several hundred feet both ahead of them and behind them. With the eyes of the dead on them, they shouldered their packs, jumped from the SUV, and ran to the bar. Emily pulled on the back door, but it was locked.

"No, no, no," Emily cried as they ran around to the front, desperately hoping to find it open. Anna reached the door first, and with anticipation of it being locked, she pulled so hard that it flew open and hit the outside wall with a loud thud. The zombies were still more than a hundred feet away in either direction, so the women hurried inside and pulled the door closed. Anna quickly bolted all three locks. The heavy door was windowless and pushed open from the inside. The zombies outside didn't know how to pull a door open, let alone such a heavy door, and they definitely couldn't bypass the locks. The front entry was secure.

Emily ran to double-check the back door while Anna ran for the windows. She quickly discovered that there were only a handful of windows, and they were set about head high. They were heavily tinted, and the zombies couldn't see through them even if their faces were pressed against the glass.

Emily checked the locks on the rear door and put the drop bar in place. It was only then that she realized she could smell death inside the bar. There was a thumping noise coming from somewhere near the restrooms. Before going to confront the noise, she had to make sure that Anna was okay upfront. As she approached the bar, she saw Anna removing her knife from the head of a zombie on the floor behind it. Its legs had been so badly torn up that it had been unable to stand; otherwise, both women would have seen it as soon as they had come through the front door.

"You okay?" Emily asked.

"I'm fine. It was a crawler," Anna said. "We'd better clear the rest of this place. Something is thumping around back there."

"The restrooms are back there, and I'm assuming some kind of office and a supply room," Emily said.

"Well, unless something jumps out at us, let's clear one room at a time," Anna said.

Knives out and ready, they walked toward the restrooms first. There was no noise coming from the ladies room, so they cleared it first. It appeared clean and normal, at least as clean as one would expect the ladies room in a bar to be. They found the men's room to be the same, albeit dirtier. There were two doors left. The first one held a sign that said 'private' on it. They listened and heard a thumping noise coming from the other side of the door. Emily carefully opened the door as Anna stepped through it with her knife in one hand and her gun in the other. A lone zombie was sitting at the corner desk, seemingly stuck in place. When the door fully opened, it turned its head to reveal nasty bite wounds to its neck and shoulder. It tried to stand up but didn't seem to comprehend that it had to push the chair back from the desk to stand. Anna quickly took advantage and thrust her knife through its ear before it could find the coordination it needed. The rest of the office was clear. There were a couple of filing cabinets, the large beat-up corner desk stacked high with papers and a computer, and an extra chair sat near the door; otherwise, the room was empty.

They could still hear another thumping sound as they carefully made their way to the last door, which was presumably a supply room. This time, Anna opened the door as Emily walked into the room. The room was slightly larger than the office and was brightly lit, with several sets of shelves lining the walls. Two zombies were shuffling toward them, trying to make their way around a few stacks of cases of beer in the center of the room. A twenty-something blonde wearing short shorts and a tiny halter top that had slipped below her chest bore a ring of bite marks down one arm, and her mouth, chin, and hands were stained with dried blood. A middle-aged man with salt and pepper hair, glasses, jeans, and remnants of what was once a concert t-shirt followed her. There was a golf ball-sized chunk of flesh missing from his neck, several holes in his arms where large lumps of fat and muscle had been torn free, and his abdomen was so nearly empty that his ribs and spine were visible. It was incredible that he was still walking. With no blood around his mouth and so much around the little blondes, it appeared that she had eaten him alive.

With the beer barrier between them and the two zombies, Anna and Emily easily made quick work of both of them. To their amazement, there had been only four in the building. Free from any further threats, they took a quick look through the supplies on the shelves. One wall of shelves held liquor, mixers, and glasses. Another smaller set of shelves was full of bags of bar mix, chips, peanuts, and more beer mugs. One corner held mops, buckets, rags, and cleaning supplies. Next to the supplies was a metal ladder bolted to the wall leading to an access panel to the roof, most likely for access to the AC unit and a place for employees to take smoke breaks. On the last wall, there were bottles of beer and beer kegs.

"Plenty of alcohol and snacks," Emily said. "Let's check the office and the bar."

Anna led the way into the office. Looking closer than she had the first time around, she still didn't see anything of interest. All she saw was desk supplies, paperwork, keys, and a computer, all of the usual stuff one would expect to find. She knew there had to be a safe somewhere, and after looking in all of the likely places, she realized it must be under the desk where the dead zombie sat on the chair. She gave him a shove, and he slid right down to the floor. She bent down and found the safe, but it was so small that there wasn't likely to be anything of use inside it. It had a combination lock, so she left it alone.

"Let's check out the bar. Then I think we should move the dead into the office, so they're all in one place out of the way," Anna said, and Emily agreed.

49

A closer look around the bar revealed a jukebox, pool table, dartboard, a few pub-style tables and chairs, and the bar itself. Behind the bar, they found the expected alcohol, mixers, mugs, beer coolers, taps, a working double-sided sink that still ran fresh water, an oversized flashlight, and a shotgun. There were a few other expected odds and ends. And, of course, the dead zombie Anna had killed.

"This guy's a mess. I'll grab his arms, and you grab his feet. Let's try to lift him, so we don't smear blood everywhere," Anna said as she hefted the top part of his body. It took a few minutes, but they managed to carry him to the office before dropping him.

"Might as well finish up and get Blondie and her boyfriend from the storage room," Anna told Emily. "Keep all of the germs and hopefully most of the smell in one place. If the power goes out, the AC goes with it, and it'll get pretty awful in here pretty fast."

It took them a good fifteen minutes, but they finally had all four bodies moved to the office and closed the door. They knew the building was surrounded by at least two hundred zombies and probably a lot more. They tended to follow each other. With nothing to do for the moment but stay hidden, they got the mops and cleaning supplies out to clean up where the dead bodies had been. An hour later, and they had both areas as clean and sanitized as they were going to get. They both drank some water then went to look out the windows to see just how bad their situation was. It was four in the morning, and they knew they weren't going anywhere anytime soon. Anna was frustrated as hell that she managed to get herself stuck in the bar while her daughter was still out there somewhere but held out hope that Camille was holed up someplace safe.

Chapter Six

Day 4

Camille awoke with a start. The sun shone brightly on her face causing her to squint as her eyes adjusted to the light and her surroundings. She was lying in the most comfortable bed she'd ever been in. It was queen-sized, soft, full of oversized and decorative pillows, and she was covered in a satin-down comforter. She stretched then a quiet cry escaped her lips at the pain that seemed to assault her entire body. Every muscle felt strained from all of the running she had done. Her hands were scraped up from using them to catch herself when she had taken a nasty fall on a rocky path. Clean gauze was neatly wrapped around both of them. Her knee was sore from an awkward twist she'd made when she had jumped over a small creek and fallen down on the other side. There was a room-temperature ice pack on the bed next to her leg. It had been cold on her knee when she had fallen asleep but had warmed as the hours had passed. As she sat up, her muscles screamed in protest, and she let out a soft groan.

She was in a brightly lit room with one full wall constructed of floor-to-ceiling windows that overlooked Lake Erie. She could hear waves lapping the shore of the beach behind the house. Listening closely, she also heard the raspy moans of the dead coming from outside. The memory of the events of last night came crashing back to her as she remembered how she came to be in this place.

Camille remembered running endlessly with the horde of thousands following behind her. The noise of the horde drew in more zombies from all around her. She kept watching for a place she could dart off to so she could hide and rest, but with all of the zombies joining the group, she had trouble finding an opening. The further she ran, the further the horde fell behind her, and fewer zombies came from other directions toward the noise. Before she knew it, she had run more than two miles. Exhausted, scared, hot, and tired, she finally took a left turn and ran north toward the lake. She ran through a small park and stumbled, trying to jump over the creek that ran through it. She winced, remembering how she'd hurt her knee.

The horde had been far enough behind her that they hadn't seen her turn, but there were dozens of zombies nearby that turned to follow her. She swatted at their grabby hands and shoved them when they got too close. She zigzagged as she continued running north, but she still maintained a strong following. Where there had been dozens, there were now a hundred. Zombies came wandering from houses and yards as she passed by. She couldn't seem to shake them long enough to slow down and rest. Her lungs were on fire, pleading with her to take a break. Her knee throbbed with every step she took. She felt like she couldn't possibly keep going, but the raspy moans all around her pushed her further than she ever thought she could go.

As she approached Lake Road and the mansions that stood between her and the lake itself, she decided to try to make one last push past the mansions and to the beach. The homes had private beaches, and many of them had boat docks with pleasure craft moored alongside them. If she could just make it to a boat and push off into the water, she might survive. She chose a path between two incredibly large mansions and ran for the beach behind them. One of them had a boat, but about a dozen zombies were blocking her way. Her heart sank, and she decided to just run into the water. She was a strong swimmer. If she could swim out a little way, she could let herself float. It had to be better than running.

With nearly two hundred zombies shuffling slowly but persistently behind her, she ran through the sand with a worsening limp, getting closer to the water when she heard a voice. A middle-aged man with graying hair who looked to be at least ten years older than her dad held open one of the back doors of the striking mansion and motioned for her to come inside.

"Hurry, they're coming," he yelled to Camille.

Seeing the possibility of refuge and a chance to finally rest, Camille didn't hesitate. She turned away from the water and ran for the door dodging three zombies on her way. The man immediately closed and locked the door behind her, and within seconds zombies were pushing against the door. She glanced around and saw that she was in a great room that was nearly the size of her whole house. She had a few seconds to catch her breath before the man beckoned her to follow him upstairs. Camille saw a woman she presumed to be his wife standing near the top of the tall staircase waving them up, so she forced her legs to keep moving. She nearly fainted when she reached the top and tried to force air into her lungs.

"It's okay sweetie, we've got you," The woman said in a kind and gentle voice. "I'm Elizabeth. That's my husband, Bradford."

"Camille," she gasped, unable to say more. She glanced around at her surroundings to see that they were in an upstairs foyer of sorts. Several rooms and hallways branched off in various directions. Looking down at the great room below on the first floor, she took in the expensive décor and the full-sized grand piano. From her vantage point, she could see most of the lower level of the house, and it appeared to be designed solely for entertaining. Extravagant furnishings, paintings, sculptures, and light fixtures filled the space. A long, beautiful polished bar filled an entire corner, with matching pub-style tables and chairs spread throughout the area. The piano sat on a luxurious marble floor with open space all around it for dancing. Plush sofas and chairs were interspersed with small tables adorned with vases and floating candles. A giant crystal chandelier was centered over the area. Striking original art pieces hung on the walls. The entire rear wall of the house was constructed of floor-to-ceiling glass, which would have been a beautiful sight if zombies hadn't been pressed up against it. With the high ceilings and expansive space in the house, she felt like she was up much higher than just the second floor. She looked down with wonder at the space twenty feet below. If the back wall hadn't been made of glass, the house looked as if it would be secure indefinitely against the zombies lingering outside. Her thoughts were interrupted when the husband spoke.

"You're safe now, Camille," Bradford started. "The zombies shouldn't be able to get through the doors. We have plenty of food, solar power, and a private water line from the lake. There are plenty of bedrooms and bathrooms on this floor and a few more upstairs."

Camille was momentarily speechless. Of all the places she could have run to, she never could have dreamed of such a safe location. That is if the wall of windows held against the zombies. Elizabeth returned to her side with two bottles of water.

"Don't drink those too quickly," Elizabeth said. "It might come right back up if you do."

Camille couldn't help but chug most of the first bottle of water before she slowed down and started sipping it.

"What about all of the glass? It looks like the entire back wall of the house is made of windows," Camille said.

"The glass is thicker than it appears. We're hopeful that the zombies won't be able to push through it," Bradford said. "If they do, we'll block off the stairs. From what we've seen, they're rather clumsy. Hopefully, they wouldn't be able to make it up here."

"Honey, Camille is clearly exhausted. Why don't we go sit in the living room so she can relax? She must have been running for a while to have amassed such a following," Elizabeth said. She turned to lead them down one of the hallways.

After hours of running, Camille had been standing still for the last ten minutes. As she moved to take a step forward, her knee gave out, spilling her to the floor, and she let out a pained yelp.

"Oh dear, I didn't realize you were hurt," Elizabeth said. "Honey, please grab my medical bag while I help her into the living room." She helped Camille up then put her arm around her to offer support as she limped down the hallway, which opened up to an oversized sunken living room overlooking the lake at the rear of the house. Camille sat down on the closest couch and let out a sigh of relief.

"I'm a doctor, sweetie," Elizabeth said as Bradford returned with her bag of medical supplies. "Let me take a look at your injuries."

As Elizabeth tended to her wounds, Camille began to explain how she ended up at their house. She told them about the horde and how she'd had no choice but to run to protect her family. How she had to keep running because more and more zombies came after her even when she tried to zigzag around to lose them. And also of her last-ditch plan to swim out into the lake to escape and stop running. They had saved her life.

Camille winced as Elizabeth finished examining her knee. "Nothing's broken, and nothing seems to be torn. I think your ligament was just stretched a bit. Some rest, ice, and pain medication should take care of everything," Elizabeth told her as she handed her two pills. "Take these. They'll help with the pain and swelling."

Camille accepted the medication gratefully. Her aches and pains were becoming more intense since she'd sat down.

"You must be starving. I'm so sorry I didn't think of it sooner." Elizabeth said, then went to make Camille a plate of food. She was back a moment later with a big sandwich and a bowl of strawberries.

"Thank you so much," Camille said as she started in on the food. She was surprised to find herself so hungry. She looked out the windows at the view of the lake outside. The zombies below were just out of her line of sight. She shuddered, thinking about how close she had come to dying and thought of her family and how worried they must be.

"I appreciate everything you've done for me," Camille started. "But I have to get back home to my family."

"It's getting dark outside, dear, and right now, what you need is to get some rest. You're in no condition to go anywhere. You need a nice hot shower and some clean clothes. I'm sure I have something you can wear. When you're done, I'll get your hands bandaged up and an ice pack for your knee, then get you settled into one of the guest rooms," Elizabeth told her. "Tomorrow, we'll figure out what we can do about getting you back home."

"Thank you," Camille said with a yawn. She knew Elizabeth was right. With all of her adrenaline long since spent, she was exhausted and wanted nothing more than to go to sleep.

"Let me show you to your room and your bathroom. I'll leave some clean clothes on the bed for you," Elizabeth said.

She led Camille down one of the hallways to a huge bedroom with an attached bathroom and laid out a robe and fresh towels for her.

"I'll leave you to it, dear," Elizabeth said. "When you're done, just press the button on the intercom by the door, and I'll be up to give you something to help you sleep. I don't want you walking around any more than you have to."

Camille thanked her as she closed the door. She looked around, amazed at the view of the lake from the wall of windows on one side of the room. The bed looked so comfortable that she wanted nothing more than to lie down and go to sleep, but she knew she needed to wash off all of the sweat and grime first. The bathroom was as big as her bedroom at home. The shower had multiple shower sprays coming from both the ceiling and the walls. A huge sunken bathtub sat next to it. There was a mirror covering one wall and a smaller mirror was hung over the sink and vanity with a plush chair sitting in front of the counter.

Camille dropped her filthy clothes to the floor and placed her knife on the vanity. She carefully stepped into the shower while favoring her knee. As the hot water washed over her, she relived the events of the day. She thought of her mom and how worried she must be. She knew that her brother would want to go searching for her. She wondered where her dad was and if he was still alive. She thought of Lucia and hoped she made it to safety. She worried about whether or not the entire horde had continued to pass by her house, whether her plan had worked or if the zombies had gone after her family. She felt the tears coming and soon her body was wracked with her sobbing. She cried for herself. She cried for her family, and she cried for the unknown. When she was finally all cried out, she turned off the shower, dried off, and pulled on the plush robe. She walked into the bedroom to dress in the clothes Elizabeth had left out for her and found that they fit comfortably. She wanted to sleep but knew she needed to press the intercom button so Elizabeth could wrap her stinging hands and give her ice for her knee, so she limped lightly over to the door and pressed the button.

A moment later, Elizabeth came in to take care of her. Afterward, she fell asleep almost immediately.

Chapter Seven

Day 4

Max downed his third energy drink in as many hours as the sun rose brightly. The fire he'd started back at the gas station burned out of control, consuming the entire block. He sighed and hoped that the flames hadn't endangered any families hiding in their homes. He couldn't think of anything he would have done differently. It was just a fluke that the flames spread to that first garage. After that, it jumped from house to house until the entire block was burning.

There was still no word from Damon about Camille or Anna. His wife and daughter were both still out there somewhere. He couldn't stop looking until he found them. He hadn't seen Anna's SUV anywhere, so it was reasonable to hope that she was still out there searching herself.

He glanced down at the gas gauge and saw that he was driving on fumes. He adjusted his route to take him to a nearby gas station. He weaved around the occasional zombie but hadn't had to deal with any large groups over the last few hours. As he approached the intersection with two gas stations on opposite corners, he slowed his speed to a crawl. He wanted to see how many zombies were shuffling around the area before he committed to one of them. To his surprise, both were relatively free of the dead, so he pulled into the one on his right. It seemed unlikely that the pumps would still accept his card, but he scanned it anyway. There was no response on the little screen. He tried again while watching the area all around him, and still nothing. The card readers were down. He was going to have to find a length of hose to try to siphon some gas or find another vehicle.

There were plenty of vehicles around, but it was a matter of finding one with keys. Unlike the movies, people didn't stash their keys above the sun visor. He looked around the parking lot to see if there were any options parked there. Several zombies in the street were headed his way, but they moved so slowly that he figured he had about five minutes before they would be upon him. He kept a close watch anyway because more could come from anywhere at any time.

Suddenly and certainly unexpectedly, Max heard the sound of another vehicle. It was the first vehicle he'd heard since leaving downtown. He tried to pinpoint its location as the sound grew louder, then looked to the south to see a gray pickup driving at a high rate of speed toward the intersection. Max didn't hide but didn't advertise his presence either. He wanted to get a look at who was in the truck before he did anything. It slowed as it neared the intersection, zigzagging around abandoned and wrecked vehicles. To his surprise, the pickup pulled into the gas station and came to a stop near Max and his truck.

Max kept his hand near his holster out of an abundance of caution. People would do crazy things in desperate times. A man in his sixties with a shock of white hair climbed out of the pickup. Max saw the bulge of a gun at the man's back as he got out. He approached Max but slowed his gait when he saw Max's hand near his gun.

"Hey, I don't mean any harm," the man started. "You're the first person I've seen alive in three days. I was starting to think I'd never see another living person again."

Max studied the man's face for a moment and immediately noticed the strain behind his smile. The smile was forced, not genuine. Max kept his hand just above his holster.

"I'm Bill," the man said as he reached his hand out to shake Max's. Max just nodded and ignored the outstretched hand. The man seemed to sense his unease. "I'm just out trying to get some supplies."

"You came down the street pretty fast. It almost seemed like you knew I was here before you headed this way," Max said without introducing himself.

Bill's expression turned dark for a second before he plastered his fake smile back on. He glanced at Max's truck to see if anyone else was inside and looked disappointed to find it empty. His gray eyes were devoid of light. His forced smile didn't travel past his mouth.

"I thought I heard another vehicle, so I sped up to try to find it. When I got close to the intersection, I saw you standing at the gas pump," Bill said. "But hey, if you don't want to be bothered, I'll leave."

"What kind of supplies are you looking for?" Max asked.

"Uh, some water and uh maybe some food," Bill stumbled with his answer.

Max had a bad feeling about the guy. He didn't think the man was on a supply run. He suspected some kind of ulterior motive but wasn't sure what it was. He looked the man up and down and noticed zip ties bulging from one of his pockets.

"Where are you holed up?" Max asked as he watched the man closely.

"Not far from here," Bill answered vaguely.

61

Max looked a little closer at the inside of Bill's pickup and saw a lot of blood on the passenger seat. Not necessarily suspect with zombies everywhere, but the blood was pooled on the seat, fresh. Then he noticed the torn panties and discarded bra, both wet with bright red blood. His eyes met Bill's, and the man knew he was busted. Max pulled his gun from his holster and had it aimed at Bill's chest before the man realized what was happening.

"You've been out searching for girls," Max said. It was a statement, not a question.

"No, no, that's zombie blood. I just found this truck. The keys were there, so I took it," Bill said, but his eyes betrayed him. He had the eyes of a sociopath.

Max was certain that this man was evil. He knew the man had a gun behind his back, so Max made sure his hands didn't go anywhere.

"What did the girl look like? Where did you find her?" Max demanded.

"There was no girl. Look, I'll just get back in my truck and go on my way," Bill said.

Max knew that Bill wouldn't go anywhere. If he let him leave, the man would probably pull a weapon and try to kill Max.

"The girl. Tell me," Max said louder.

"I didn't hurt her," Bill said with no trace of his fake smile. "She was a twenty-something blonde, and she wanted it. A zombie snuck up on us and bit her. That's where the blood came from."

Max didn't believe a word the man said. It wouldn't matter for much longer. Max had been keeping a close eye on his surroundings during the entire encounter. Bill hadn't. Bill slowly backed up toward his pickup while he held his hands up and stared at Max. Just before he reached the door, a zombie grabbed him by the shoulder and tore a huge piece of flesh from it. Bill screamed in shock and tried to pull away from the zombie, but it had a firm grip and wouldn't let go. It tore into the side of Bill's neck, and blood spurted freely, splattering Bill's face and his truck. Max watched as the man begged for help before falling to the ground under the weight of the zombie's grip. It tore into his chest, exposing stark white ribs glistening with blood and oily lumps of fat. Max waited until Bill went still before taking out the zombie, then he thrust his knife through Bill's ear. Bill wouldn't be hurting anyone else.

Max took a closer look inside the man's truck and found several pairs of torn undergarments and a discarded shoe. The zombie apocalypse had happened, the world fell apart, almost everyone was dead, and this sociopath had seen it as an opportunity to capture and rape women. Max wasn't surprised because he knew there were more like him out there, but he hadn't expected people to go so dark so fast. He shook his head and got back into his truck. A dozen zombies were nearly upon him. He'd find another place to get some gas or find another vehicle.

Max tried to put the scene out of his head as he drove south a little way. He was heading for an intersection that had two gas stations, a coffee shop, and a car dealership. He figured he'd try for gas one more time, and if it didn't work, he'd try to find a new vehicle at a house like he'd done last night. There was less chance of getting caught surrounded by zombies if he drove down a residential street that was relatively empty of the dead.

He was about to pull into the first gas station when he noticed that the gates at the car dealership were wide open. There were very few zombies shuffling around, so he pulled into the parking lot. One of the showroom windows was shattered from the inside out. Someone had already broken into the place, which meant that the alarm had already gone off and since died. *Jackpot.* Max pulled the truck up close to the building and parked. A couple of dozen dead bodies were strewn around the parking lot, but only a few zombies were walking around. He wanted to get a better look inside the building, so he needed to take out the zombies outside first. He walked up to the closest one, a petite woman with so many bite wounds he was surprised she was still standing and thrust his knife through her ear. With one easy kill on the ground, he moved toward the next. He sighed at the sight of a morbidly obese man with blood ringed around his mouth, a gaping neck wound, and rolls of fat hanging over his waist. It was a long reach to the zombie's head, so Max kicked him in the knee, causing him to fall heavily to the ground. Before the dead man could make another movement, Max plunged his knife through its ear. The final two both wore mechanic uniforms and were shuffling slowly toward Max. He took out the first one easily, but the second one towered over him. Max tried to take it down with a foot to the knee, but the zombie stayed on his feet, so he stepped behind it and reached up to plunge his knife through its ear. With all four zombies on the ground, he double-checked the parking lot to make sure there weren't any others lurking about. Whoever had been here before him had killed a lot of them and he assumed whatever remained had followed the car as it left the lot.

With his knife in one hand and his gun in the other, he carefully crept over the shattered glass on the ground. The showroom was full of brand new cars, trucks, and SUVs.

He saw the empty spot where someone had taken the vehicle that had been closest to the window. There were at least half a dozen dead zombies on the floor and dried blood was streaked around the large room. Max quietly made his way toward the back wall and a row of light switches. The electricity in the area was still on, so he flipped several switches to light up the showroom. In broad daylight, the lights wouldn't draw the attention of any of the dead. Near the light switches, the oversized door to the mechanics bay was closed and locked, so he didn't worry himself about checking out the rear half of the building. He could hear scraping and shuffling noises coming from the back, but the heavy door was secure.

He listened carefully for any noises coming from adjoining offices but heard nothing. Not willing to risk a stray zombie surprising him, he took a quick peek in each empty office then closed their doors. The door of the final office stood wide open, and Max saw a large key safe on the back wall. It had already been broken into, and it held the keys for all of the vehicles in the showroom.

Max took another look at the vehicles on display. There was so much to choose from that he felt like a kid in a candy store. Sports cars, SUVs, and trucks filled the once pristine showroom. A huge silver pickup truck with a snowplow, an extended cab, oversized bumpers and tires, and a towing winch caught his eye. It was the biggest thing in the place and would offer much more protection than anything he'd driven so far. He went back to the office to find the keys then walked over to the truck with a grin on his face. He didn't want to drive through the broken glass if he could avoid it, so he looked around for door openers. He found one on the side not far from where the truck sat on display. He pressed the button, and the door slowly lifted into the ceiling. Max went back outside to collect his bags of water and weapons then lugged them into the new truck. He climbed in, turned the key, and with another stroke of luck, saw that the gas tank was full. He steered around one new car in the showroom then drove out through the open door. He turned left onto the main road to resume his search in a westward direction.

Chapter Eight

Day 4

Michelle couldn't go back to sleep after the boys went to bed, so she sat in the kitchen looking at Jesse's phone. She scrolled through pictures and read their last text message conversations. She quietly shed tears during the first moment of privacy she'd had since Max had given her the devastating news. She was having a hard time coming to terms with the fact that Jesse was gone. They had been together for twenty years, and she couldn't imagine a life that didn't include him. Hours passed as she mourned his loss and let their lifetime of memories flood her mind.

Shortly after the sun rose, everyone else in the house started waking up. To keep herself busy, she pulled a bunch of fresh food from the fridge and cooked a large breakfast. By the time she finished cooking the bacon, everyone had made their way into the kitchen.

"Morning, Mom," Lucia came in with swollen red eyes. She'd been crying some more.

"Help yourselves," Michelle said as she pulled Lucia close for a hug.

"Smells good in here," Frank said. "Thanks for cooking. Last night was… well, I'm sorry for your loss," Frank said and introduced himself.

"Morning," Junior said. He had never felt so awkward in his life. "I'm Junior. I know you don't know us, but we're sorry about Jesse. He and Max saved our lives. We wouldn't be here if it weren't for them."

"Thank you," Michelle said quietly. "There's coffee on the counter." She didn't know what to say to these men. She didn't know the first thing about them, and she certainly didn't feel like spending time with strangers.

Damon and Joey piled their plates with food. Between them being teenage boys and their zombie-killing spree during the night, they had worked up quite an appetite regardless of their grief.

"So, how did my dad and Max save you guys?" Joey asked as he shoveled eggs into his mouth. He had seen their fire rescue shirts the night before and figured they should have been the ones doing the saving. Then he thought back to some of the news they'd seen on TV and realized he wasn't being fair.

Everyone felt the tension in the air. Only Lucia seemed oblivious, and that was because she was stuck in her own head. Michelle and the boys knew that if Jesse had planned to bring these men home, then he must have trusted them. Their grief was deep and heavy, so they weren't too keen on getting to know the two strangers.

Frank and Junior sat down with cups of coffee and started to tell the story. Frank did most of the talking. They remembered every detail, the friendly banter with their crew, and thoughts that had run through their minds but didn't voice any of those things aloud. Some details didn't need to be shared.

Frank had been twelve hours into his shift and was lifting weights in the gym at the old fire station when the watch desk sounded the alarm. At six foot three and a muscular two hundred fifty pounds, he dropped the heavily laden weight bar too quickly and from too great of a height, creating a jagged crack in the concrete floor. The captain was going to chew his ass out for that later. He hurried past the kitchen, where the tantalizing aroma of what would have been the crew's lunch caused his stomach to rumble. He jogged past Junior, who was sliding down the pole from the upper floor. Once at the truck, he quickly slipped into his gear and climbed up into his seat as the other four men on his crew did the same. Lights on and sirens blaring, the truck pulled out, heading for a multi-vehicle pileup on the nearby freeway. Two ambulances carrying two paramedics each followed closely behind.

Frank leaned his head against the window and noticed an unusually large number of people walking the streets. Before he could take in any further detail, he heard his name from one of the guys seated behind him.

"Frank, how'd things go with that blonde from the apartment fire? You know who I mean, Mount Everest?" Steve laughed, making hand motions to describe the woman's ample chest. "Shit, I would have been all up in that if I'd seen her first."

Frank laughed and shook his head. "You know damn well how it went. One look at my fine black ass, and she was begging for more."

"I heard Dan hooked up with her roommate," Shawn, their driver, chimed in.

"Fuck, you know Dan hooks up with a different chick every fire," Steve said.

"Yeah, don't forget about Romeo back here," Junior said, elbowing Jake. "That redhead that came into the office was looking for him."

"In his defense, she was leaving. She already came," Shawn ribbed. They all laughed.

Frank laughed, then tuned out the friendly banter as they turned onto the onramp. He'd had a couple of fun nights with the blonde. Heather, or Amber, or something like that. He didn't know her name then and definitely couldn't remember it now.

Raised voices suddenly interrupted his thoughts. "What the hell is going on over there?" Junior asked loudly as he pointed toward a crowd of people walking around on the highway. They were nearing the accident and saw a few dozen people walking in various directions across the right two lanes. The people took no notice of the fire truck and made no effort to move out of the way.

Shawn veered the truck to the left across all four lanes and pulled to the front of the pileup. Within seconds, both ambulances stopped behind them. Before they could climb out of the fire truck, a police car slammed into the inner wall of the overhead bridge. Another police car pulled up beside it.

Screams were coming from nearly every direction. Frank and his crew were headed for a smashed-up car that was engulfed in flames while the paramedics rushed to tend to the wounded. As they focused on getting the hose ready to start on the fire, a few dozen people shuffled toward them from behind the accident.

"Where are all of these people coming from?" Frank hollered. The people weren't involved in the car accident, so his confusion grew as he saw that everyone heading their way had horrific bloody injuries. The walking wounded had chunks of flesh missing or torn from their faces, shoulders, arms, hands, and even some abdomens. It looked like a bomb had gone off.

The paramedics from one ambulance had strapped in a man who was injured in the car accident. Before the driver could close the rear doors, a middle-aged man in a business suit stumbled up to him, grabbed him by the arm, and bit into his neck. Blood spurted wildly from the gruesome wound, and the stunned paramedic dropped to the ground. The man in the suit went down with him and tore more flesh from his face and throat until the first responder went still. The suit stood up and bit into the foot of the injured man strapped to the gurney in the back of the ambulance. The second paramedic, confused and shocked, tried to push the suit away and got his hand bitten in the process.

The other two paramedics went to check on the police officer in the wrecked car. They found him strapped in his seatbelt with fatal injuries, yet the officer pressed his face up against the window and snapped his jaw at them. Unsure of what to do, and before they could do anything, four people who were dead closed in on them. Three women and one man reached for them and brutally bit into both of them. The screams were gut-wrenching, but they were cut short as the paramedics were bitten on their faces, necks, and hands.

Shawn yelled for everyone to get back in the fire truck. Jake and Steve quickly jogged toward the truck but were overcome by half a dozen zombies before they could get there. They went down fighting. Their heavy uniforms, gloves, and helmets offered protection, but they didn't understand what they were dealing with and were overwhelmed by the weight of so many bodies pulling them down. Heavy jaws painfully clenched down on Jake's arms but couldn't penetrate the heavy material. By sheer luck, two zombies managed to pull off one of Jake's gloves and immediately mangled his hand with their teeth. As he fought to push them off, his helmet came loose, and his ear was ripped from his head within seconds. Four of the dead lumbered over Steve, and one managed to bite a bloody chunk out of his neck. Within a minute, Jake and Steve were both clumsily back on their feet, looking for a meal for themselves.

As the driver, Shawn didn't wear a helmet or jacket, just his heavy uniform pants, suspenders, and a thin t-shirt. He hadn't seen Jake and Steve go down, so when he got close to them, he yelled for them to get back to the truck. He saw their dead eyes just before they both locked their hands onto his arms and shoulders. Shawn yelled and kicked and hollered, but together Jake and Steve were too strong for him to fight off. Jake nearly ripped Shawn's bicep from his arm, leaving stringy sinew and bloody detritus around the stark white bone. Steve bit into Shawn's shoulder then clamped down on Shawn's fingers so hard that he severed nearly his entire hand. He held them up to his mouth to eat like chicken wings. Shawn passed out from the pain and blood loss, only to rise again as one of the dead only moments later.

Frank and Junior had heeded Shawn's order for everyone to get back to the truck with only seconds to spare. Of the five firefighters, four paramedics, and two police officers on the scene, they were the only two men to make it back to safety.

"What the fuck is going on?" Junior yelled. From within the safety of the truck, they watched as more and more people fell to the dead. Within minutes, fifty zombies were roaming the area. People got out of their trapped cars to try to run down the hill alongside the highway, but not one made it without suffering at least one bite wound. Most of them went down screaming before coming back as zombies. A handful kept running, unknowingly spreading the infection further as they fled the area.

"Holy shit," Frank said and pointed at the rest of the crew. Shawn, Jake, and Steve were scattered within the crowd shuffling around looking for a fresh meal.

More cars came to screeching stops as they reached the accident and found themselves blocked in. Frank watched as a dozen zombies surrounded a small red compact and pressed against the windows as they sought to reach the stunned woman in the driver's seat. They pushed against the windows until they formed spider webs of cracks then pushed the glass into the car. The woman screamed and tried to fight them off, but several zombies grabbed hold of her hands and arms and started feasting. Her scream died off as she became one of the dead, and the zombies turned away, looking for another living meal. The dead woman remained in her car without the mental capacity required to open her door, so she reached the remains of her arms and her head out of the broken window, grasping at the air.

As scorching flames left unchecked roared through one of the cars in the pileup, the fire gradually spread to the other smashed-up cars. The torrid heat found its way to the gas tank of the second car, causing an explosion that sent shrapnel everywhere and shook the firetruck on its axis.

"Damn it, we've gotta get out of here!" Junior said. He climbed into the driver's seat and tried to start the engine. "It's not starting." The stress in his voice was evident.

"Look," Frank said. "There's smoke coming from the engine. We must have taken some damage from that explosion. I don't think we're getting out of here unless we go on foot."

"There's nowhere to go on foot. The zombies are everywhere," Junior said. The truck was quickly becoming surrounded as more and more of the dead made their way toward the accident. The explosion seemed to draw in at least a hundred more.

"I think they know we're in here," Frank as he watched a lot of the zombies shift their focus to the truck. "We're sitting up high enough that they shouldn't be able to reach us." He wasn't sure he was right, but he hoped he was. The zombies were slow and uncoordinated. He watched the dead that remained strapped in seatbelts in their cars, seemingly unable to unbuckle themselves or open their doors.

"So we just sit here and wait?" Junior asked.

"I think so. Maybe something else will grab their attention, and they'll wander off. Whatever this is, it's happening lightning fast. I don't think anyone will be coming to help us."

"We'll fucking die of heatstroke sitting in here," Junior said. "There's what, a few bottles of water? That might keep us cooled down enough for a couple of hours. Then what are we going to do?"

"Damn it, I don't have all the answers. I'm seeing what you're seeing. All I know is that right now we're stuck, and we're not going anywhere," Frank said with anger creeping into his voice.

With nothing to do but sit and wait, they watched more of the horrifying carnage all around them. From their vantage point, they could still see a few living people trapped inside their cars. A man on a motorcycle suddenly came within view, weaving and dodging the zombies that reached for him. He made it about a hundred yards past the fire truck before his luck turned, and he hit a zombie head-on. The man flew off his bike, and the second he hit the ground, he was swarmed. The dead ripped his helmet off, gorged on his face, and ripped his nose clean from his face. A young teenaged girl tore his fingers from one hand while an old man in Bermuda shorts ripped into his abdomen. A woman in yoga pants bit into his neck repeatedly, causing blood to spurt wildly. She moved down to his chest and started pulling on his organs. Two of them were on their knees, pulling on ropes of glistening intestines. Another nearly scalped him with one hand while the other pulled his eye from his socket. They did enough damage that the biker didn't rise again as one of them. Their meal finished, the small group of zombies slowly shuffled back toward the fire truck.

"Shit, we're going to need a really big distraction if we're ever going to get out of here," Junior said. "Hot as hell or not, I'm not getting out of this truck." Frank nodded in agreement.

Over the next few hours, they saw the last of the trapped drivers succumb one by one as the zombies pressed against their car windows with enough force until the glass broke free. Then it was just Frank and Junior. Every last zombie on the highway gathered around the fire truck. The crowd was nearly ten deep all the way around.

Resigned to being trapped, Frank and Junior settled in and tried to get comfortable in the heat. The zombies couldn't reach the windows, so they broke two of them to try to get some fresh air circulating. The slight breeze carried smoke and the noxious smell of hundreds of freshly dead bodies.

"We're sitting in a truck full of water, and we're going to end up dying from dehydration and heatstroke," Frank said with a little laugh.

"Better that than the zombies. Well, at least zombies would be a fast death," Junior said with a laugh of his

75

own. "I'm not giving up, though. Someone is bound to come around, or something is going to distract them."

"I hope so, but do you think something is going to distract so many of them? Maybe if a semi plowed through here," Frank said without expecting an answer.

They had two bottles of water left. They were already dehydrated from sitting in full gear in the heat of the truck, and they had to make the water last.

"I'm taking my gear off. If we see anything coming, I'll throw it back on quick," Junior said.

"Good idea," Frank said. They'd been keeping it on in case they had a chance to escape, but they weren't going to survive the oven inside the truck if they didn't find a way to cool down.

As night fell, the dead never lost interest in the fire truck. They listened to the nonstop raspy moans of a couple of hundred zombies surrounding them. The two broken windows gave them some desperately needed fresh air. They split one of the two bottles of water between them and planned to save the last bottle for as long as possible. Both men had been up for more than twenty-four hours at this point, so Frank told Junior to try to get some rest while he kept watch. There was nothing to do but watch and wait, hoping that someone would come their way.

Throughout the night, in groups of twos and threes, more zombies gradually surrounded the truck. Frank sighed at the hopeless situation. He couldn't believe that his life was going to end this way.

Frank had married in his mid-twenties, but the marriage fizzled out fast after he became a firefighter. They had started life together happy, had two toddlers, and had planned to add to their family, but he found that no matter how hard he did or didn't try, he couldn't turn down all the women that threw themselves at him. As soon as women saw the uniform, they were all over him. He'd been young and dumb and couldn't say no to any of them. He made it work for a few years until his wife had wizened up and given him an ultimatum.

Fifteen years ago, she'd left him after she'd caught him cheating on her one too many times. She'd taken their boys and moved across the country. After she left, he started drinking a little too much. Between her wanting distance, the job, and his drinking, he'd gradually fallen out of touch with them. He thought about her and his two boys and wondered where they were now if they had somehow survived. Even if he could search for them, he'd have no idea where to even begin to look. He resigned himself to the fact that he would never know.

He liked to think of himself as a changed man, but he never settled down again, and he hooked up with at least one new woman every week. Firefighting and random flings had been his life ever since the divorce. Looking out at the crowd of zombies and knowing he was going to die soon, Frank was full of regret. His biggest mistake had been letting go of his boys. He shed a few silent tears over the things he'd done and the things he'd lost.

The screech of fingernails along the bottom of his window pulled him from his recollections. An immensely tall zombie had its arms reaching straight up, and its fingers were grazing the window. The eerie sound somehow stood out even with all of the raspy moans and shuffling feet.

"Well fuck," Frank muttered, wishing he could do something about it. The noise woke up Junior, who had somehow managed to sleep over the last six hours or so.

"Damn Frank," Junior said when he saw the time. "You should have woken me earlier."

"Nah, I was good," Frank replied. "I'll try to get some sleep now. Wake me if the sun doesn't." It was just past 4:00 in the morning. The sun would be up in a couple of hours.

"You got it boss," Junior said. As Frank tossed and turned, Junior watched the hundreds of zombies keeping them company. He'd watched so many that none of their appearances surprised him anymore. He was just glad that he wasn't up close and personal with any of them.

He checked his cell phone and saw that the internet was working. It seemed crazy to him that he couldn't make a phone call, but he could go online. It wasn't long before he regretted checking the news. He watched one terrifying, horrific video after another, quickly learning that most if not all of the country had fallen to the dead if the news reports were right. He put his phone away and resumed watching the dead around the truck.

Junior Martinez was twenty-five and single. He came from a large family and had more cousins than he could count. His mom had a family dinner every Sunday and, without fail, nagged him about when he was going to settle down and give her grandbabies. His siblings had already given her a half dozen and showed no signs of stopping, but she wouldn't be happy until she had at least a dozen grandchildren to spoil. He smiled to himself, thinking of her voice and the loud house at Sunday dinners. His family was sprawled out all over the eastern suburbs and beyond. They might as well be a thousand miles away since everything went to shit. As much as he wanted to, he didn't see how he could try to get to any of them if he ever escaped the firetruck. The thought of his parents possibly being killed brought tears to his eyes. If ever there was a way to get to them, he would, but it just didn't seem possible. Hell, he couldn't even get his ass safely out of the damned truck.

The sun rose brightly, promising another scorching hot day. The inside of the truck had cooled to a barely tolerable temperature during the night, but with the morning sunshine, it was already heating up. Frank awoke to the sun on his face and the sounds of raspy, moaning zombies shuffling and stumbling around the truck. He looked out the window to see that the crowd was about the same size it had been before he'd fallen asleep.

He was so thirsty that he felt a bit lightheaded and his lips were cracked and dry. He looked over at Junior to see that he appeared no better. "How about we each drink about a quarter of that last bottle of water?"

"Sounds good to me. We're never going to make it through today if we don't get more," Junior said, knowing they had no way to get more. If it wasn't so hot, they could make it last longer, but that wasn't an option. He took the bottle from Frank and relished the few gulps of warm water, wishing desperately that he could drink more.

They debated busting out the rest of the windows. The tallest of the zombies could only reach the bottoms with their fingertips, so they felt safe letting more air in as long as they didn't sit right next to the broken windows. The stench from the dead was putrid, but they needed the air so they wouldn't overheat completely. Throughout the morning, they made small talk and watched the zombies all over the highway. By noon, they were both feeling sick from the heat. They were tired, their mouths were as dry as sandpaper, and dizziness came and went. They decided to finish the last bit of water since it was the only thing they could do to help themselves.

As the afternoon wore on, they talked of their fallen brothers. Neither of them had seen the guys getting attacked, but they had seen them after they had become zombies. They didn't know what had happened and hoped they hadn't suffered too badly. All that mattered was that they were dead. Watching them mingle within the crowd of zombies was a painful thing to see. Steve and Jake both had dried blood on their faces and mouths, but Shawn looked like he hadn't yet found a meal. They knew he would though, and just hoped that it wouldn't be them.

"I can't see any way out of this truck," Frank said. "We die of heatstroke and dehydration or we get out and get torn apart by zombies."

"Choices, choices," Junior said with a weak laugh. "I haven't seen one car or truck or hell, even a living person since yesterday. I don't think any kind of help is going to come our way."

"I watched for headlights in the dark last night. I didn't even see any off the highway. I didn't hear anything but the fucking zombies," Frank said.

They both zoned out while watching the dead, feeling disturbed each time they saw one of the guys. There was no sign of the paramedics, but they weren't wearing stand-out firefighting gear. They knew they were in the crowd somewhere.

Junior was watching one particularly pathetic zombie hobbling around on the outer edge of the crowd. It had a knife stuck in the middle of its throat, causing its head to bob up and down with every movement. His eye was drawn back to the middle of the crowd by a couple of charred zombies. They were badly burned, resembled ashy charcoal, and pieces of them flaked off as they stumbled into other zombies. Their eyes, ears, noses, and lips were gone, and he couldn't imagine how they were still standing. They looked like skeletons sheathed in black cloaks.

A sudden movement in the distance caught Frank's attention. "Holy shit!" he said. "I think there's a truck coming this way."

Junior jumped up to look out the window. There was a white pickup driving down the highway headed in their direction. "Gear up, Frank. Looks like we might have a ride," Junior grinned as he quickly pulled on his uniform and grabbed his equipment. Frank was ready just as fast.

They both jumped at the sound of gunfire. With no other noise other than that of the zombies, each gunshot sounded like an explosion. They saw where the truck was pulling up along the left side of the truck and quickly smashed out that window. Before the truck had come to a complete stop, both Frank and Junior had jumped from the firetruck down into the bed of the pickup.

Frank slapped the top of the cab with his hand and yelled, "Go, go go!"

Focusing back on the gazes of Michelle and the boys in the kitchen, Frank said, "And that's how they saved us. We would have died up in that firetruck if Max and Jesse hadn't come along."

Chapter Nine

Day 4

Anna and Emily had both dozed off and on during the early morning hours. There wasn't a single place to get comfortable in the entire bar, and the moans of the dead outside were relentless, so neither of them slept well. Every now and then, Anna looked out one of the small darkened windows and saw nothing but zombies. She couldn't be sure, but she thought the crowd outside had probably doubled in size. She went behind the bar to rinse her face with some cool water, then filled a glass and drank the whole thing. Emily was stretching on the pool table and doing some yoga. She said it helped to center her and helped to clear her mind. Anna thought it was pretty weird but kept that thought to herself.

"We've gotta find a way out of here," Anna said for the hundredth time.

"Unless and until something draws the zombies away, I don't see what we can do," Emily said. They'd had this discussion so many times that she didn't know what else to say.

The bar was fully surrounded by hundreds of zombies. There was no way to shoot their way out. They didn't have a waiting vehicle outside. Unless something else drew them away, they would probably surround the bar indefinitely.

"I'm going to try that ladder to the roof. At least I can get a better view of what we're dealing with," Anna said. With no way for the zombies to get inside the building, they didn't need to keep watch at all times, so Emily decided to go with her.

"I'll go too," she said. "I wouldn't mind getting a look for myself."

They went to the storage room, and Anna climbed up first. She had difficulty opening the square panel at the top that granted rooftop access. She didn't see any kind of lock on it, but the hinges were rusty, and it didn't appear to have been opened for some time. She pushed on it some more until finally, it snapped open. Anna stepped out onto the roof with Emily right behind her.

"Holy fuck," Anna said. There had to be five hundred zombies surrounding the building. Less concerning was a fire burning in the distance. The fire couldn't have been more than a mile or so away and appeared to cover an entire block of houses.

"What happened?" Emily said, not expecting an answer.

"Maybe the zombies will get distracted by the fire," Anna said.

"Maybe, but I don't think so," Emily said. "Maybe if there was an explosion, it would draw them away. Otherwise, I don't think they'll leave when they know we're here. I mean, look at them. They're just staring straight at the building. None of them are even looking at the roof; they think we're still inside."

"Damn it, I don't know what the fuck to do," Anna said in a frustrated voice. "My daughter is out there, my husband is out there, and I'm stuck in this damn bar."

They looked around and saw a couple of large trees near the rear of the building with branches nearly touching the roof. The ends of the branches were way too small to climb or try to jump to. Even if they could somehow do it, the zombies below were at least ten deep. They would just end up stuck in a tree.

Anna slumped down and sighed. It wasn't in her nature to give up, but no matter what she tried to come up with, there was just no way out of the bar. She needed some kind of distraction.

"Emily!" Anna said suddenly. "We've got a bar full of alcohol which means we're sitting on a building full of fuel. Maybe we can use it to distract them."

"Wait, you want to start more fires to try to get out of here? We could set the whole building up in flames. It would take a hell of a lot to distract them," Emily said.

"It's worth a try, though," Anna said with determination in her voice. It was killing her that she couldn't look for Camille. She was willing to try just about anything.

"Anna, no, it's not," Emily said firmly. "There's got to be at least five hundred of them down there. Do you think you're going to make Molotov cocktails or something? You'll end up killing us too." Emily was just as adamant as Anna was.

"Well, I don't know what the hell else to do," Anna said.

"We wait. We have food, water, and shelter. We have to wait for some kind of opening," Emily said.

The faint sound of an engine approaching in the distance gradually filled the air. It was hard to hear over the noise the zombies made, but with no other competing sounds, they both realized that the vehicle was heading their way. Both women looked around eagerly, hoping that this might finally be their chance. Then they saw it. A gray pickup truck was speeding down the road, driving far too fast, and headed for a specific place. No one would drive

84

that fast with zombies around unless they were hurrying toward someone or something. Anna and Emily both yelled and waved their hands, but the driver seemed to be focused on the road ahead of him and never glanced their way. Even if he had, it would have taken a lot of luck for him to see them on top of the building. They sighed with frustration as the pickup sped out of sight.

"Maybe the zombies will follow it," Anna said hopefully.

As they watched, some of the zombies between the bar and the road turned toward the noise of the retreating truck. It was an agonizingly slow process, but gradually about a hundred of the dead stumbled and shuffled about in the direction the truck had gone. Some of the zombies around the front of the building were drawn by the moving crowd and started to follow as well. Within an hour, about half of the zombies that were surrounding the bar had left to follow the others. They were left with about a hundred or so to contend with.

"This may be our chance," Anna said. "There are only about a hundred of them, and they're spread out around the building."

"What's the plan?" Emily asked. "We still can't just run through them, and we don't have a vehicle."

"Maybe we shoot our way out the front door then run around the corner to the houses back there. We're bound to find a car at one of them."

Emily shook her head, and a shiver ran up her spine. She'd run through plenty of zombies during her initial escape from the beach. She was worried about the gunfire drawing too many of them in and having to run through a thicker crowd without a clear path of escape.

"If we can fight past the crowd, where are we running to?" Emily asked and waved in the general direction of the house-lined street behind the bar. "We should pick a house now. Preferably one with a vehicle in the driveway."

"They're all going to be drawn to the gunfire, and most of them will come after us. But remember, they're slow as fuck. If we have a solid plan, I think we can make it," Anna said. "I say we run between those houses until we're on the next street over, then find a house over there. It'll give us a few minutes of breathing room to find a car."

Emily walked around the roof of the building, looking at the zombies down below. Some of them shuffled about aimlessly, seemingly confused as to whether or not there was still a meal awaiting them inside of the building. The others remained pressed up against the walls and front door. The back of the building was far less crowded, with only a dozen or so zombies lingering near the rear door.

"All right, I think you're right. It's time. There are only about a dozen around the back of the building," Emily said. "I think we may be able to do this without using our guns. If we can run around them, I don't think the others will see us or follow."

"Let's get moving," Anna said as she started down the ladder back into the storage room. She didn't want to wait another minute.

Emily followed her back down to the storage room. Their backpacks were still full of supplies and ready to go. They both wore guns on their belts and readied their knives. When Emily opened the door, Anna was going to charge out first to kill any zombies blocking their exit with Emily following behind her.

"Are you ready?" Emily asked. She'd removed the drop bar and unlocked the other two locks on the door,

86

prepared to push it open as soon as Anna gave her the word.

"Open it," Anna replied.

As Emily pushed the door open, it hit two zombies that had been standing directly in its path. The first fell to the ground while the other was wedged in place and became a doorstop. Unconcerned with closing the door behind them, they quickly darted around both zombies. Before the remaining dead could react, both women took off, running for the street behind the bar. They dashed between houses and shoved a few zombies out of the way. They continued forward until they were two streets over, hoping that the zigzagging between houses was enough to throw the zombies off their trail. They stopped to catch their breath and get a good look at the area. There weren't any zombies nearby, but further down the street, a couple of dozen zombies shuffled aimlessly.

"Let's cut over at least one more street, maybe two," Anna said quietly. She didn't want to do anything with that many zombies so close to them. They carefully cut between the two closest houses and found both had fenced yards. Anna took a quick look at the gate to see that it was unlocked then quietly opened it. They crept silently through the yard until they reached the rear of the chain-link fence. With no gate in sight, they had to climb over it. Seeing no zombies nearby, they climbed over the fence as quietly as they could, landing in another backyard that was free of zombies. They slowly made their way to the side of the house to look at the street in front of it. There weren't any dead in sight, so they stopped to take a better look around and decide where to go next.

"What do you think? Look for a car here or keep going?" Anna asked.

"Let's look around here. For all we know, the next street could be full of zombies," Emily said. There weren't any zombies shuffling around nearby, and knowing the closest that they'd seen were two streets over gave them some time to find a car and figure out what to do next.

"Let's look for a house with an SUV or truck in the driveway," Anna said.

They kept low as they moved from house to house. When they were three houses down, four zombies seemingly came out of nowhere and crossed their path. One was a tall man with a muscular build and his cheek torn halfway off his face but with no other visible injuries. Another was a child no more than ten years old. She had numerous bite marks up and down her arms. A morbidly obese woman in a torn summer dress splattered with dried blood pushed past the child in her eagerness to consume a fresh meal. A thirty-something woman missing a chunk of her neck completed the pack of four.

The tall man immediately reached for Anna and managed to grasp her arm with his hand. She was surprised by his brute strength and the pain that his grip caused. Unable to pull her arm away, she started to panic. A glance to her left told her that Emily was struggling with the obese woman and the other two zombies were about to close in on them. With no other option, Anna pulled her gun from her holster and fired directly into the face of the zombie that gripped her arm. He went down instantly, but his fingers still grasped her arm. She turned and fired three shots at the obese zombie bearing down on Emily with the third round striking it in the head. The last two zombies were close enough to bite, so Anna quickly shot them both.

"Are there any more?" Anna asked, gasping as she tried to pry the dead fingers from her arm.

"Not yet, but there will be after those shots," Emily answered. She was absentmindedly rubbing at a cut on her hand as she looked around.

"Holy shit Emily, were you bitten?" Anna asked worriedly when she saw the lightly bleeding cut on Emily's hand.

"No," Emily said. "That bitch scratched me while I was trying to fight her off."

"Are you sure? Let me take a look at it," Anna said.

"It's just a scratch, Anna," Emily said, annoyed. "We've gotta move now before all of the zombies around here home in on us. You can look at it once we find a place to stop."

As Emily spoke, zombies started to appear up and down the street, coming out of houses and from places unknown. Knowing they had very little time, Anna and Emily hurried across the street to cut between the houses there. As they neared the rear of one house, a zombie came around the corner. Anna shoved it out of her way, but it was replaced by another, then another. They had no choice but to take out all three zombies. Since they had already made so much noise shooting the other zombies, Anna fired at all three of them. Nerves frayed, even at such close range, it took six shots before all three were down.

"Damn it," Anna said. They were going to have to go further to find a vehicle because there were too many zombies around that had been drawn by the sound of gunfire. She quickly reloaded just to be safe in case she had to use her gun again before they found a place to stop.

They continued past the three dead zombies on the ground and into the backyard they had been heading for. It was a small enough piece of land that they could see that there were no zombies, so they rushed through to the rear of the yard. The back of the garage bordered the rear of the yard, so they dashed behind it for a moment as they looked around to see where to go next. Both backyards they faced were clear of the dead, so they continued to move forward. They were very careful as they reached the sides of the houses to make sure they weren't caught by surprise again by zombies coming their way. They eased their way toward the fronts of both houses and saw dozens of zombies in the street ahead.

"Fuck," Anna said. "Let's get back behind this house."

They eased their way back to the rear of the house and checked to make sure that the yards were still clear.

"I'm going to take a look inside the patio door," Emily said just before sprinting away. Anna watched and was amazed when the door slid open freely. She hurried over to Emily, and they carefully made their way inside the house. Finding themselves standing in a dark kitchen, they both stood silently to listen for any noises coming from within the house. After about two minutes of silence, they crept their way through the house. It was a small ranch-style home sparsely furnished with very few decorations. The kitchen counters were bare, and the dining room held nothing but a table and chairs.

Emily opened the fridge to find it empty then turned on the faucet to get a drink of water, but no water came. The living room was nearly as empty. It all felt very strange until Anna braved a quick look out the front window and saw the 'FOR RENT' sign on the front lawn.

"Of all the houses we could have tried," Anna started as she shook her head. "There's definitely no vehicle here."

"At least there aren't any zombies," Emily replied. "And we're not surrounded for a change."

Anna looked out the front window at the numerous zombies in the street. They were wandering aimlessly and didn't know that the women were inside the house. About half a dozen houses down across the street, she saw a red SUV parked in a driveway. If the zombies continued to shuffle about as they were, they would probably continue to make their way down the street and beyond until something new caught their attention. Once that happened, Anna wanted to head for the house with the SUV. They couldn't do much without transportation.

"You're right. We're not surrounded, and they don't know we're in here," Anna said. "Once they finish making their way down the street we can leave and try for that SUV."

They both opened bottles of water from their packs and sat quietly as they waited.

Chapter Ten

Day 4

Max's stomach was rumbling, and he didn't remember when he had last eaten. There was a convenience store in a little plaza coming up on the left, so he decided he'd run in and grab whatever food he could find. Four zombies shuffled around the parking lot, but they were spread out. He didn't know what he might find inside the store, so he thought it was best to take out the zombies before he went inside. It didn't take much effort for him to put down all four of them. He took another look around to make sure the area was clear before walking up to the glass door of the store.

Looking through the door, he didn't see any of the dead stumbling around. He opened the door slowly then swore when a little bell at the top of it rang to announce his presence. He took another glance behind him then walked inside. He heard the telltale sound of raspy moans, but it sounded like there were only a couple of them. A quick look down the end of each aisle revealed nothing, but at the rear of the little store two zombies were stumbling out from the office and storeroom area. He kicked one in the knee to knock it off balance but it stayed on its feet after a little stumble. That was all the time he needed to kill the first one before taking care of the second. There was a thumping sound coming from somewhere in the back, but he didn't feel the need to clear the storage room since this was a quick stop. He walked back to one of the little food aisles and grabbed an armful of beef jerky. Eyeing a display of trail mix, he grabbed a couple of bags from behind the counter and filled them to the brim with jerky, nuts, and trail mix. With the electricity still on, he grabbed a couple of bottles of cold soda and a few more energy drinks. It was plenty to hold him over for a while so he wouldn't have to make another stop like this. He had a full pack of water in the truck but grabbed a case on his way out the door anyway. He thought of Frank and Junior being stuck in the firetruck with no water and shuddered. He wasn't going to get himself stuck anywhere without supplies, and the day was already heating up to be another scorcher.

Max pulled out onto the street and thought of the pharmacy coming up at the next intersection. Knowing that medications were soon going to be hard to come by, he decided to make a stop. With his wife being a nurse, Max knew that she would want a stockpile of various medications in case of illness or injury. He pulled into the parking lot and parked near the door. A half dozen zombies were lingering nearby, and he knew he should take them out before he went inside, or else they might draw a larger crowd. The zombie closest to him was a frail fifty-something man dressed in what was once a nice shirt and tie before it became blood-splattered when the man had lost a chunk of his neck to a zombie bite. Max quickly and easily grabbed the man and thrust his knife through his ear. Close behind was a teenage girl wearing very little clothing. Both hands were missing fingers, and several bite wounds ran up her left arm. Max took a handful of her hair to hold her in place, then plunged his knife in. A little further away, two twenty-something male zombies shuffled toward Max. They both wore tattered jeans with concert t-shirts and shared the same curly blond hair, making Max believe that they had probably been brothers.

93

He generally didn't notice or care about those details because they were all zombies, but the matching hair stood out to him. They were both built pretty solid with minimal visible bite wounds to impede their movements, so Max figured he'd better separate them before trying to kill them. He shoved the one on the left, causing it to stumble backward a few steps as he took those precious seconds to kill the blond on the right. He turned back and killed the first blond as it regained its footing, but before it could lay a hand on Max. He looked around to make sure no other zombies had wandered into the area before taking down the last two. Both were fast, easy kills.

The store was unlocked and well-lit, which wasn't surprising given that the zombie apocalypse had started on a Friday afternoon. He stepped inside and stood by the door for a moment to see if he could hear anything moving within the store. There was a faint tapping sound coming from the rear of the store and a pair of shuffling feet somewhere nearby. Max looked up at the nearest security mirror to see a zombie about to round the corner toward the front door. Max met the zombie halfway and dropped it to the floor with a quick thrust of his knife. Looking around, he could see that the store had already been ransacked. Smears of dried blood coated the counter by one of the registers, and a dead body lay on the floor behind it. Full displays of chips, sunglasses, and candy were knocked to the floor. Blood was smeared throughout the front of the store, with several more bodies scattered around. Max silently crept past the end of each aisle to make sure there were no surprises in store for him. At the fourth one, he found a legless zombie crawling toward him at an agonizingly slow pace. He walked over to it, bent down, and put it out of its misery. Looking around,

94

he didn't see anything else other than the mess of store goods knocked onto the floor throughout the store. There was still a tapping sound coming from the direction of the pharmacy, which sat just out of sight in the far corner after a small curve in the wall. Max used the security mirrors hanging near the ceiling to help make sure that the area was at least relatively clear. When he finally rounded the corner toward the pharmacy, he saw several dead zombies on the floor, and the security door to the pharmacy itself stood wide open.

The tapping sound was coming from somewhere beyond that door. Max quietly stepped through the open doorway and looked around. The pharmacy had been ransacked. Baskets filled with bags of prescriptions had been knocked to the floor, and several shelves stood empty. He followed the tapping sound to the controlled substance area. What should have been locked up to protect the drugs from would-be thieves was freely exposed. The tapping sound Max had been hearing was coming from the pharmacist turned zombie who was wedged in by the door for controlled substances. Pen in hand, the mindless zombie moved his hand up and down with the pen hitting the door, creating the tapping sound. Before looking any further, Max put down the pharmacist. A slight noise from the corner grabbed Max's attention. Sitting on the floor with his back against the wall was a twenty-something guy bleeding freely from a large bite wound on his arm. Max looked closer to see if the guy was armed but saw no weapons of any kind.

"Hey man," the guy said quietly.

"You alone?" Max asked. He wasn't sure what he was dealing with yet and wanted to make sure no surprises were going to jump out at him and that the guy didn't have friends with him ready and waiting to make a move.

"Yeah," he said with a gasp. "I was an idiot trying to get into the narcotics and didn't see the pharmacist until it was too late."

"The pharmacist bit you?" Max asked.

"I thought the pharmacy was clear, so I didn't even have my knife out. When he clenched down on me, he ripped out my bicep. It was all I could do to shove him behind that door."

"You have anyone out there waiting for you?" Max asked.

"Nah man, I'm on my own. Shit, I should have never left my house. I'm David," he introduced himself.

"Max. Can I do anything for you? You want some water or something?" Max looked closer at the wound and knew that the guy didn't have much time left.

"Keep me company for a few? I don't want to die alone, man," David said. His face was so pale it was nearly white.

Max took another look around to make sure everything was still clear before he answered.

"Yeah, I'll stay," Max said.

David nodded his thanks as his breathing grew more labored. He never said another word before his head dropped to his chest and the last bit of life left his body.

"Shit," Max mumbled to himself. He crouched down and thrust his knife through David's ear. The guy had survived the first few days of the apocalypse then died because he went looking for a quick high. Max just shook his head. What a waste.

He stood back up and looked over at the controlled substances. He grabbed a few bags and cleared an entire shelf of painkillers, then quietly walked around the pharmacy looking for antibiotics. Most of the medications were foreign to him, and he had no idea what they were for. Finally, he found a section filled with some familiar names of antibiotics. He grabbed various bottles until he had a bagful. He looked around some more, then grabbed steroids, the allergy and cold medications kept behind the counter, and a few other random things that he was unfamiliar with. He didn't know if or when any of those items might come in handy but figured it was worth grabbing what he could while he was there.

As Max took one last look around the pharmacy, he jumped when he heard a loud slapping noise coming from his left. A quick look revealed a few zombies pressed up against the glass of the drive-through window. He let out a sigh of relief and figured he'd better get moving before he drew a crowd. He went down the regular store aisles and filled a few bags with first aid supplies, peroxide, and alcohol. Not wanting to push his luck any further, he quietly made his way back to the front of the store. He looked out the door to see a handful of zombies shuffling around the parking lot but none near the door. He hurried out, and put all of his overflowing bags in the back seat, then got into the truck. A few more zombies had turned toward the store and were headed his way, so he quickly pulled out of the parking lot to put some distance between them and resume his search for Camille.

Chapter Eleven

Day 4

Camille eased herself out of bed then slowly walked to the bedroom door. Her knee protested as she put her weight on it, but she made herself keep moving. Once in the hallway, she heard the voices of the family who had taken her in. She followed the sound to find them once again in the living room at the rear of the house.

"Good morning, Camille," Elizabeth said warmly, although Camille thought she sensed some tension in her voice. "How are you feeling?"

"Much better, but a little sore all over," Camille said.

"A little more rest and some ice should help quite a bit," Elizabeth said as she handed her a bottle of water and two pills to help with the pain. "Sweetie, sit down on that recliner so you can keep your knee elevated. I'll be right back with some breakfast and a fresh ice pack."

She returned a moment later with a plate of cinnamon rolls and fresh fruit in one hand and an ice pack in the other. Camille accepted both gratefully and started eating.

Elizabeth and Bradford sat down and got comfortable on plush couches. Camille couldn't help but notice that the noise from the zombies was louder than it had been the night before. She thought Bradford and Elizabeth both seemed a bit stressed.

"What's it like outside?" She asked. The couple exchanged a quick glance before speaking.

"Well, the house is surrounded by a few hundred zombies, but they're mostly focused on the rear of the house," Bradford decided to be blunt with his answer. "I don't think they'll be able to get inside, but with so many of them out there, I just don't see a way to try to get you back home, at least not yet."

Camille sighed. She was grateful to be safe and felt she couldn't have stumbled upon a nicer, more generous family to take her in, but she desperately wanted to get back home to her own. She also worried that the sheer number of zombies surrounding the house would cause the wall of windows to break. She shivered at the thought of hundreds of zombies making their way inside.

"Do you really think the weight of so many zombies pushing up against the house isn't going to cause the windows to break? What about the doors? With so many of them out there, you don't think they're going to manage to push or break the doors open?" Camille asked.

"The doors and doorframes are reinforced with steel. I honestly don't think they can get through," Elizabeth said. "I think the glass is thick enough that it will hold as long as they don't all pile up against it." That was exactly what Camille was afraid of; that the zombies would all pile up against the glass. At least the zombies couldn't see them up on the second floor, or else they would have been in a feeding frenzy.

"The yard slopes downward toward the beach. That should help keep too many of them from pushing up against the windows. If the ground were level, I'd be much more concerned," Bradford said, then sighed. "A fire started up last night in Westlake and has burned through two entire blocks of houses. We're hoping it will eventually burn itself out before it spreads any further."

"We're just keeping a close eye on things right now," Elizabeth said.

Neither of them had to say any more for Camille to understand that they were potentially in a precarious situation, but she thought that they were far enough from Westlake that it wasn't likely to become a problem for them.

"I've been packing up bags of supplies, so we have some things ready to go just in case we have to leave in a hurry," Bradford said. "We packed some extra things for you."

"But you said there are hundreds of zombies surrounding the house. How would we get through them?" Camille asked.

"I'm trying to come up with a plan for that, but honestly, I'm not sure yet," Bradford said. "We'll just have to figure things out as we go."

"In the meantime, you need to rest that knee as much as you can," Elizabeth said. "I don't think that we're going to end up running around on foot, but if you need to move quickly, your knee needs some time to heal. Don't get up, sweetie. If you need anything, just let one of us know."

"I understand how badly you want to get back to your family, but I don't think we're going to be able to do anything about it today," Bradford said. "So just listen to my wife's advice; she's a fantastic surgeon, and she knows what she's doing."

Camille appreciated their care and refuge but knew she couldn't wait another day to try to get home to her family. Before she could put her thoughts into words, Elizabeth picked up a remote and turned the TV on. The screen was so large that it filled nearly half of one wall. It almost felt like a mini-movie theater. Camille thought she was going to flip through channels to see if any of them were still on the air, but instead, the screen split into more than a dozen smaller frames. Each frame showed live security footage from views all around the outside of the mansion, covering every entrance as well as each side of the home, the driveway, and the beach.

Nearly every camera captured close-up images of zombies surrounding the house. Elizabeth pressed some buttons to zoom out on the view outside. There were indeed at least a few hundred zombies surrounding the house and covering the beach, but there weren't very many at the front of the house.

Camille perked up a bit when she saw the views of the front of the house and the street. She had already run through smaller crowds of zombies, much like what she was viewing on the monitor. Where the family that had rescued her saw hopelessness, she saw a possible opening.

She glanced at Elizabeth and Bradford and saw the strain evident on their faces. She wondered if either of them had come face to face with a zombie yet. Somehow she thought it was unlikely that they had. With the safety of their home, they would have had no reason to. She tried to imagine the two of them using knives or guns to fight off the dead, but the image seemed ridiculous in her mind. She wondered what kind of weapons they had or if they even had weapons.

"Do you have guns and knives ready if we have to fight our way out?" She asked as she double-checked that she still had her knife on her belt. Knowing it was there was reassuring.

"We have some guns for self-defense as well as some hunting rifles, and I have half a dozen good knives," Bradford said. "I've put them with our supplies."

Elizabeth visibly blanched at the thought of using a knife or firing a gun.

"I've had to kill some zombies. You may have to mentally prepare yourself for it, especially if you have to use a knife. The easiest way to kill them is to plunge the knife through their eye or ear. It's gross, and the smell is horrible, but if you hesitate…" Camille trailed off. She was a guest in their home but felt that she was better prepared to fight the zombies than they were. "We've avoided using guns since they're drawn to sound."

"If we're forced to leave due to the fire, perhaps some of them will be distracted by the flames. Maybe we won't have to go through so many of them," Elizabeth said hopefully.

"For now, we're just going to make sure we're prepared for a worst-case scenario," Bradford said. "We may be lucky. The zombies could get distracted, and the fire may burn out before it reaches this far."

Camille turned back to the monitors to get a better look at what the front of the house looked like. She was already so accustomed to zombies that the images didn't disturb her much. As she looked at the various screens, she noticed that some of the zombies got carried away into the water, unable to maneuver where the waves gently lapped the shore. As more zombies went into the water, others that surrounded the house made the push back toward the water.

The medication, ice, and rest were all helping to relieve the pain in her knee. She felt she could use it, but it would be a long walk home, and if she had to run, her knee might give her trouble. She wondered if the kind couple would let her take one of their cars. She didn't know how to drive, but how hard could it be? There were no other drivers on the road; she'd just have to dodge zombies and abandoned cars. All she could think about was getting home to her family. She knew her mom had to be out of her mind with worry, and her dad and Jesse could be home by now. She was sure they were out searching for her, but how could they possibly find her? They didn't know where to look and could be anywhere. They didn't even know which direction to search in. She'd put quite a bit of distance between herself and the horde and had run further than she ever would have thought possible. She was interrupted from her thoughts when Bradford commented on the zombies getting carried away into the water.

"I know, I've been watching the monitors, and there are fewer zombies in front of the house than there were just a little while ago," Camille said. "A lot of them are getting washed out into the lake."

"You're right," Bradford said as he looked at the screen. "There don't seem to be many new ones taking their places out front."

"I need to get home to my family. Depending on what kind of route I can take, it's probably about three miles. I can walk it as long as I can avoid any hordes, but I'm worried my knee might give me a problem if I have to run."

"Sweetie, even if we could figure out a way to get you out of the house, I don't think you're up for a three-mile trip. You know it won't be an easy three miles, and who knows how many detours you'll have to make?" Elizabeth said. "It could take you a day or two to get home if there are hordes out there."

"Well, I wanted to ask you something," Camille hesitated a moment. "Would you let me take one of your cars? I don't have my learner's permit yet, but I wouldn't have to worry about other drivers on the road. I would just have to avoid zombies and deserted cars."

Elizabeth looked at Bradford, and after a moment, he nodded his head.

"We have more vehicles than we can use," he said. "Even if we have to leave here ourselves and we take two, there's still two more in the garage, although the sports car wouldn't do you any good. You could take one of our SUVs, but there are still way too many zombies out front. You would never get through them before they surrounded you."

"There's not that many. I think I could get through them pretty easily," Camille said. "And the sound of the car may draw away most of the zombies around your house. Once they're distracted, they'll forget you were ever in here, and you'll be much safer." She was starting to get excited about the possibility of heading home to her family.

"I suppose most of the dead will try to follow you. You could make your escape, and we wouldn't have to worry about being surrounded anymore," Bradford was picking up on Camille's excitement and started to feel optimistic himself. They could give this poor girl a shot at getting back to her family while in the process making their house more secure. He and his wife could survive for months, if not a year, without having to leave their home for supplies. If the zombies followed Camille, they would be about as safe as they possibly could be.

"Well, if we're doing this, I'm going to make sure you have any supplies you might need," Elizabeth said. "I'm going to grab the bag we'd started packing for you and top it off with some other things." She went to the kitchen to add bottled water and food in case Camille didn't make it home right away. She worried about the young girl leaving on her own but knew there was nothing she could do about it. The girl needed to get back to her family, and Elizabeth understood how important family was. She returned a few minutes later with a nearly full backpack.

"Camille, I added some protein and granola bars for you. They'll be light to carry if you end up on foot and will hold you over until you get home. I'm also adding some mild painkillers and anti-inflammatory pills for your knee. Don't take the pain medication unless you have to; it might dull your senses. But if you find yourself stuck hiding somewhere and you need it, then take it," Elizabeth said.

"Thank you so much," Camille said. "You and your husband have been so wonderful to me."

"From what you've told us about your family, they would have done the same thing," Elizabeth said.

Bradford added a sheathed knife to the bag, knowing that Camille already had one on her but wanted to make sure she had a spare. He held a small handgun with several boxes of ammo.

"Do you know how to use this?" he asked.

Camille took a closer look at it. It was the same as the one her brother had shown her. "Yes, well enough at least. Thank you," she said as she put it inside the backpack.

"Are you ready for this?" Bradford asked as he took a quick look at the security monitors.

Camille nodded. She was starting to feel a bit overwhelmed, but the feeling was surpassed by intense anticipation. Elizabeth unexpectedly pulled her into a warm hug. "Be careful out there. Get home safe to your family," she said.

"I will," Camille said, then turned to Bradford. He was ready to take her down to the garage while Elizabeth stayed by the monitors.

She found that she could walk on her knee fairly well, even down the long flight of stairs. He led her to the garage and one of the luxury SUVs inside. He went over the basics and got her settled in with the seat and mirrors adjusted, then showed her the remote for the garage door opener.

"I'll be in the garage next to the door leading into the house. When you're ready, just press the button on the garage door remote. If any zombies try to get into the garage, I'll take them out, and then I'll close the door after you pull out. Drive fast down the driveway and into the street and make the first turn you can. That should keep you from becoming surrounded," Bradford said. "After that, just get yourself home as quickly as you can."

"Thank you so much for everything," Camille said sincerely. She might make it home to her family soon. The thought of seeing them again caused her to tear up, but she managed to pull herself together. She watched as Bradford walked over to the door to the house. She waited until he was ready, then she took a few deep breaths, put the SUV in drive, and then pressed the button on the garage door opener.

Chapter Twelve

Day 4

Between looking for gas and going to the dealership, Max found himself several miles south of the area he wanted to search. He didn't think there was any way Camille had made it this far to the east, let alone five miles to the south, so he drove a little way before starting another grid search. He kept his eyes open for any signs of life as he slowly drove along and ate some jerky. It wasn't long before he started running into larger groups of zombies. Most of the streets were two lanes and had wrecked or abandoned cars on them. He wound his way around and dodged as many zombies as he could. When he rounded one corner, he found about a dozen zombies blocking his way. He could have braked in time, but he thought it was as good a time as any to see how the plow on the truck handled them. He drove straight through them, with several falling to either side of the truck, one cartwheeling over the top high into the air before slamming into the ground and two falling underneath. The truck handled the minor beating so well that it was almost as if he'd just hit a pothole or two.

He continued driving until he came across a multi-car pileup that filled an entire intersection. With deep ditches on either side of the road, it wasn't worth trying to find a way past it, so he turned around and cut through another housing development. Almost everywhere he looked, he saw dead bodies, scattered shoes, dried blood and entrails, discarded limbs, and pieces of clothing. The road was covered with a thin layer of blackish-red zombie slush, indicating that a horde of some size had come through recently. It was still wet and shiny even in the heat of the day. Soon he came upon some crawlers and realized that he wasn't far behind the horde. Max didn't want to draw their attention, so he made the next possible turn and backtracked until he was in another development. He was surprised by how many hordes seemed to come through, but he supposed it didn't take much to gather their attention.

He noticed the smoke trailing high in the air in the distance. The fire he'd started was spreading a little further, and billows of smoke hung in the air just a mile or two away. He wondered if the horde had been drawn to the fire. He'd seen plenty of burned zombies, and the flames didn't kill them, but they were ashy and seemed to shed layers of their bodies as pieces flaked off. He hoped that they were all going to the fire and that they would burn badly enough that they would at least lose the ability to walk. He figured that once they got ashy and flaky that they probably didn't last much longer, at least not on their feet. It would be nice if one good thing came from the burning neighborhood. The fire was still miles east of his home, but he planned to keep a close eye on it. It didn't seem likely that it could burn to his house, but he'd seen much of downtown Cleveland go up in flames. With no rain and nothing to stop them, who knew how far it would spread.

As Max drove slowly down yet another street, he saw a house in the distance that was surrounded by zombies. He knew the odds of finding his daughter inside were small, but there was someone trapped in the house. He thought about it for a moment then decided to try to drive them all away. He put his hand on the horn and fired his shotgun a few times. That was all it took to turn the heads of most of the crowd. He hit the horn again and slowly drove past the house. He crept along at less than five miles an hour to give the zombies a chance to follow him. He kept making noise and watched in his mirrors as the dead seemed to leave the house as one in pursuit of a new meal. He led them nearly a half-mile away before turning and speeding back toward the house. When he pulled up, there were only a half dozen left in the yard, all of them slowly making their way toward the street. He saw curtains move in the living room window, so he pulled into the driveway, got out, and started killing the remaining zombies. When they were spread out, it was pretty easy to take them down. Less than a minute later, he dropped the last zombie and looked at the house.

He was surprised that no one came rushing out the door and into their vehicle to escape. He saw the flutter of curtains again, and his curiosity got the better of him. He approached the front door, prepared to lightly tap on it. He didn't want to make enough noise to get the attention of any zombies that might be lingering in the area. Before he could knock, a fifty-ish woman opened the door. Her short hair was graying, crow's feet extended from both eyes, and smile lines around her mouth gave the impression of a woman who had experienced a lot of joy in her life. She was dressed sensibly in jeans and a t-shirt with hiking boots.

"Thank you for leading them off. I'm Maggie," she introduced herself.

"Max. You doing okay in there?" he asked. "I was kind of surprised that you were still here when I circled back. I thought you might have taken the time to escape to somewhere else."

"Well, I don't know where else might be safer," she said practically. "I was boarding up my house to hunker down when I attracted too many of the dead. Somehow or another, I got lucky, and they didn't get in."

Max looked at the front of the house and saw some cracked boards on the ground, damaged by the zombies that had surrounded the place.

"Looks like they messed up most of your plywood," Max said.

"I reckon they did. I have a little more in the garage, but I'm not sure if it'll be enough," she said while she looked around to assess the damage. "I'm used to being by myself and didn't have anywhere to go, so I figured I'd try to make the place safe and stay home."

"Where were you while your house was surrounded?" Max asked.

"In the basement. I bolted and blocked the door. There's an extra fridge and a bathroom down there, so I was going to be okay for a while. When I heard your shotgun, I hurried upstairs to see what was going on. I didn't think anything was going to make the dead leave," Maggie said.

Max was torn. He needed to get a move on, but there was something about this woman that he liked. He wanted to help her if he could.

"Look, I can help you board things up if we move fast," He hesitated, then made up his mind and said, "Or you can come with me. My house is well fortified and a little off the grid. My son's there, my best friend's family, and two firefighters we found a couple of days ago."

"Your wife?" Maggie asked gently, assuming the worst.

"She's missing. So is my daughter. I'm driving around searching for them. It's a long story," Max said.

110

Maggie seemed to be able to read Max about as well as he was able to read her. Her gut told her that he was a good man and she should take him up on his offer.

"Do you mind if I pack up a few things?" she asked.

"Not at all. Do you need any help?" Max responded.

"I've got a full pantry if you want to grab some things. I just want to gather up some clothes and a few odds and ends if there's time," Maggie said.

Max took a look around to make sure there weren't any zombies nearby, then said, "Lead the way."

While Maggie packed up the things she wanted to take with her, Max checked out the pantry. It held enough food to feed a family of four for a month. He laughed to himself, thinking that Maggie shopped just like his wife did. He filled one large recyclable bag after another and put them by the front door. Several cases of water and cold drinks from the fridge topped everything off. With each trip to the door, he took a good look around outside to make sure everything was still relatively clear. He didn't see a single zombie. It seemed that all the zombies in the neighborhood must have followed him when he had led them away earlier.

"Wow, you work fast," Maggie said when she met him at the door with two duffle bags.

"Have to nowadays," Max said. "It's clear out there, so let's go ahead and get everything loaded so we can get out of here."

It took him half a dozen trips to the truck before he had all of the groceries and water loaded, and they were ready to go. They both got settled into the truck, and Max backed out of the driveway before they resumed talking.

"Have you been in your house since the start?" Max asked.

111

"Yes, I worked from home and set my own hours, so I was lucky enough to be inside and relatively out of harm's way for that first day. The dead weren't too bad until I started boarding up the house. I didn't realize how many had heard me until there was nothing I could do about it," she said. "I had to kill a few of them. I used a knife. Seems to work pretty well."

Max was relieved to hear that she'd already killed some zombies. He didn't want to try to teach her everything he'd learned so far if he didn't have to. As he slowly drove back toward his house, they talked and got to know each other a little better. Maggie had been widowed about ten years back, and she and her husband had been unable to have children. Between that loss and her working from home, she was used to being alone most of the time. Max gave her a shortened version of his story from the last few days and told her about Anna and Camille.

"I can keep you company while you search," Maggie said. "We don't have to go back to your house just yet. I'm capable, armed, and can kill the dead. I can also take over driving if you need a break." She came across as a very practical, no-nonsense woman. "I may be old enough to be your…"

"Big sister," Max said.

"Right, big sister," Maggie said, and they both laughed. "But I can take care of myself."

"Well, how about we continue my grid search for a while until we get near my house. I don't know exactly what I'm looking for. Some sign of life at one of these houses or someplace surrounded by zombies," Max said. "But it can get really bad out here really fast. I lost my best friend trying to get home from downtown, and I lost a new friend last night. There are hordes of zombies out here and no way of knowing when you might run into them."

"I'm up for it, Max," Maggie said. "I'd like to help you find your wife and daughter, to feel like I'm doing something useful."

Max nodded then resumed his search. He didn't mind having some company, and Maggie might see something that he missed. His eyes darted with worry back to the heavy smoke only a mile or two away. It looked like it was burning up an entire neighborhood, but he couldn't tell if it was still spreading.

Chapter Thirteen

Day 4

Anna watched anxiously as the zombies slowly made their way down the street. She could see the tail end of the group, and she was eager for them to pass by. It had been hours already, and this wasn't even a horde. They must have been drawing in more zombies as they shuffled along, growing their ranks as they passed. She hoped the house with the red SUV was going to be free of zombies once they were finally able to make their way over to it. She'd seen zombies stumble out of quite a few houses on the street to join the group passing by. They still didn't seem to be able to open doors, and most of them got tripped up on porch steps. The zombies that came from the houses left through doors that were already open.

"Anna, you should eat something," Emily said. "It looks like we're going to have an opening soon, and you need to get some food in your stomach."

Anna hadn't had much of an appetite since the zombie apocalypse had started, and what little appetite she did have completely vanished after Camille disappeared. The last thing she felt like doing was eating; however, she was a nurse and knew that she had to eat to keep her strength up.

"Thanks Emily," Anna said as she accepted an energy bar. Anna sat with her back against the wall as she ate and watched Emily at the window. The blonde woman was strikingly beautiful, and, as Anna was learning, she was truly kind and selfless. There was no reason for Emily to have risked her life helping Anna search for Camille other than the fact that she had a huge heart. Anna realized she was quite lucky that their lives had intertwined and vowed to try not to be so snappy with her. She felt a little guilty for questioning Emily earlier about the scratch on her hand. The poor woman had seen her brother die after a zombie's tooth had barely grazed him; she would never have lied about a bite. Anna had such a hard time trusting new people, but the world was different now. She would be more cautious than ever, but she would trust those who had proven they were trustworthy.

Emily watched the tail end of the zombies as they passed by the house. They were achingly slow in their movements. Another half an hour, and they should be clear to make a move. She watched the zombies shuffle down the street and took in their appearances. Most of them had horrible bite wounds to their faces, necks, arms, and hands. Here and there, a zombie walked along, displaying stark white ribs with empty abdominal cavities or lengths of intestines slowly falling out. She noticed that some seemed fresh while others were just starting the beginning of the slow decaying process. It seemed that most people died or turned that first day, but there had to people hiding or trapped in various houses and buildings. Emily knew that their small group was hardly the only group of people still living in the area. Until they had left Anna's house to search for Camille, they had done their best to stay hidden, so she imagined others were doing the same. The sheer number of zombies they had encountered was terrifying, though. Between the huge horde that had passed by yesterday and all of the dead they'd seen since then, she wondered just how many people did survive. For there to be so many zombies meant there could only be a small number of survivors.

She looked over at Anna, who had resumed watching from her spot at the window, and thought about how lucky she was that Michelle and then Anna had taken her in. From her brief time with them, the two women seemed as much like sisters as they did best friends. They were so much alike in personality. Physically, Michelle was a petite little thing with long black hair and gorgeous eyes that were nearly black. She was strong, stubborn, no-nonsense, had a fearless attitude, and was a fierce protector of her family. Anna was taller with long dark hair and piercing green eyes. Like Michelle, she was strong and stubborn but also impatient, slow to trust, and just about the scariest woman Emily had ever met when it came to her children.

"Emily, I think we're in the clear," Anna said suddenly. "The last few zombies just left my line of sight."

"Are there any in the street at all? Any shamblers?" Emily asked.

"Nope. I don't see anything," Anna said with a grin. Her natural impatience, coupled with her worry for her daughter, made all of the time waiting for the zombies to pass by nearly unbearable. Seeing that their wait was finally over, she couldn't help but smile.

"Let's go out the front door then. Stay low, dash behind cars and stay out of sight until we get to that red SUV," Emily said. "Please let the house be empty and the keys easy to find," she muttered.

Anna opened the door, and they quietly walked down the front steps. She looked around and didn't see any zombies. They carefully walked along the front of the house, paused at the corner to make sure no surprises lay in wait between houses, and then continued past the next.

They walked until they were across the street from the home with the red SUV in the driveway. With their path clear, they crossed the street then crouched down next to the SUV.

"The front door is closed," Anna said quietly as she studied the front of the house. "Hopefully, it's unlocked." They crept up to the door while keeping an eye out for zombies but didn't see any. Anna tried the doorknob and found that it was locked. Looking up and down the street, they hadn't seen any other vehicles worth trying for, so she decided to check for a hidden key for the door. Both women checked the planters and rocks but found nothing.

"Let's try the back door," Emily suggested. "We could still get lucky."

Anna nodded in agreement. They walked past the front of the house around the corner of the garage and found the way clear. Within seconds they were at the back door, and this time the knob turned freely in Anna's hand. Knives at the ready, she slowly opened the door and stepped inside with Emily right behind her. They stood still for a moment to listen for the telltale sounds that zombies were in the house. Hearing nothing, they fully entered the kitchen and started looking for a key rack or a key ring on one of the counters but found nothing

"Of course, it couldn't be that easy," Anna sighed. They moved further into the house and entered a large dining room. There was some mail and clutter strewn about on the table but no keys. Off to one side sat a family room with a sectional couch and a big-screen TV. On the other side, a hallway ran off the dining room, presumably leading to the bedrooms and bathroom, which seemed the most unlikely of places to find keys. Straight ahead of them was the living room at the front of the house.

"What do you think? Living room?" Emily asked. "There could be key hooks or a little table by the door."

"Probably, I'm not sure where else to look," Anna answered as she headed for the living room. The room was neat, with nothing out of place and no sign of keys anywhere. She double-checked the area by the front door but found nothing. Annoyed, she turned back to Emily, "Where the hell else should we look?"

"You check the family room, and I'll check the master bedroom. If we don't find them there, they're probably not here," Emily was irritated too.

Both women went through and checked the rest of the house. Having wasted a good twenty minutes searching for keys that didn't seem to exist, they returned to the kitchen feeling frustrated. They were going to have to find another vehicle at a different house.

"Well, I guess we head down toward the other end of the street. There's bound to be something there," Anna said. "Let's go out quietly and make sure it's still clear out there."

They went out the back door and silently walked around the side of the house to the front as they checked the area for zombies. There was one stray zombie in the middle of the street, unfocused and standing still. They decided to slowly move past the houses one by one until they found another with a suitable vehicle in its driveway. Three houses down, they stumbled across a lone zombie standing near some bushes. It was a young brunette woman in shorts and a tank top. Several large rings of bites lined one arm, and a small chunk of flesh was missing from her neck. She turned toward Anna with outstretched arms, but Anna was easily able to thrust her knife through its ear before the zombie could grab hold of her. They continued further down the street until they saw a black SUV in one of the driveways.

"Let's try this again," Anna said as she walked toward the small front porch and up the five stairs to the door. The screen door had tinted storm windows in it and opened outward. Looking through the darkly tinted glass, she couldn't tell if the main door was open or not. The screen door was unlocked and opened freely when Anna pulled the handle. The main door behind it was wide open, and before either woman knew what was happening, zombies poured out the door and onto the porch. Anna jumped back from the reaching arms and stumbled backward down the steps landing on her tailbone on the walkway. Wincing, she struggled to get back to her feet before the zombies fell on top of her. Emily had darted to the side as the dead came out and was immediately caught in the grasp of what had been a middle-aged woman in jogging clothes. The woman had a bandage on her hand but otherwise appeared whole and had a very strong grip. Emily fought to free herself, but it was futile. The zombie's strength was greater than that of her own. Unable to find an angle to use her knife while the zombie grasped both of her arms, Emily twisted around and attempted to knock the woman down the stairs. The woman fell, but she took Emily with her. Anna had just gotten back to her feet and plunged her knife into the zombie's ear before its teeth could reach Emily's arm. The zombie's grip didn't loosen with its second death, and Emily was unable to pull herself free or get to her feet. Terrified, she kicked the dead body and pulled as hard as she could, but the dead hands remained locked around her arms, holding her in place. At least six more zombies had come out through the door and all of them stumbled down the steps toward Anna and Emily. As Emily struggled to break free, she twisted, turned, and kicked the approaching zombies. She was completely vulnerable and nearly helpless down on the ground.

A large man wearing the bloody remnants of a shirt and tie came lumbering toward them next. He had several bites of flesh torn from his arm and one of his hands. Just behind him was a teenaged boy in shorts and a t-shirt. His mouth was covered with dried blood, his shirt was stained crimson, and he had a dirty bandage wrapped around his arm. Anna shoved the man, hoping to knock him down. He was so tall that she couldn't reach anywhere near his head. He stumbled backward but didn't fall. He regained his footing and reached for her, his hand grazing her shoulder. Anna thrust her knife upward under his chin but only succeeded in causing brackish blood to drip onto her hand and arm. She tried to push him away, but his sheer size prevented her from moving him even an inch. Starting to feel desperate, she tried to kick him as hard as she could in the knee but hit his shin instead. He leaned down to grasp her arm and pulled it toward his mouth. His fingers wrapped around her arm with unbelievable strength and brought a crushing pain that she felt down to the bone. In his eagerness to try to make a meal of her, he leaned forward just enough for Anna to thrust her knife at his head. She stabbed him in the nose and cheek before finally plunging her knife through his eye. He fell to the ground hard.

Emily was trying to take down the teenaged boy as he sought her out. Unable to move freely, she laid on her back on the ground with the dead woman next to her, still holding her arms. The boy leaned down toward Emily's face, so she used every ounce of strength she had left to kick him in the knee to try to knock him back. Instead of falling backward, he fell on top of Emily. With his gnashing teeth just inches from her throat, she tried to force her knife upward and sliced his ear off. Undeterred, the boy leaned closer to take a bite when Emily managed to thrust her knife through his eye. The fetid milky fluid dripped onto her face, and his full body weight dropped on top of her. Thoroughly trapped, there was nothing else Emily could do but hope that Anna was able to kill the rest. The other zombies were nearly on top of them. Anna saw that Emily was trapped and knew that she was on her own. A blonde woman in jean shorts and a tank top displayed sickening bite wounds with most of her face cleanly ripped away to reveal her bare teeth, which formed a snarl as she reached for the women. Anna was able to grab her by her long hair and thrust her knife through the woman's ear, then immediately lunged for the next zombie. With the woman out of the way she was faced with two more teenaged zombies and an elderly man, all reaching for her at once. She shoved the old man and tried to kick one of the teens out of the way as she focused on the closest teenager. As she plunged her knife through his eye, she felt hands becoming entangled in her hair from behind, pulling her backward. She felt clumps of hair being pulled from her head as the old man tried to pull her closer while she pulled away. With no time to spare, she pulled her gun and shot the teenager point-blank in the face. She couldn't see the old man behind her but fought against his grip on her hair. She had no idea if his teeth were about to sink into her or not, so she forcibly turned her head sideways, painfully losing more of her hair in the process, and tried to shoot him in the head. Her first shot went wild, but with him partially within her field of vision, she nearly emptied her gun until a bullet finally found its way into his head. When his body dropped, she fell with him as her hair was still wrapped around his hands.

Her long dark hair fell a few inches shy of her waist, so she was able to twist her body just enough to start cutting her hair off with her knife. The knife was so sharp that it sliced her hair off quickly. With blood running down her neck and back and bloody patches around the back of her scalp burning intensely, she stood back up to look around and make sure that no more zombies were coming. None came from the house, but in either direction down the street, small groups of the dead were slowly shuffling in their direction, no doubt having been drawn by the gunfire.

"Emily, are you okay? Were you bitten?" Anna asked frantically as she struggled to pull the dead teenaged boy's body off of her.

"I'm okay. He didn't bite me, but I can't get these damn hands off of me," Emily said as tears filled her eyes. Anna had seen how Emily had become trapped and started sawing the dead fingers off of Emily's arms. Dark purple hand-shaped bruises circled both of her arms. "It's just my arms. I couldn't get free. Anna, you're bleeding pretty badly. He must have pulled out chunks of your scalp."

"I can't worry about that right now," Anna replied. "More zombies are coming this way; we've got to get moving." She said as she helped Emily up.

"Holy shit," Emily said as she stood up. "We've got maybe a minute. I'm going to check inside the front door for keys. There might be a table or key rack right there."

Anna nodded and kept watch as Emily briefly went inside. The first groups of zombies were closing in and were less than a minute away. Emily came back out the door with keys in her hand, and they ran for the SUV. Emily jumped into the driver's seat as Anna rushed around to the passenger side. The vehicle started and displayed a nearly full gas tank. Emily immediately backed down the driveway and turned into the street, dodging zombies as she went. She made it to the end and turned left to take them further north and further away from the two areas they had been forced to fire a gun, knowing that more zombies would have been drawn to the sound.

Anna pulled open her backpack and reached for one of the bottles of peroxide she had grabbed from the gas station back when Emily had some of her hair ripped out. She pulled down the visor and looked in the mirror. Zombie blood had splattered on her face mixing with some of her blood from her bleeding scalp. Her hair was cut jaggedly and fell just past her shoulders. She could feel the heaviness of the blood on the back of her neck and running down her back. She grabbed a bottle of water and washed her hands with it. She wiped away as much of the zombie blood from her hands and her face as she could. Turning her face upward, she poured the entire bottle of peroxide over her hair and down the back of her head. It stung like pure alcohol. She let it do its job and settled back into her seat as Emily drove. She knew she might need a few stitches, but there was nothing she could do about that right now. She'd keep the wounds as clean as possible and get them bandaged up later.

"Anna, I think we should make a quick stop at your house. We need to treat your head, so you don't get an infection. I know you're the nurse, but it looks pretty bad," Emily said. Her injuries hurt, but they were just bruises, so there was nothing she could do about them.

123

Anna didn't want to waste any more time and wanted to resume their search for Camille, but the nurse in her knew that she needed to treat her head. Even if stitches were unnecessary, her scalp needed a much more thorough cleaning. Who knew what kind of germs had gotten into the wounds and what kind of infection they could bring on.

"I hate this. I hate stopping even for a little while," Anna started. "But you're right. That old man did some damage, and I have what I need to treat it back at the house. Besides, we haven't checked in since we left yesterday. Camille or Max and Jesse may have made it home."

With that, Emily adjusted her course and headed for Anna's house.

Chapter Fourteen

Day 4

As the garage door opened, Camille saw that there were a few more zombies than she had anticipated. Having never driven before, she depressed the gas pedal too hard, and the SUV shot out of the garage, plowing through half a dozen of the dead before her foot found the brake. Luckily for her learning curve, the zombies had all fallen to the side without causing any damage to the vehicle. The driveway consisted of a large circular loop that was wide enough for at least two cars all the way around and had two openings leading to the street. After hitting the brakes hard enough to come to an abrupt jerking stop, she hurriedly steered toward her right to follow the loop out onto Lake Road. She turned right to head in the general direction of her home. She was surprised to see so many wrecked and abandoned cars along what was once a busy two-lane road. When she'd been running for her life the day before, she had been too preoccupied with avoiding zombies to notice all of the vehicles.

She eased up on the gas pedal to drive at a snail's pace because she was afraid of hitting one of the many cars. There weren't many zombies on the road in front of her, but without fail, every one of them turned in her direction. Even at her slow pace, the zombies were still too slow to catch up to her. She didn't dare exceed five to ten miles an hour, at least not until she found a more open stretch of road. She was so nervous behind the wheel that she found herself shaking. Thinking of her family and the possibility of seeing them soon helped to calm her nerves. She focused on the road in front of her as she carefully weaved around cars and stray zombies. A small opening up ahead was void of cars but held half a dozen of the dead. She slowed for a moment, then saw more of the dead entering the road from a mansion on the right and decided to try to drive right through them before the rest could walk into her path. As she sped up, she veered to her left and managed to hit only two zombies on the edge of the headlight, both of which were knocked to the side.

She was coming up on the first main street when she saw a multi-car pileup at the intersection. She brought the SUV to an abrupt stop as she considered her options. An experienced driver would have been able to go around the wreckage without much difficulty, but Camille was afraid she would hit one of the cars. She didn't want to turn left yet if she didn't have to because it would force her to go through what would have been a busier area. Lake Road was busy enough, and she had hoped to go further west before turning into the suburbs. She very carefully veered around the accident using the shoulder to avoid hitting any of the cars, and her confidence went up a notch.

She had another half mile to go before making her first planned turn. Zombies seemed to come from everywhere at the sight of the SUV, but they were slow as hell. As long as she drove faster than they walked, she thought she would be okay. There were so many cars on the road ahead that she slowed to a near crawl as she made her way past them. With her inexperience behind the wheel, she had trouble judging distances between her vehicle and the others. She gasped when she loudly scraped the side of a vehicle on her right but forced herself to keep going as she tried to veer slightly left, only to scrape yet another car on her left. The road ahead was nearly gridlocked, but she kept going forward, ignoring the scrapes and noises as she grazed other cars. She knew all of the noise was drawing more zombies toward her, but there was nothing she could do about it.

She was coming up on Bradley Road when she saw another multi-car accident. Five cars were wrecked in the middle of the three-way intersection. Two of the cars held zombies still fastened in by their seat belts. The windows were smeared with gore from the zombies pressing their faces and hands on the glass. The sight didn't faze her as she had become so accustomed to seeing zombies. It only seemed logical to her that a lot of the cars would have zombies inside of them. Camille slowly crept forward to the intersection, trying to find a way around the accident. The shoulder was grass, and there was no curb, so she decided to turn onto Bradley while driving partially on the grass. After successfully negotiating the turn, her confidence in her driving abilities grew a little more.

About a block down, a dozen zombies were shuffling around in the street. Camille wasn't sure if she should try to drive through them or turn around. She didn't want to have to negotiate her way around the accident behind her again, so after a moment's thought, she decided to speed up to try to go around them. She veered to the right hoping that she wouldn't hit them, and pressed hard on the gas pedal. Again she went faster than she had intended to, not realizing that she had pressed the gas pedal to the floor. The SUV jumped forward and slammed into three of the zombies head-on. One somersaulted over the car, another was sucked underneath, and the third landed on the hood. The dead man's face was bloodied, and his left arm was ringed with bite marks, but it didn't stop him

127

from reaching toward the windshield. Before his hands could find a grip, Camille hit the brakes hard. The zombie flew off the car instantly while Camille's seatbelt dug painfully into her shoulder. She winced slightly but kept her focus as she put her foot back on the gas. She couldn't believe that she had just driven through three zombies without any apparent damage to the SUV. She was well aware of the fatal damage that a single zombie could cause to the vehicle, but she had thought she could pass by them and had been afraid of trying to backtrack.

She continued for another couple blocks until the next pileup. It was another three-way intersection with four cars long since wrecked and abandoned. Once again, she brought the SUV to a stop so she could figure out what to do. She desperately wanted to keep going straight as it was the most direct route to her house, but she was afraid she might have to turn right. Turning right would add at least a couple of miles to her trip while taking her through busier streets and intersections. As she looked ahead to see if she could pass the cars and continue on her heading, there was a sudden thump on the rear of the SUV. Camille nearly jumped out of her seat in surprise and fear. Unaccustomed to driving, she'd completely forgotten about her mirrors. A glance in the rearview showed several zombies from the group she had driven past that had caught up to her as she sat there at a standstill. One of them had hit the rear window with its hand.

Out of time and with fear making her decision for her, she hit the gas and drove around the left side of the accident to continue straight down the street. The SUV clipped a truck, and the passenger side mirror was torn off, but she managed to get past the wreckage without being forced to make the turnoff. Her heart beating out of her chest, she breathed a sigh of relief and vowed to herself that she would keep an eye on the remaining mirrors. She had almost learned the hard way that coming to a complete stop could be a death sentence.

For the next two blocks, the road ahead was free of zombies. Camille drove painfully slow and very carefully around abandoned cars but didn't have to worry about any of the dead for a few minutes. She saw a handful of zombies coming from homes on either side of the street, but she was well out of harm's way before any of them could reach even the sidewalks. Her nerves were frazzled, but she was becoming slightly more confident in her driving. She was testing the gas pedal to slow down and speed up to avoid another sudden accidental burst of speed when she came upon another group of zombies. There were only five or six of them, and having already learned her lesson about coming to a complete stop, she sped up slightly and drove around the group missing all but one of them. The lone zombie glanced off one of her headlights, and she kept going.

Camille was amazed at how long it was taking to drive such a short distance. She'd left the mansion nearly an hour ago, and she still hadn't made it to her planned second turn. She wondered if this was how it had been for Michelle, Joey, and Lucia back on the first day and desperately hoped that it wouldn't take her two days to get home.

She drove the equivalent of another block when she saw that the road up ahead was completely obscured by both vehicles and zombies. A huge multi-car accident mixed with dozens of zombies shuffling around made it completely impassable. To her right were the start of several side streets and about six blocks that she could cut through to try to go around and come back out on the other side of the accident and the dead. She made a wide unpracticed right turn onto the first street, nearly jumping the curb. The way ahead was mostly clear. There seemed to be just the usual parked cars on either side of the street and only three zombies within her line of sight. She drove to the end of the block and then stopped to make sure the way was clear before she turned left. A few houses down, she saw dozens of zombies surrounding a home. She figured that there must be someone trapped inside but didn't think she could do anything to help. She could barely drive and was afraid she'd wreck the car. She slowed to a crawl to give herself a moment to think. A few of the dead noticed her and turned their heads her way. When she realized the SUV itself could be enough of a distraction, she looked ahead to make sure the street was wide open for the rest of the block then made a decision. She hit the horn a few times, feeling terrified as the crowd slowly turned toward her and away from the house. She hit it twice more then drove past them and down the street. This time she remembered to keep an eye on her rearview mirror and glanced at it every few seconds. The zombies moved achingly slow, but they left the house and followed her. Camille had no way of knowing whether or not she had helped whoever might have been inside the house, but she felt good about leading the zombies away. As she increased her speed, the dead fell further behind and were soon nearly a block behind her.

Camille decided to drive a little further before trying to turn left to make her way back over to Bradley and around the zombies and wrecked cars that had blocked her way.

Chapter Fifteen

Day 4

After hearing Frank and Junior's story, Michelle decided to go lay down for a bit. She was glad that Max and Jesse had been able to rescue them, but she wasn't up for any more conversation. With her heart aching so badly that she didn't know what to do with herself, she tried to sleep to pass the time. Her presence wasn't needed for anything. The men and the boys had everything covered with the house and were doing perimeter checks. Lucia had decided to join her brother and Damon because she wanted to learn how to protect herself against the zombies.

Frank and Junior left Michelle to herself to grieve while they tried to make themselves useful. After what had happened the night before with Damon and Joey, they felt they should take on more of the risk to relieve some of the boys' burden of protecting their families, so they started making regular perimeter checks. They were also doing the cooking and cleaning up afterward. Working for the fire department, they both had plenty of experience with making nice home-cooked meals.

Joey and Lucia were both devastated over the loss of their father but understood that there was too much for them to do to sit around crying, and they both found it helpful to keep busy. They did cry and would certainly cry some more, but they were learning to compartmentalize their emotions so they could focus on whatever task was at hand.

Lucia carried tremendous guilt over Camille's absence. She felt that had she not frozen in fear, she might have been able to help Camille kill the neighbor zombies, and Camille wouldn't have had to take off running to lead the horde away from the house. Damon and Joey tried to reassure Lucia that there was nothing she could have done, but Lucia knew better. She kept picturing Camille's face as her eyes pleaded with her for help. There was work to be done, and they all needed a distraction, so they decided to spend a good part of the day next door at the Wright's house. Four days into the apocalypse, Mr. Wright and his granddaughter's body were growing ripe in the heat of summer.

"We're going to have to pull these bodies out of the house," Joey said as they walked into the living room. "That smell is going to stick to everything."

"Yeah, I'd much rather let them rot outside before this place is overrun with bugs, rats, and who knows what else. Our supplies could end up being damaged," Damon said in agreement.

Lucia wore a horrified expression on her face, but she had vowed to herself that she would do better. She wanted to be an asset instead of a liability and was trying to make up for the guilt she felt over Camille. "Okay, let's do this. With all three of us, we may be able to lift the bodies instead of dragging them, so we don't leave a bigger mess on the floor."

Damon and Joey shared a quick look, both surprised but proud of Lucia.

Mr. Wright's body was closest, so they decided to move him first. Lucia and Joey each grabbed an arm and shoulder while Damon grabbed the feet, and they lifted as one. To their surprise, the deadweight was much more difficult to lift than they had expected.

"This isn't going to work," Joey panted with exertion. "Why don't we roll him onto a sheet? Then we can drag him outside."

"That's a good idea," Damon said. "Kind of like when my dad had to move the old fridge out. Once he had something underneath it, it was pretty easy to move."

"I'll go find something from the closet in the hallway," Lucia said as she left the room. She was freaked out from touching the old man's body and was relieved when her brother had thought of a different way to do it. The linen closet was full of sheets, blankets, comforters, and quilts. She chose two thin blankets and brought them back to the living room.

"Perfect," Joey said. He and Damon had already pushed the coffee table far to the side so they had easier access to both bodies. He laid the blanket on the floor and, with Damon's help, rolled the body over onto it. The boys grabbed the end and started pulling it across the floor quite easily. As Lucia reached out to help out, Damon shook his head.

"Open the front door and make sure we're clear. We've got this," Damon said. Lucia checked the yard to find it was empty other than what remained of Mrs. Wright's body. The boys made quick work of dragging both bodies out then went back inside the house. They were hot and sweaty, so they went to the huge farmhouse-style kitchen at the back of the house to get some water.

"Do you think we should board up the big window in the living room?" Joey asked. It had been broken since day one, but since they were counting on being able to use the

133

house and its supplies as needed, it was worth consideration.

"I doubt anything or anyone is coming in here," Damon replied. "But I suppose it couldn't hurt. I don't think we need to fortify the house or anything, but yeah, we could board up that window and fix the front door, too."

"There's enough wood in the garage here," Joey said. "I don't think we need to grab anything from your house." He turned to Lucia. "Can you keep an eye out front? We're going to be making a little bit of noise, and I don't want any zombies getting the jump on us."

"I can do it," Lucia gulped. "Can you please help me with my knife? I mean, I know how to hold one, but I don't know if I can stab one of those things the right way."

"Yeah, let's go practice on the bodies we just dragged outside," Joey said. "It's gross, but there's no risk."

"I'll grab the wood and tools from the garage while you guys do that," Damon said.

Joey spent the next ten minutes teaching Lucia how to stab through the eye and ear of a zombie while Damon gathered supplies for the window and the front door. The front yard and the street remained clear of zombies, so Joey left Lucia to keep watch while he and Damon went to work.

Lucia was so nervous that she was shaking, but she vowed to herself that she would stay at her post in the front yard. After about five minutes, two zombies slowly lurched into sight. The minimal noise that the boys were making was enough to draw their attention. Lucia was so eager to prove to herself that she could handle things that she didn't call on Damon or Joey for help. One of the zombies was dragging a badly damaged leg behind him. He was dressed in the uniform of a mail carrier and still carried a bag over his shoulder. Dried blood ringed his mouth, and his abdomen was torn open, exposing decaying entrails. With the other zombie a dozen feet behind the first, she decided to take on the former mailman by herself. She had yet to kill a zombie herself, and her adrenaline started pumping as she closed in on him. He was about her height, so she decided to try to grab him by his hair then go in for the kill. She wrapped her hand around a wad of the hair on the back of his head and tried to stab his ear. Her knife missed and sliced off the bottom of his ear as his teeth snapped near her face. Undeterred, she aimed again and successfully plunged the knife through his ear. When he didn't drop immediately, she pushed the knife further and gave it a twist causing the zombie to finally fall dead to the ground.

By then, the second zombie was only a couple of feet away. A teenage girl in a swimsuit with rings of bites up one arm leaving just strings of flesh holding her muscles in place, tottered toward Lucia with her arms outstretched. Lucia grabbed one of her arms, causing the flesh to shift and a muscle to plop out and onto the ground with a wet slap. She tightened her grip and thrust her knife into its eye. Milky putrid fluid poured from the eye as she drove her knife in deep. The zombie girl dropped to the ground before Lucia could pull her knife back out. Gagging, Lucia bent down to retrieve her knife and wiped it clean on the grass. She quickly stood up to take a good look around to make sure there weren't any other zombies closing in. She breathed a sigh of relief when she saw that everything was clear. She nearly jumped out of her skin when Joey came running up from behind her.

"Holy shit, Joey," Lucia said. "You scared the crap out of me."

Joey was busy looking at the two bodies on the ground. "Why didn't you call for help? You didn't have to take them out all by yourself."

"Yes, I did," Lucia said firmly. "Now I know that I can do it."

"For fuck's sake, Lucia," was all Joey could say before he pulled her in for a hug. He was proud of his sister but wanted her to know that she had nothing to prove to anyone. "Next time, let someone help you. No more unnecessary risk, okay?"

Lucia nodded. She'd done what she needed to do and promised Joey that she wouldn't take chances like that again.

Damon walked up, having just finished with the repairs. "You did good, Lucia," he said, then took a look around to make sure the area was still clear. "Let's go inside and finish searching the house for supplies."

The three of them went inside and quietly closed the front door behind them. They finished exploring every nook and cranny to find every possible supply they could use. They loaded up the car and the truck in the Wright's garage. If they had to leave in a hurry, there were two vehicles stocked and ready to go. They had collected additional supplies and left everything in the mudroom off the garage for quick and easy access.

After they finished, they went back over the fence to Damon's house. Frank and Junior had left a spread of home-cooked food on the kitchen counter, and the three of them were famished. They ate second and third helpings until they were stuffed. The firemen went out to do a perimeter check so the kids could have some space.

"Oh, I ate too much," Lucia moaned.

"You practically ate a whole damn cow," Joey teased. "I think you ate more than me and Damon combined."

"Shut up, dumbass. My stomach hurts," Lucia threw back at him.

"Well, it should. You didn't leave anything for anyone else to eat," Joey said. "Shit, now you're going to have to cook, and everyone's going to be in trouble." He made fake gagging sounds at the thought of eating her cooking.

Damon just sat back and grinned. He was happy to see Joey and Lucia starting to act more like themselves again. Their constant teasing and bickering was their normal, and it felt good to watch them go at it.

After their food settled, Damon and Joey decided to spend a few hours introducing Lucia to guns. It would be a while before she was truly comfortable using them, but at least she was no longer afraid of them. They couldn't exactly take her out for target practice, so they patiently taught her as much as they could over a few hours and planned to continue to teach her more each day. They wanted to help her get a few zombie kills, but firing a gun was like ringing the dinner bell for all of the zombies in the area. When the time came that they would have no choice but to use guns, they hoped to have taught her enough that she would be able to handle herself.

Their earlier plan had been to teach her how to kill a zombie with a knife the next time they saw just one or two lingering in the street. It would have been a fairly controlled situation, so the risk would have been minimal, but after her two kills earlier that afternoon, they could see that she had gained some confidence in her abilities.

With the day's gun lesson complete, they settled in to eat some dinner. Frank and Junior were keeping to themselves for the most part, but they were making sure that freshly cooked food was ready whenever anyone was hungry.

Everyone was worried about Max, Anna, Emily, Vince, and Camille. Zombies popped up everywhere, hordes appeared from out of nowhere, and there wasn't any truly safe place. Damon worried that he might lose his entire family and hated staying at the house while they were all out there somewhere separated from each other. He was voicing his concerns to Joey when he heard a vehicle in the driveway.

"Someone's here," Damon said and quickly rushed to the door with Joey on his heels.

Chapter 16

Day 4

An unfamiliar black SUV pulled up to the garage, and Damon saw his mom and Emily climb out. It was immediately evident that Camille wasn't with them. He was out the front door and the door of the enclosed front porch before they could take two steps toward the house.

"Holy shit, mom," Damon exclaimed. "What the hell happened?" He saw that her hair was jaggedly and unevenly cut short, and blood stained her head, neck, and shirt. He glanced at Emily and saw purple hand-shaped bruises on both of her arms and bloodstains on her shirt as well. He took his mom's hand and led her toward the house while Joey grabbed their backpacks of supplies from the car. Joey looked at both women worriedly. It was clear they'd been through a lot.

"Has your sister come home?" Anna asked though she knew in her heart that she hadn't.

"No. Not yet," Damon said. "But dad made it home last night." Before he could say more, Anna started questioning him.

"Dad's home? He's okay?" Anna's eyes teared up with relief, knowing that her husband was safe and at home.

"He came home but left again to search for you and Camille," Damon started. "Mom, Jesse's dead."

"Oh my god," Anna gasped, then looked at Joey. "Joey, honey, I'm so sorry." She let go of Damon's hand and pulled Joey in for a hug. She hugged him so tightly that he dropped the backpacks. When she finally pulled away,

Damon grabbed the backpacks and ushered everyone into the house.

"Dad brought three other guys home with him. A man named Vince, and two firefighters, Frank and Junior. Vince went back out with dad last night to search," Damon said. "Frank and Junior are here, and they've been doing perimeter checks and keeping everyone well fed."

"What about Michelle and Lucia?" Anna couldn't believe that Jesse was dead. A hundred questions ran through her mind. She was worried sick about her best friend losing her husband and was upset that she couldn't have been there with Michelle when she found out. She felt like she was in shock herself, finding out that Jesse died and that Max had come home but left again. She was terrified that she was going to lose both her husband and her daughter. She shook her head, trying to fight back the tears that threatened to overflow.

"My mom is in pretty bad shape," Joey said as tears filled his own eyes. "She's been in bed all day. Once she realized that the guys had things covered and she wasn't needed, she took a sleeping pill and hasn't been up since. I'm worried about her."

"Lucia's in the kitchen. She's having a hard time, too," Damon said. "She feels guilty about Camille and thinks it's all her fault that Camille had to take off running the way she did. She blames herself. Between that and losing her dad, she's having a rough time of it. She's pretty tough, though, Mom. She killed her first two zombies today."

"That poor girl, it's not her fault," Anna said as she shook her head. She was surprised to hear that Lucia killed a couple of zombies but supposed she should get used to the kids maturing and growing up overnight.

"We've been teaching her about weapons, and we finished going through the Wright's house. We just finished eating, so she's cleaning up the dishes. She'll be okay," Joey said. "It's just going to take some time. For all of us."

"I've gotta check on Michelle," Anna said.

"Anna," Emily spoke up. "We have to clean you up first."

Anna was so caught up in everything the boys were telling her that she forgot all about her head. She nodded, and they headed for the kitchen instead. All of the first aid supplies were gathered up on one of the counters with the rest of the supplies that they had bagged up.

She saw Lucia and immediately pulled her in for a hug. "I'm so sorry about your dad, sweetie." Lucia nodded, and tears filled her eyes, but she fought them and pulled herself together. "Thank you," Lucia said as she wiped her eyes. She would let herself cry some more later on. She stepped back to allow the others more room to move around the kitchen.

As Anna looked through the first aid supplies, Joey started refilling the backpacks from the car to make sure Anna and Emily were well stocked when they went back out.

"What happened to you?" Damon asked. He was really worried about seeing his mom injured and bloody.

"I'm fine, kiddo," Anna said. "A zombie ripped out a few handfuls of my hair, that's all. I just need to clean up the wounds, so I don't get an infection. Emily has nearly the same injuries from a different zombie that got a hold of her last night. Mine are just a little bloodier. We should clean yours up again too, Emily."

141

"Why don't you lean over the sink?" Emily said. "Let me rinse away as much as I can, and then I'll pour peroxide over your whole head." Anna leaned over the sink while Emily cleaned her up. The peroxide burned so badly that it felt like straight alcohol, but she held back from letting out a yelp. She didn't want to worry her son any more than he already was.

"Damon, grab some scissors for me," Anna said. While she waited, she cleaned up the wounds on Emily's head and checked the bruises on her arms. "Ouch, those bruises look pretty bad. How severe is the pain?"

"It feels like my bones are bruised. That's how much it hurts. I wouldn't mind an aspirin, but I don't want any painkillers that might cloud my head," Emily said.

Anna nodded and grabbed a bottle from one of the bags. She took a few for herself then handed the bottle to Emily as Damon returned with the scissors.

"Would you like the honor?" She asked Emily with a grim smile as she held out the scissors. Her once beautiful, long dark hair was now just past her shoulders but the length varied by inches in some spots because of the rough knife cut she had to do. She was too stressed and worried about everything else to care about her hair anymore. She just wanted a quick chop straight across, and then she'd pull it back in a short ponytail. Emily made quick work of it then asked Anna to cut hers off.

"Are you sure? We can just pull your hair up in a bun or ponytail," Anna said as she looked at Emily's beautiful long blonde hair.

"Yes. Same cut as yours. I don't want either of us nearly getting killed again because of our long hair," Emily said resolutely. As Anna was making the quick cut, she was startled by the voices of two men as they walked in the front door.

"It's okay, Mom," Damon said. "It's Frank and Junior. They were doing a perimeter check."

She finished chopping Emily's hair off as the two men entered the kitchen.

"Hi, you must be Anna. I'm Frank, and this is Junior," Frank said. "We heard the car pull up when we were checking the perimeter and figured it had to be you or Max."

"Yeah, and this is Emily," Anna said quickly.

"Hi," Emily nodded to Frank and Junior. "So you guys are firemen? I dated a fireman once. He worked downtown somewhere."

Frank and Junior shared a glance, chuckled, and both said, "Dan!"

"That's right," Emily perked up. "We had a fun time. Did he make it?"

Junior started to tell the story, but Frank interrupted, "Don't know, ma'am. He worked at a different station."

"How has the perimeter been?" Anna interrupted, picking up on Frank's cue.

"Well, the boys had a close call late last night and took out a good seventy zombies in the yard behind yours. Since then, we've killed half a dozen," Frank said.

"What the fuck? Damon!" Anna started. "What the hell happened? Are you okay? Why the hell would you go up against so many zombies by yourselves?" She was shocked to learn that Joey and her son had been in such mortal danger.

"We're fine, Mom," Damon said with a sigh. He could tell his mom was going to lose it and tried to head her off. "We didn't realize how many were back there until it was

143

too late. Some guy helped us, but he ended up getting bit. We made it through without a scratch."

"We didn't lose any hair, either," Joey said with a grin knowing that Anna was either going to laugh or tell him off.

"Funny," Anna said with a little laugh, and the boys breathed a sigh of relief. Her laugh faded, and she turned to Frank and Junior with venom in her voice. "Where were you? Letting the boys take on so much risk out there like that."

"We didn't know, or we would never have let them go out there," Junior spoke up. "We've taken over doing the perimeter checks since it happened."

"It's not their fault, Mom," Damon said. "After dad came home, and we found out about Jesse… we needed to get out and kill some zombies. We never would have gone over the fence if we'd known the yard was full of them."

"I needed it," Joey said as his expression darkened thinking of the memory of finding his mom sobbing on the floor in Max's arms. Anna read Joey's face and decided to let it go.

"We've gotta get back out there," Anna said. "Camille is still out there somewhere."

"Mom, wait, I almost forgot," Damon started. "We have a radio. Dad and Vince stopped back home last night to give us one, and he kept the other so we could call him if you or Camille made it home."

"We have a radio? Where is it?" Anna asked quickly. Her mood lifted considerably after finding out they had a radio. She couldn't believe that she had a way to contact her husband and that she would finally hear his voice.

"Here you go, Mom," Damon said. "It's already on the right channel."

Anna tuned out her son and everyone else around her as she pressed the button to call Max. "Baby?" she said into the radio.

Chapter Seventeen

Day 4

Max was driving around, continuing with his search, when he suddenly heard Anna's voice come from the radio. Stunned and elated, he immediately picked it up and responded.

"Anna, holy shit babe, I can't believe it's you," Max said.

"Baby, I've missed you so much," Anna said, her voice full of emotion.

"I've missed you too," Max said heavily. "You have no idea."

"Are you okay?" Anna asked. "Damon told me about Jesse." She held back a sob. Saying the words aloud made it feel more real.

"I'm just fine babe," Max said.

"I love you so much, Max," Anna said. "Where are you?"

"I love you, too. I'm just a couple of miles away. I should be there in twenty minutes," Max answered.

"Emily and I just stopped home to clean up some minor injuries. I've got to get back out there to look for Camille," Anna said. "I can't waste another minute."

"You can wait twenty minutes, baby," Max said. "I need to see you. I need to see for myself that you're okay."

"I'm fine, Max. I just lost a few chunks of hair to a zombie with a good grip. I'm all cleaned up, the boys restocked our bags, and we're getting ready to head back out," Anna said.

"Wait until I get there. It's been twenty-four hours; another twenty minutes isn't going to make a difference."

"Max…," Anna started, then hesitated a moment. She desperately wanted to see her husband, but every second that she wasn't out searching for Camille was killing her. She was so afraid that she would never find her.

"Anna, please wait. I know she's your baby girl, but I need you to wait for me," Max said.

"Damn it, Max, fine, I'll wait. Twenty-one minutes and I'm gone," Anna said with a little laugh.

"I love you, babe. I'll be there as fast as I can," Max said with a grin on his face as relief flowed through him.

He set the radio down and focused solely on the road in front of him. He increased his speed since he was temporarily suspending his search and heading straight for his house. He glanced at Maggie and the small smile set on her face.

"She sounds pretty tough, like she can handle herself," Maggie said.

"She is, and she can, but I would feel much better if I knew she was safe at home while I was out searching. It's the same reason I wouldn't let my son help me look for Camille. Knowing he's safe, I can focus fully on looking for my daughter. Now that I know that my wife is safe, with her going back out again, I'm going to be worrying even more about both her and Camille," Max said. "She's smart, stubborn as hell, and she's fiercely protective of our kids. There's no way I'm going to be able to get her to stay home." He sighed in resignation.

"Maybe the two of you can search together instead of going off separately," Maggie suggested.

"That's my plan. If she won't stay home, then I want her with me," Max said, but he knew it would be a battle to get Anna to agree. Sometimes she was too stubborn for her own good.

He weaved around a few zombies in the middle of the street then sped up a little more.

"You afraid she's going to leave if we're not there in twenty minutes?" Maggie asked with a grin.

"Shit, with Anna, who the hell knows," Max said with a little smile. He honestly was a little concerned that she might take off before he got there if he didn't make it home quickly.

Up ahead, a few dozen zombies filled the street, so Max made a quick turn to avoid them. Cutting down the little side streets was always risky because if he came upon a big enough crowd of zombies, he could get caught up and have to ditch the truck. He made a couple more turns, dodging abandoned cars, zombies, and bodies in the streets, before getting within a half-mile of his house.

"We're almost there," Max said excitedly. He drove around half a dozen zombies, then turned onto his street. Zombie slush still covered the road. Blood, guts, arms, legs, feet, entrails, shoes, clothing, and occasional dead bodies covered the road from one side to the other. Not much had changed since last night other than things seemed to be a bit more dried up. He made a slow pass by his house while looking everywhere for the dead. He had to make sure there weren't any up the street or in neighboring yards that might see him pull into his hidden driveway. Several houses down, three zombies stumbled about in the middle of the street.

"Shit," Max said. "I've gotta stop and take these out, so they don't follow us. Keep a lookout to make sure there aren't any more in the yards or anything."

Maggie nodded and kept a sharp eye out for more zombies as Max got out of the truck.

The three zombies were walking close together, which made them a little bit harder to take down, but Max had killed so many that he knew how to use caution while killing them quickly. One was an old man that looked pretty frail. He wore ripped striped pajamas with bare feet. Several large chunks were missing from both arms. The second zombie looked like he'd been a middle-aged businessman of some sort with the suit, tie, and dress shoes he wore. Dried blood ringed his mouth, and one visible bite wound exposed tendons under stringy flesh where his neck met his shoulder. The third looked like he'd been a twenty-something bodybuilder in a bloody wife-beater and torn jeans. His muscular arms bore several bites with dried brackish blood, and tattered pale flesh hung loosely. Max went for him first, giving him a solid kick to the chest to knock him backward while he took down the two easier kills. A quick thrust of his knife and the old man dropped to the ground. He gave bodybuilder another kick while he grabbed the former businessman and plunged his knife into his ear. The bodybuilder was relentless but much easier to take out once the other two were down. When he reached for Max the third time, Max plunged his knife into his eye. He bent down and wiped his knife off on the stained wife-beater, then stood back up to look around for other threats. Seeing nothing, he looked at Maggie, and she shook her head.

With no other zombies in sight, Max backed the truck up to his driveway and made the turn. He hopped out to unlock the gate, pulled forward, locked the gate, and pulled down the driveway until he reached his garage.

"Wow," Maggie said with wonder in her voice. "You weren't kidding when you said you were a bit off the grid. I would never have found this house on my own."

"Home sweet home," Max said, feeling a bit giddy about seeing Anna. "Let's go."

As Max walked toward the enclosed front porch, Anna met him at the front door. He climbed through the bars then walked inside with Maggie following closely behind him. He wrapped his arms around Anna, and they stood there embracing for a moment. As they let go, he got a good look at her and saw that her hair was chopped short and blood stained her shirt.

"Are you okay babe? What happened?" Max asked with concern.

"I'm fine. A zombie got a good hold on my hair, that's all. I had to cut it off with my knife to get free of its grip, even after I killed him," Anna said dismissively. She didn't want Max worrying about it. "You almost missed the twenty-minute mark," she said with a grin. "I was just about to take off without you."

"No you weren't," Max laughed at her grin. They were both ecstatic to see each other. If their daughter wasn't missing they'd be having an entirely different kind of reunion. Seeing her did wonders for his state of mind.

"Who's this?" Anna nodded toward the fifty-ish woman standing just behind her husband.

"I'm Maggie. It's a pleasure to meet you, Anna. I've heard so much about you," Maggie said.

"Hi Maggie," Anna said simply, then turned back to Max. She knew she was coming off bitchy, but she wasn't in the mood to deal with new people.

"Her house was surrounded, and I managed to drive off all of the zombies. They'd done too much damage for

150

her to finish securing her house, so she packed a bag, we emptied her pantry, and she's been helping me search for Camille," Max said. "How is everyone doing here? I haven't checked in since last night."

"Michelle's sleeping, the kids are making themselves useful, and the guys have been doing perimeter checks. Firemen make good cooks, too," Anna said.

They headed for the kitchen since that was where everyone was waiting. Max wanted to make a new game plan that would involve some of the others. Upon seeing his son, he pulled him in for a hug, then looked to Joey and Lucia and asked them if they were doing okay. They both nodded in response.

"Boys, we have a ton of supplies in the truck outside. Can you go unload it? Leave some but bring in most of it. I'd hate to lose everything if I have to ditch the truck," Max said.

"No problem, Dad," Damon said as he and Joey headed for the door.

"Where's Vince?" Frank asked with trepidation.

"He didn't make it. We ran into a bunch of zombies last night, and three of them came through the windshield," Max said sadly without giving further details. None were needed.

"Damn," Junior said softly. He'd really liked Vince.

Frank nodded and looked away. He was tired of losing people.

"You must be Emily," Max offered his hand to the twenty-something blonde standing near the sink.

"Hi Max, it's good to finally meet you," Emily said.

"Everyone, this is Maggie," Max said as everyone introduced themselves.

"Great, everyone knows everyone now," Anna was growing impatient with all of the introductions and wanted to get back on the road. "We need to get going."

Max had a plan, but he didn't think Anna was going to go along with it, which was why he wanted to talk with everyone all at once.

"Anna, I would feel better if you stayed home, at least for a while," Max started. "I can put all of my focus into searching for Camille if I'm not worried about you being out there in harm's way." Before he could say another word, Anna cut in.

"There's no way in hell I'm going to stay at home while my daughter's out there," Anna said firmly, leaving no doubt in anyone's mind that she was going to go back out there.

"Then let's go together," Max said. "You and I can search for her together."

"Max, we can cover twice as much ground if we go separately," Anna said. "We're already wasting enough time as it is standing around here talking."

"We can help," Frank offered. "Junior and I would be happy to join the search."

"What, and leave the boys here alone with another mess? Leave them to protect everyone on their own?" Anna demanded. Seeing Max's confused expression, she continued. "Damon and Joey took on seventy zombies all by themselves last night. We're lucky they weren't killed. Your new friends here let them go out on their own when they should have been out there helping them." She glared at Frank and Junior.

Damon and Joey had just entered the kitchen laden down with supplies from the truck outside. "Mom, we told you, it wasn't like that," Damon said with a sigh. He turned to his dad. "The yard behind us was full of zombies. We thought it was just a few, or we would never have gone over the fence. We didn't get hurt. Frank and Junior have taken over the perimeter checks since then, and they wouldn't let us go again if we wanted to," Damon explained.

Max considered what was said for a moment. He knew Anna was slow to trust new people, and she was worried sick about Camille. It made sense that she would be angry with the two men even though they hadn't done anything wrong.

"Alright, Anna, what if one of them helps with the search? The other can stay here to help protect the house," Max said.

"How the hell are they going to help? They don't know Camille. They don't know what she looks like," Anna said. "If Camille saw them, she'd probably hide from them." Her temper was starting to rise.

"Okay," Max decided to try a different tactic. "How about you take one of the guys with you? At least consider that. I'd feel much better knowing that one of them was with you in case things get bad out there."

"I've already been through the bad, and I don't know them," Anna said. "I know Emily. We've been through plenty together, and I trust her." Earning Anna's trust wasn't easy, and Max knew it. He was going to lose this argument because his wife was stubborn, but that was part of her nature and one of the things he loved about her.

"Max, we need to get going. Every minute we waste talking about this is another minute my baby is out there missing," Anna said.

Max nodded in agreement because he knew that Anna wasn't going to change her mind. "You take my radio. If you get into trouble, you can call the house for help. I'm not budging on this," Max said firmly as he read her expression. "We're going to drive east to Crocker. You search half a mile north, and I'll search half a mile south, and then we can meet up at Bradley to check-in. That's gotta be it, Anna. It's the safest way to do things, and we can keep track of each other."

Anna hated nothing more than being told what to do, but she knew Max meant well and that his plan was solid, so she nodded. She grabbed his hand and led him to the other room.

"Are you okay? I'm so sorry about Jesse," Anna said as tears filled her eyes.

Max's whole expression darkened. "I'm as okay as I'm going to be. I just don't know how to go on living life without him. It's always been us, then the four of us, the kids…" he trailed off. "I'll get through it."

"I love you so much, Max," she said. "Be safe out there. I can't lose you."

"I love you too, Anna. We're going to find our girl," Max hugged her. "If we somehow lose track of each other out there, let's check back in at the house around midnight."

"Okay," Anna said. "It's time to go."

As they went back to the kitchen to grab Anna and Emily's restocked backpacks, Max quickly told the guys that he would be fine on his own.

"It's better if you're here to protect the kids and the house," Max said.

Frank and Junior agreed to stay, but Maggie spoke up. "I'm going with you, Max. I'm not needed here. You shouldn't go alone, and I'm a second set of eyes," she said.

He didn't argue. It was time to get moving, he didn't mind the company, and it was always safer to travel in pairs.

Chapter Eighteen

Day 4

Max drove to his search grid while hoping desperately that Anna would stick to hers. It was difficult trying to go street by street and impossible to hit every single one. He hoped they would be able to meet up as planned but knew that realistically it was unlikely. Very few things had gone according to plan since the zombies made their first appearance. He liked having Maggie along for the ride. She seemed to know when he was in the mood to talk and when he needed silence. She was very easy to get along with, and he felt he could trust her to be a reliable second set of eyes.

The fires in the distance didn't seem to have spread any further. With any luck, they would start to burn themselves out. They hadn't jumped north over the highway or moved further west. Finally, there was one less thing to worry about. That was the first time he'd had that thought since the zombie apocalypse had started.

There were some large shopping centers in their current search area. A huge outdoor mall set up like a little village with countless high-end stores, restaurants, outdoor vendors, salons, a movie theater, and parking garages were mixed in with a few luxury apartment buildings. The area was so large that it had little streets of its own and traffic lights at some of the mini intersections. Max decided to pull in and drive past all of the storefronts on each little street to see if anything was surrounded by zombies. There was no way or reason to search each store, but he figured that if anyone was alive in there, a crowd of zombies would let him know. There were more zombies in the shopping center than he expected. By their manner of dress and the bags still mindlessly held in their hands, he assumed most of them had been shoppers and had been in the area since day one. He slowly cruised down the first street, seeing nothing to indicate that anyone was alive there. He turned left at the first light and immediately wished that he hadn't. There was a long, wide grassy strip in the middle between the rows of buildings on either side of the street. The grassy area held a playground and splash pads for children to play in the heat. Dozens of young children in summer clothes, swimsuits, and even diapers were now slowly staggering around like zombies. He'd seen plenty since that first day downtown in Public Square, and he'd seen dead children walking but nothing like this. It was a devastating sight that brought tears to his eyes. They bore vicious wounds just as all of the other zombies had. Thinking of the agony all of those innocent children had suffered was almost more than he could take. He wished there was some way he could put all of them out of their misery.

"Just look away, Max," Maggie said gently, interrupting his thoughts. He was so caught up in the tragedy before him that he'd forgotten that she was in the truck with him.

He had no words, and he didn't trust himself to speak, so he nodded and tried to look straight ahead and avoid the horrors to his right. The images were forever burned into his mind, though; he knew that without a doubt. It was truly the stuff of nightmares. He tried to push the thoughts from his head so he could concentrate on his search.

Max continued driving ahead then made the turn to the next little street within the shopping center. About halfway down, a storefront was hidden from view by the dozens of zombies that were pressed up against it. He sighed, wondering what to do. There were so many zombies spread around throughout the whole shopping area that he wasn't sure he could lead them off without becoming surrounded by others. Someone had to be alive in there, so he couldn't let it go. The sound and movement of the truck had been drawing in zombies since they'd arrived, but they couldn't keep up with him as he drove down the little streets and made turns. He decided to press his luck and hit the horn. Nearly every zombie gathered at the storefront turned its head at the noise, and then their bodies followed suit. He hit the horn a couple more times to make sure that they followed him then made the next turn. He would go around the block of stores and come back around to see if anyone needed help or came out of the store.

Two turns later, he came upon several dozen zombies wandering in the street. They homed in on his truck but he was able to speed up and veer to the side to avoid most of them. A few of them flew over the truck as it struck them, but he cleared most of them. Without fail, every single zombie followed him as he passed, but like all of the others, they were slow as hell. He made the final turn to come back up by the block of shops and found that all of the dead had left the storefront that had held their interest just twenty minutes ago. He pulled up alongside the door to see if anyone was there but couldn't tell from inside his vehicle.

Max turned to Maggie. "I'm going to have to make a quick run inside. Someone is or was in there or the dead wouldn't have been so interested," he said. "You stay here. If too many zombies get dangerously close to the truck, hit the horn. Backward thinking, I know. But I'm pretty sure I'm going to have to use my gun anyway when I come back out. There are just too many scattered around here. If I hear the horn, I'll come back out here faster."

"Be careful," Maggie said as Max opened his door and got out. He had plenty of firepower on him if he needed it; he just didn't use it in most situations because the dead were also drawn by the noise.

Max quickly killed a lone zombie standing in front of the store then walked toward the door. The windows of the store weren't tinted, but the display items sitting in each one obstructed his view. He tried to open the door but found it was locked. He debated for a moment whether he should break the door open. If someone was set up inside and intended to stay there, he could be threatening their safety by destroying the lock. He looked intently through the glass as he was coming to a decision when a zombie shuffled by inside about ten feet away from the door. A woman with a bandage on her forearm appeared otherwise unmarred until he looked at her dead eyes. There was no visible blood on her body or face, but the bandage, the eyes, and the shambling gait told Max all he needed to know. The woman had gone inside to treat a bite wound, locked the door behind her, and then turned into a zombie. The dead that had surrounded the store had seen a live person go inside and must have been there since day one because their minds couldn't comprehend anything else. They stayed until they were distracted by Max and his truck. There was nothing for him to do here, so he turned back to the truck. Several zombies were within a few feet of him, but he was able to dodge a couple of them and shove another, then got into the truck.

"There was a zombie inside," Max said upon seeing Maggie's expectant expression. "The dead are too dumb to tell the difference. They saw a living person go in there a few days ago and stayed until I distracted them."

He put the truck in gear and drove down another little street of shops. There were dozens of zombies, but they were spread out all around the area. He continued and passed a parking garage. Upon seeing the garage, Jesse and their initial escape from the dead downtown crossed his mind. Max pushed the thought aside so he could focus on what he was doing. Up ahead, the luxury apartment buildings appeared to be surrounded. The front façade of the building was mostly made of glass. There had to be several hundred zombies in front of the building and countless others on the sides and presumably the rear. The buildings had high security in place, so no one could enter unless they lived there. Max thought it was highly unlikely that Camille had found her way into one of them. Someone would have had to let her in, and he doubted that she would have run through the entire zombie-filled shopping center and into one of them. Still, the zombies surrounding the buildings meant that there were probably people alive inside.

Seeing Max's expression as he studied the apartments, Maggie said, "You can't save everyone, Max. I know how much you want to, but we don't know who or what is inside. For all we know, some people could be using the place for safety."

"Yeah, it looks like a pretty secure place to hole up since the glass front doesn't start until the second floor. If anyone's in there, they're surrounded by places to scavenge whatever supplies they need," Max agreed. "But maybe I should try to draw the zombies away, just in case. We could be someone's only hope."

"Well, you can always hit the horn again and try to get them to follow us. If anyone in there is waiting for an opening, that ought to do it," Maggie said.

With that, Max decided to create a distraction and try to draw the dead away. He hit his horn a few times until it looked like most of the dead were at least turning their heads his way. He laid on the horn for a few seconds, then slowly pulled forward away from the apartments. He quickly gained hundreds of followers both from the buildings and from the shopping area. Zombies started popping up in every direction he looked. If they weren't slow as hell, he would be in some serious trouble. As it was, he'd put himself and Maggie at risk. He hadn't expected so many of the dead to be drawn in and had to find a way to maneuver around them and out of the shopping center complex. He sped up to put some distance between him and the zombies from the apartments, but there were easily another two hundred coming toward the truck from other areas.

"Hold on tight," Max said as he shot forward and mowed down half a dozen zombies. The oversized truck's snowplow took the hits well without any apparent damage. He weaved around as many as he could but had no choice but to hit some of them. He plowed through another dozen or so zombies as he sped up, and most of them were flung over the truck or fell to either side. One lone zombie landed on the hood with a loud thud. Maggie jumped at the intrusion and let out a little yelp. Max slammed on the brakes, and the zombie went flying. He'd had too much experience with zombies coming through the windshield to take any chances, so slamming the brakes felt like his best option. He was grateful it worked and looked ahead to try to find his best way through the crowd. The streets were narrow, with many cars parked alongside the curbs. It didn't leave him much room to maneuver. With barely a yard to spare between him and a row of parked cars, he took the next right and found his opening. He passed a high-end grocery store and another parking garage before finding himself at the rear of the complex. There were large open areas and loading docks for semi-trucks to make their deliveries, and most shoppers never ventured to the area. It looked like very few zombies had made their way back there either. He saw a handful here and there, but nothing compared to what he had just escaped. He breathed a sigh of relief, seeing what looked to be essentially a safe area.

"Holy shit," Max said. "That was pretty close back there."

"You're telling me," Maggie started. "That was the scariest situation I've been in since this whole thing started. Nice driving, Max."

"I'm just glad I found this truck at the dealership. Almost any other vehicle, and we wouldn't have made it," Max said. He followed the roads that delivery drivers used behind the shopping center, making his way toward an exit on Detroit Road. Once he got to the main road, he was able to turn left to head toward Bradley to finish his search area before meeting up with Anna. There weren't any residential areas to check; it was all small business buildings, a few restaurants, and a small shopping strip. Time seemed to drag and fly by at the same time as he drove around. Without even realizing it, they'd been at the luxury shopping village for hours. It was almost time to meet Anna. He desperately hoped that he'd find her there when he arrived.

Chapter Nineteen

Day 4

Camille started to grow tired as the hours passed. All of the driving was fraying her nerves. The darkening sky had slowed her down. There weren't enough streetlamps, and she had never driven at night before. She drove so slowly that she thought even a zombie might be able to keep up with her. She didn't dare speed up for fear that she would hit something. She had eventually driven around six blocks or so before she headed back to Bradley and found herself about half a block south of the huge car accident and group of zombies that she had originally taken the detour to get around. The drive had been grueling but had been worth it as the zombies were now behind her. If she could just get to her next turn, she'd feel like she was on her way home.

When full darkness had fallen, she was afraid to drive at all. She thought about pulling over or pulling into the driveway of one of the many houses she passed, but she was afraid she would become surrounded or trapped. Zombies had a way of showing up just about anywhere at any given time. She was also aware that her fuel gauge was getting low, and she didn't have any way to refill the gas tank. She was going to end up on foot again soon, only this time in the dark and that seemed much scarier to her than what she had gone through the day before.

She perked up when she finally came upon the street she had wanted to turn onto. Originally she'd planned to go all the way to Detroit Road, but after passing so many wrecks, she thought she would be better off cutting over on a smaller street. Railroad tracks ran parallel to the street, so the area wasn't heavily populated. It was mostly lined by businesses that she had never heard of or paid any attention to. Camille hoped her decision to take this route would turn out to be a good move. She figured there would be far fewer zombies and little to no gridlock. As she made the right turn, she was relieved to see the open road in front of her. The lighting was poor, so she fumbled for a moment to figure out how to turn on her brights. Doing so lit up the entire street in front of her with no cars or zombies in sight. As she slowly passed business buildings on her right, she saw an occasional zombie stumbling around while the railroad tracks to her left were empty.

Camille relaxed a bit at finally having an open stretch of road without having to constantly dodge zombies or weave around cars. Going down the little street to cut over to the next road would normally have been about a two-minute drive but took her twenty minutes because of her overabundance of caution. With the fuel gauge on empty and the gas light on, Camille began to accept the fact that she would soon have to abandon the SUV and finish her journey on foot. She made it to the next road and turned left. She was only a mile or so from home and teared up a little bit, thinking about seeing her mom again. As she wiped her eyes with her arm, a lone zombie appeared on the road directly in front of her. She swerved to avoid it but turned the wheel too hard to the right, and before she could try to correct herself, she slammed into a telephone pole with a loud crash.

The front of the SUV caved in, and steam rose from under the hood. The airbag deployed, throwing her back against her seat, and her seatbelt dug painfully into her

165

shoulder. She was stunned and shaken but tried to clear her head to take inventory of her injuries. Her shoulder was throbbing, and her left wrist was sore, but the rest of her body seemed to be okay. She was trembling from head to toe, but she knew that was just from the shock of the accident. Suddenly she remembered the zombie in her path that had caused her to run off the road. She quickly looked at her rearview mirror, but it was so dark outside that she couldn't see anything. Not knowing where it went was scaring her, but there was nothing she could do until he caught up to her. She was definitely going to go looking for him in the darkness, and if he were to show up at her door, she would just go out the passenger side.

She grabbed her backpack from the passenger seat and painfully pulled it over her shoulders. She quickly chugged a bottle of water and forced herself to eat a granola bar because she knew she was going to need to keep her strength up. She removed her knife from her belt to carry it in her hand.

Another look out the rearview mirror showed nothing, but a glance at her driver's side mirror showed that the zombie was just a few feet away from the car. It was a middle-aged man in jeans and a t-shirt stained with blood. Most of his throat was missing, and his head wobbled around loosely because of another huge bite taken from the side of his neck. *At least he'll be an easy kill,* she thought to herself. She opened the car door, took a step toward the zombie, and plunged her knife through his ear. She sighed and looked around to make sure there weren't any others, then started her long walk home.

It was so dark outside that a zombie could come within a few feet of her without her seeing it, but she hoped to be able to hear the dead before they got too close. She heard the sound of crickets chirping as she kept her focus on the area directly in front of her when a new noise began to fill the emptiness of the night. It sounded like a car or truck was coming up the road from behind her. She briefly considered her options trying to decide whether she should wave down whoever it was or if she should move off to the side where she wouldn't be seen. At the last second, just before the lights from the truck came within sight, she stepped back when she heard raucous laughter and yelling coming from at least a few guys. The headlights weaved back and forth as the driver carelessly swerved to either side of the road. The sudden incredibly loud noise of a shotgun blast caused her to duck down into a ditch as she tried to make herself invisible. She shook with fear and desperately hoped that no one had seen her. Just when she thought the truck was going to pass by her completely, it slowed to a stop at the house next door to the one she had hidden in front of.

Various men's voices spoke loudly and drunkenly over one another, with laughter interspersed as they all climbed out of the truck. Camille thought they had to be drunk to carelessly make so much noise but was certain of it when she heard slurring and incoherent speech. One of them was yelling something about his boss's house to the laughter of the others. The whole group approached the front door of the house, and a couple of the men fired shotguns. The house was dark and appeared unoccupied to Camille. It was difficult to understand everything they were saying, but her impression was that they were going to hurt the boss if he was in his home. She wanted nothing more than to take off running, but she was afraid of what would happen if one of the men saw her. The bright lights of the truck would probably expose her if she moved, but if she stayed in the ditch, they were unlikely to see her. It took every ounce of her willpower for her to force herself to stay still.

She listened as the men loudly broke into the house and were yelling complaints that they hadn't found the man that they had been looking for. She heard something about a fire, and the next thing she knew, they were trying to burn the house down. They must have found gasoline in the garage because the smell of it assaulted her nose. Then a barrage of gunshots rang out as it sounded like every single one of them fired their guns all at once, followed by cheers and shouts as the house went up in flames. Camille could feel the heat of the fire, and the area was quickly lit up with flames shooting up into the dark sky. She ducked down lower and hoped against hope that they wouldn't see her with the night now better illuminated from the burning house.

A pain-filled scream suddenly interrupted the drunken cheering and laughing. "Shoot the fucking thing," someone yelled as a second man started crying out in pain. She heard gunshots and peeked to see just how bad the situation had gotten. The dumbasses had brought at least two dozen zombies down on them, and that was just what she could see from her hiding place in the ditch.

"Shit," Camille said quietly. Zombies were probably homed in on them and coming from every direction. She had to get out of there. She glanced at the truck but didn't know if the driver had left the keys in it. If he hadn't, there were too many men nearby that would probably come after her once they saw her, and they were closer to the truck than she was. At least half a dozen men had been in the bed of the pickup, and two or three had been in the cab. From what she could see, only two had been bitten.

She found herself hoping that the others would fall to the zombies as well. Never could she have imagined herself thinking such a thing, but the whole group was bad news.

She decided to stay where she was instead of risking being seen or shot by a stray bullet. These idiots were clueless about survival, and she hoped their foolishness didn't lead any zombies toward her in the ditch. They kept firing their guns as they made their way back to their truck. A third man went down screaming as he was attacked by a zombie, while his friends jumped into their truck, leaving him to suffer instead of putting him out of his misery. As they backed out of the driveway, there were more whoops and hollers, and the truck ran over two zombies in the road. By the time they turned and went on their way, there were at least three dozen zombies visible due to the flames lighting up the sky.

Camille breathed a big sigh of relief when they drove off without seeing her. She noiselessly climbed from the ditch, but her silence didn't matter much with so many zombies around. Scared to death but knowing she had no choice but to get moving, she started running down the road. Within a few seconds, she managed to run right into a zombie at full force, taking them both to the ground. Before she could stop herself, she screamed in terror but managed to hold onto her knife and plunged it through the zombie's eye. With not a moment to waste, she was back up on her feet and running before any of the others could get too close to her.

She was starting to feel like she was repeating her escape run from yesterday, only this time it was in the dark, making it that much more difficult and terrifying. She picked up the pace and ran, dodging zombies as she saw them, often at the very last second. Others she shoved out of the way, and occasionally one was right on top of her forcing her to stop and use her knife. She cut down the next side street she came across, running as fast as she could, then turned left down another. The path was taking her away from the worst of the zombies and closer to home. She ran for twenty minutes before she found herself clear of the dead that had been drawn in by the assholes in the truck. There were still zombies around but in smaller numbers, and they weren't coming at her from every direction. She had run far enough to find the dead shuffling around aimlessly again with nothing holding their interest. It was much easier to sneak past them when they weren't focused on anyone or anything.

Camille returned her focus to getting back home. She was so close now.

Chapter Twenty

Night 4

Anna and Emily had thoroughly searched their area over a few hours. It was mostly businesses with very little residential mixed in. They'd found no signs of Camille or any buildings surrounded by zombies. Anna's heart ached with worry for her daughter, and hopelessness crept in. It was getting close to midnight and nearly time to meet Max.

"We should try to meet Max now," Emily said. "We're nearly out of gas, and it's just about time to meet him."

Anna sighed and headed for the pharmacy at the corner of the intersection where they had planned to meet. "I appreciate your help, Emily. You've been putting yourself in harm's way all this time when you don't even know my daughter. It means a lot." It was unusual for Anna to open up to someone she hadn't known and trusted for ages, and Emily knew it.

"I wouldn't have it any other way, Anna," Emily replied warmly. She wanted to find Camille almost as much as Anna did.

They pulled into the parking lot and saw the doors to the pharmacy were shattered from the outside, presumably by looters. By necessity, everyone was a looter now, so it didn't mean the looters had been bad people.

"Max isn't here yet," Anna started. "I'm going to go inside and check the pharmacy. There are so many medications and first aid supplies we may need, and they're probably going to be hard to come by pretty soon."

"If you're going, I'm going," Emily said. When Anna started to protest, Emily continued. "If Max arrives while we're inside, he'll see our SUV. You know it's safer to do everything in pairs."

"You're right. Just make sure you have your knife ready," Anna said.

They got out of the SUV and silently walked toward the door. The store was fairly dark with just its overnight lighting turned on. They could see well enough as long as they moved slowly and carefully, but it would have been easier if all of the lights had been on. They must have been on an automatic timer since the power was still on. Once inside, they paused to look and listen for zombies. There was a slow shuffling noise toward the back of the store, but they didn't hear anything else. Looking around from where they stood just inside the front door, they could see that someone had thoroughly trashed the place. Displays were knocked down and destroyed, and bullet holes stood out prominently on the counters near the registers. Coolers full of drinks near the registers to their left were broken, the glass having been shot out. So many things were broken that it was apparent that someone had trashed the store for no reason. There weren't blood trails on the floor or dead zombies lying around. There were no signs of a struggle, just destruction. Broken glass from a counter full of makeup and perfume covered the aisle to their right. A wall of cosmetics was knocked to the floor.

"Whoever did this is gone," Anna shook her head with disgust. "I get coming in and taking what you need, but I don't understand the idiots tearing up the place.

"I have a feeling we're going to be seeing a lot of this," Emily said.

"You're probably right. Let's double-check these aisles to make sure there are no surprises," Anna said. "Then we'll take out the zombie in the pharmacy."

The store wasn't very big, so it only took a minute to look down each aisle. From pantyhose to dog treats, it looked like someone had gone through the place with a baseball bat knocking things to the floor in every aisle. The beer case was empty, but the small wine section was untouched. They headed to the pharmacy at the back of the store and found a lone woman in a nurse's uniform mindlessly lurching back and forth. She had numerous bite wounds up and down both arms and was missing several fingers. As Anna approached, the dead nurse leaned across the pharmacy counter, making it easy for Anna to grab her hair and plunge her knife through her ear.

"All clear," Anna said as she hopped across the counter. "Why don't you grab basic first aid supplies, cold medicines, and all of the other general over-the-counter stuff. I'll look through this mess," She gestured toward the pill bottles that were scattered all over the floor of the pharmacy as she grabbed a handful of bags for Emily to fill.

"I'm on it," Emily replied. She began to pick through the mess left on the shelves and the floor in the aisles in front of the pharmacy. She grabbed every package of gauze, tape, bandages, and antibiotic creams that she could find before moving onto medications.

Anna went through the pharmacy and found some areas untouched. Whoever had ransacked the place hadn't paid much attention to some of the most important medications. She filled bags with antibiotics, medications for blood sugar, blood pressure, thyroid, pneumonia, bronchitis, eye drops, and a few other things. She assumed the narcotic pain killers had been wiped out but checked anyway. All of the stronger prescriptions were gone, but she found a large supply of lesser-known drugs, mild pain killers, and muscle relaxers. She'd filled half a dozen plastic bags by the time she was done with the pharmacy. She looked out to see that Emily had nearly a dozen bags herself.

"Let's take all of this to the front of the store," Anna said. "Then we can come back through to pick through anything else we can use." She grabbed two bottles of bleach from a shelf as she walked by it. If they needed to purify water, later on, the bleach would do the trick.

Together they carried all of the bags to the front door and looked outside to see if there was any sign of Max or zombies. Seeing neither, they went back in to do a little more shopping. Anna filled bag after bag with canned foods, energy drinks, instant coffee, and prepackaged ready-to-eat foods before heading over to the candy aisle. Thinking of Camille and Damon, she filled several bags with their favorites then added a few of her own. Just the thought of chocolate becoming a thing of the past made her fill a few more bags. There was no such thing as too much chocolate.

Emily stepped into the aisle, saw the bags full of candy then laughed. "I was about to stock up on chocolate, but you have us covered."

"I feel like a kid in a candy store," Anna laughed. "I was just imagining a future without chocolate and went a little crazy, I guess." She still wore a big grin on her face. She looked at Emily's bags and was thankful that she was a little more sensible in her shopping. Emily had taken what looked like every last package of batteries, lighters, flashlights, and boxes upon boxes of feminine products.

"You sure did shop a bit smarter than I did," Anna laughed again. "At least one of us was thinking clearly."

"Oh, I threw in some frivolous stuff, too," Emily grinned. "But then I thought about not having tampons and changed gears."

They lugged all of their bags toward the front door of the store. They had so many bags that they were going to nearly fill the SUV, but to them, it was worth it. They took a look around for zombies and saw only two at the far end of the parking lot. The dead were so slow that it would take a good five minutes to get over to them, so the women began to quietly load the SUV. It was nearing midnight, and Anna felt a twinge of worry about Max. They had planned to meet at this intersection after finishing their search grid, but if they missed each other, they were supposed to meet at their house at midnight. They had both known going in that it might not be possible to meet up, but she was going to do her best to catch him at the house. After all of the bags were loaded, she decided to give him a few more minutes.

The two zombies had slowly staggered toward them as they loaded up the car and were now close enough that they had to be killed. Both were women dressed in torn and bloodied summer clothes. One still wore sandals while the other was barefoot with her skin sloughing off from walking. Anna took the one on the right while Emily took the one on the left. Anna thought that sometimes it seemed almost too easy to kill them, but that was a dangerous line of thinking, and she knew it. She reminded herself that just one mistake or one moment of carelessness was all it would take. Even if she did everything right 100% of the time, it still didn't mean she would survive. She mentally scolded herself for taking the situation too lightly, even if it were only for a moment.

"We might as well get going. Max could be at the house already," Anna yawned. Her eyes were red and stung from lack of sleep. She had been up for the better part of forty-eight hours, and it was wearing on her. She pulled out into the street and headed home. She had to dodge wrecked and abandoned cars, but the road was mostly free of zombies. They were back at the house in less than fifteen minutes. Max's truck was nowhere to be seen.

"It's okay, Anna," Emily said. "He's probably on his way here now."

"You're probably right," Anna replied, even though she couldn't help but worry about him.

"We should get some of this stuff unloaded while we wait for him," Emily said.

"Better yet, we should have the guys come out and unload it," Anna said. "I'm so tired."

They went inside the house where Damon had been waiting and had opened the door for them. Anna pulled him in for a tight hug. "Are you doing okay, kiddo?" she asked him.

"I'm good Mom," Damon said. "I've just been worrying about you guys. Everyone's in the kitchen and family room. We knew you might be checking in with dad here at midnight, so we've been hanging around waiting."

Anna saw Frank and Junior standing off to the side. "Would you guys mind unloading the SUV? We did some major shopping at the pharmacy," Anna said.

"No problem, we've got it," Frank said as Junior nodded. They headed right out the door to start bringing the bags in.

Anna was surprised to see Lucia, Joey, and Michelle in the kitchen. At the sight of her best friend, her eyes immediately filled with tears, and she rushed over to hug her.

"I'm so sorry, Michelle," Anna said as they embraced. Michelle's body was quickly racked with sobs as she hugged her best friend and let it all out. She felt like she would never run out of tears for Jesse.

Damon, Joey, Lucia, and Emily moved to the family room to give them some space. Joey and Lucia couldn't stand seeing their mother cry; seeing her raw grief caused both of them to tear up as well. Damon tried his best to comfort his best friend while Emily pulled Lucia close as the tears fell.

The loss of Jesse was felt heavily by everyone, and it would be a while before any of them would feel normal again. Michelle feared she would never feel like herself again but knew she needed to be strong for her kids. She'd taken a day for herself to grieve and try to sleep through the pain, but she knew that her time to cope with the initial shock of their loss was over. She would shed many more tears and would always have a hole in her heart, but her kids had to come first from this point forward.

Voices coming from the front door pulled everyone out of their grief for the moment. Frank and Junior had brought all of the bags and left them just inside the door, hoping not to disturb the family, but when Max and Maggie walked in the door, they all started talking at once.

Max hurried to the kitchen and family room area and was relieved to see Anna in one piece with no new injuries. He immediately noticed everyone's red eyes and realized he had interrupted some grieving time, but everyone pulled themselves together quickly. It seemed to be the new normal that they were all being forced to grow accustomed to. Everyone said their hellos then they were ready to plan for whatever was next. He looked around the room with pride as his eyes met those of each person, and without fail, he saw determination and strength on every face. It was time to make a new plan, and he felt confident that each one of them would do their part and do it well.

Chapter Twenty-One

Night 4

"How are the perimeter checks going?" Max asked Frank and Junior.

"They're going well," Junior said. "The yard hasn't been breached yet. The connecting back yards have been free of the dead, too. We've killed about a dozen or so zombies in the street out front just to be safe. We don't want any to linger near your house or the Wright's place next door, so we've been taking them out."

"None of them have shown any interest in either place," Frank added.

"Good to hear," Max said. "As long as they don't discover us in here, we should be safe for a little while. I'm not sure how much longer the power will last, so it could get uncomfortable once we lose the AC, but as long as we're safely hidden, we'll figure out how to deal with the heat when the time comes."

"Frank and Junior have been keeping everyone well fed," Damon said. "You and mom should eat some real food before you head out again, Dad."

Max nodded his thanks to the guys then turned to Anna. "Before we head back out, Anna, we should talk about it for a minute. We need to make another plan for how and where we're going to search, and you need a break. You can barely keep your eyes open, and you've been up for two days straight," Max said.

Anna immediately disagreed, saying, "We're all tired, Max. Imagine how tired Camille must be out there. You know I can't rest until my baby is home safe."

"I'm not saying that you should just stop searching and stay home. I think you need to eat something, maybe take a shower, and sleep for a couple of hours before you head out again. If you and Emily keep going without getting at least a little bit of rest, you're more likely to make a mistake out there," Max said. "You could run off the road, get surrounded, and anything could happen. I can't lose you, Anna." Max pleaded.

"What about you? We can't just all take a break," Anna insisted. "We have to keep searching."

"I had a nap yesterday, and you know me, I don't need much sleep," Max said. Desperate to get Anna to agree to take a break, he said, "Eat, sleep, do what you need to, and I'll be back in four hours to switch places. I'll rest up when you head back out."

"I just can't, Max," Anna started, then yawned.

He gave her a look, then smiled, "You can't even argue with me without yawning. Please, Anna, stay home and take a quick nap." He watched her expression closely as she came to a decision and felt instant relief when she nodded.

"You promise me you'll be careful out there," Anna said.

"You know I will. I love you, baby," Max said.

"I love you too, Max," Anna said as she stifled another yawn, and he grinned.

"Damon, I don't know if Emily is familiar with the showers or bedrooms," Max said. "Get her set up, will you?"

"Sure thing, Dad," Damon said.

"Then you kids need to get some sleep, too," Max said. "Michelle and the guys can handle everything else until I get back."

"Until *we* get back," Maggie said. "I'm still your second set of eyes out there." Max nodded.

With everyone settled or about to be, Max gave Anna a hug and a kiss. "I'll see you soon. I love you," Max said. "Thank you for staying. I mean it, thank you," he said as he took her face in his hands, stared into her eyes, and kissed her. His wife was so stubborn and so protective of their children that Max was almost surprised that he had talked her into getting some rest.

"You're welcome, but in four hours, I'm leaving whether you're back or not," Anna said with a trace of a smile. Max just shook his head because he knew without a doubt that in four hours and one minute, Anna would be back on the road.

"Ready Maggie?" Max asked as he took the radio Anna held out to him.

"Let's go," she answered, and they headed out the door.

Anna and Emily both grabbed a quick bite to eat then retired to their showers and beds, leaving the kids, Michelle, Frank, and Junior in the kitchen.

"I appreciate you guys doing all of the cooking today," Michelle said. She was used to being in the kitchen herself. It almost felt strange to her to have someone else feeding everyone.

"Happy to do it," Frank said.

"I'll take over in the morning," Michelle said. "Between feeding everyone and doing perimeter checks, have you guys gotten any sleep?"

"We napped here and there," Junior answered. "We're used to it at the fire station. We keep odd hours and sleep when we can."

"I don't mind doing the next perimeter check if you guys want to get some rest," Michelle offered.

"No can do, ma'am," Frank said. "We do everything in pairs now. We can't have you going out there alone, especially not at night."

"It's Michelle, no need to call me ma'am," Michelle said. "I've slept all day, so after your next round, why don't you guys get some sleep? I'll keep an eye on things. By then, Anna and Emily will be up, and Max should be back."

"That sounds good to me," Frank said.

It was nearly 1:00 in the morning, but the kids weren't ready for bed. All three of them were heaping plates full of food leftover from a late dinner. Michelle realized she hadn't eaten all day, so she joined them. There was so much food that Frank and Junior put together another plate for themselves then everyone got comfortable in the family room to eat and hang out.

"So, do you guys have a pole at the fire station?" Joey asked.

"Most of them don't nowadays, but our station is older, so we still have one," Frank said.

"Do you leave your uniform and your gear next to the fire truck like they do in the movies? So you can just step right into it?" Damon asked.

"We do. Everything is all ready to go, so when a call comes in, we can put our gear on, get in the truck and go out the door as fast as possible," Junior explained.

"That's pretty cool," Joey said. "I thought about maybe becoming a firefighter, but I guess that doesn't matter anymore."

Frank put his hand on Joey's shoulder and said, "You'd have made a fine fireman, son. We would have been lucky to have you." Joey grinned at the praise.

"So, did you climb ladders to save people from burning buildings?" Damon asked.

"We were on an engine that supplied the water, and we were the hose men," Junior said. "We'd hold the fire hose to put out the fire. We didn't ride the ladder truck, which is what you're thinking of."

"That's sweet," Damon said. "How many guys have to hold the hose? I mean, it must be pretty heavy."

"It's usually takes at least two men to control it once we turn the water on," Frank replied. "It's pretty damn heavy."

"Alright, alright," Michelle said. "It's late, and you boys need to get to bed." She looked over at Lucia and started laughing. Everyone else turned to see what had made her laugh. Lucia was sound asleep, sitting up with a plate of half-eaten food on her lap. Everyone laughed, but she slept right through it.

Just as Joey was about to startle her awake by getting right next to her ear to say her name loudly, Michelle stopped him. "Enough, Joey," Michelle said loudly. "Off to bed. I'll take care of your sister."

"Careful Mom, you're getting loud," Joey teased.

"What if there had been a zombie right outside the window when you raised your voice?" Damon joined in.

"We could be surrounded right now and not even know it all because you couldn't keep your voice down," Joey jokingly admonished her.

Michelle gave the boys a lethal look that made them both instantly shut up.

"Goodnight Mom," Joey said in an exaggerated whisper with a little grin.

Both boys turned from the room, and Damon quietly said, "Your mom's temper is back. I told you she's scary as hell."

"I heard that!" Michelle said with a little laugh, and the boys hurried down the hallway to Damon's room. It made her happy to see the boys acting like themselves. It felt good to laugh and smile, even if only for a couple of minutes.

"I'll clean up after I get Lucia to bed," Michelle said as Frank and Junior started to clear the dishes. "You two could use a break." Michelle gently woke Lucia then told her to go to bed. Lucia nodded sleepily and made her way down the hallway.

Michelle gathered all of the dirty plates and got ready to wash dishes. Frank and Junior were hanging out for a few more minutes before they had to do their next perimeter check. They didn't force any small talk on her, and she was grateful for it. They seemed to be good men, and Jesse would never have brought them home if they hadn't been. She'd just had enough conversation for one evening and was glad to lose herself to the mindlessness of washing a sink full of dishes. When she was about halfway done, they excused themselves to head outside. She was relieved to have a little time to herself. Her thoughts were focused mostly on Jesse and her children and moving forward now as a family of three. Of course, they were all family with Max and Anna and the kids, but she was the head of her little family now and knew she would do anything she had to do to keep them safe.

It was after 2:00 in the morning before Michelle had the kitchen cleaned up to her satisfaction. She checked the fridge to see what fresh food they had left since they knew the power wouldn't last much longer. She wanted to make sure that nothing went to waste. The frozen food would probably last another day or two when the time came, and she figured the men could grill it out back if the neighborhood was still quiet. After sleeping for most of the day, she felt wired and wide awake. She always took comfort in cooking and baking, so she pulled out the ingredients to bake some blueberry muffins, chocolate chip muffins, and banana bread. It occurred to her that there would be very few baked goods in their future, so she decided to make some cake, cookies, and cinnamon rolls too. By the time she finished baking, everyone would probably be waking up, and she would make them a proper breakfast. She got lost in her baking and enjoyed a couple of hours of peace and quiet.

Chapter Twenty-Two

Anna awoke to the delicious aroma of baked goods coming from her kitchen. She checked her phone and saw that her alarm was about to go off, so she hit the button. As she walked out of her room feeling recharged, she headed for the kitchen to see what smelled so good. The counters were full of muffins and desserts, and Michelle was in the middle of making several other things. Emily had been asleep in the family room and walked into the kitchen just as Anna did.

"Wow, it smells good in here," Anna said. "You're doing some serious baking."

"I just wanted the kids to enjoy as much as possible before we lose the ability to bake," Michelle said. "And you know me. Baking is my happy place." Anna walked over to hug her friend. Michelle hugged her back and didn't break down in tears. All of the time in the kitchen was doing her some good.

"Morning Michelle, Anna," Emily said with a yawn. She still felt a little tired, but that nap had done wonders for her.

Michelle handed them muffins and coffee so they could get a little something in their stomachs before they headed out again. They definitely needed the caffeine. "Eat and drink, both of you," Michelle said in the motherly way she spoke to her children.

"No word from Max?" Anna asked. He was due to be home soon. She smiled to herself, thinking of him worrying about her leaving if he was even one minute late.

She'd give him at least five minutes. She sipped her coffee and watched the clock.

"If you're worried, you can call him on the radio," Emily said. "But I'm pretty sure he'll be here on time or very close to it. He doesn't want you taking off again without him."

"I'll give it a few more minutes. When I'm done with my coffee, I'll be ready to head back out," Anna said. "Hopefully, he'll be here by then."

Frank, Junior, and the kids were all still sleeping. It had taken some persuasion on Michelle's part to get the men to take a nap. She had promised to wake them when Max got home.

"I restocked your backpacks for you even though you haven't been eating much. They were still nearly full when you brought them in. I added some muffins and a few more bottles of water," Michelle said. "You'd better start eating more." Anna just nodded in response. Michelle was in mom mode right now and was doing her best to take care of everyone.

"What all are you baking," Anna started but stopped abruptly when she heard a noise at the front door. She jumped from her chair so quickly that it nearly fell over. She hadn't wanted to admit it, but she'd started to worry about Max and was so relieved that he was home. Anna removed the lift bar, opened the door, and nearly jumped for joy.

"Camille!" Anna exclaimed. "Oh baby, I've been so worried about you." Before Camille could say a word, Anna wrapped her arms around her and held her tight. Camille sobbed into her mom's chest and hugged her back. They both cried tears of joy and relief and couldn't let go of each other. Camille had been hoping and waiting

187

for this moment for so long. She'd been so afraid that she would never see her mom again and had dreamt of her mom holding her in her arms. It was one of the things that had kept her going through it all.

Michelle and Emily were stunned and watched from the kitchen. Camille showing up at the door was the last thing that anyone had expected. Both women teared up with the joy of seeing mother and daughter reunited. Michelle loved Camille as if she were one of her own and had to force herself to wait before running over to hug her. She knew Anna and Camille needed a few minutes to themselves.

Anna finally loosened her grip on her daughter and held her back to take a good look at her. "Are you injured? Does anything hurt?" Anna asked.

"I'm okay Mom," Camille said through her tears. "My knee is sore from twisting it, and my shoulder and wrist hurt from when I drove into a telephone pole. Nothing serious."

"When you wrecked… you drove?" Anna asked in surprise. Camille had never even sat in the driver's seat before.

"It's a long story, Mom, but I'm okay," Camille replied. "I promise."

Anna had a million questions but, for the moment, settled on hugging her daughter again. She led her to the little family room off of the kitchen to sit down. Michelle brought her a glass of water and a plate of muffins. "I missed you, kiddo," Michelle said as she gave her a quick hug.

"Emily, do you mind grabbing the radio for me?" Anna asked. She didn't want to leave her daughter's side. Emily handed it to her a moment later. Anna pressed the button to call Max, and he responded immediately.

"Don't leave without me, Anna. I'll be there in five minutes," Max said over the radio. He was running a little late and was worried that she was going to take off before he got there.

"Max, listen," Anna said, then she handed the radio to Camille. "Hi Daddy," she said.

Max immediately teared up and struggled to find his voice. He honestly had never expected Camille to find her way home, not after she'd been gone for so long. "Hi baby girl," Max said as he was overcome with emotion. "I've missed you so much. Are you okay?"

"I'm fine, Dad," Camille said through tears of her own. "I just got home a few minutes ago."

"I love you, baby girl. I'm right around the corner," Max said. "I'll be there in a minute."

"We've been searching everywhere for you," Anna told Camille. "Your dad got home not long after the horde finally passed by. What were you thinking? You could have been killed!"

"You know I didn't have a choice, mom," Camille said. "I was so scared, but I knew that the zombies at the front of the horde saw me. If I'd gone back into the Wright's house or hopped the fence to ours, they would have followed me. We'd all be dead right now. I had to run."

Anna knew that was true, but it killed her that her daughter had been out there on her own for so long. "I know. You're braver and stronger than I could ever be. I'm so proud of you."

"Is everyone else okay?" Camille asked with worry evident in her voice. It was the middle of the night, so she knew that her brother, Joey, and Lucia were probably sleeping.

Anna diverted her eyes for a moment before answering. "Honey, Jesse didn't make it. He was killed when he and your dad were on their way home."

Camille's eyes grew wide and filled again with tears. "What happened? Are Joey and Lucia okay?"

"I don't know exactly, but I do know that he didn't suffer," Anna said quietly. "Joey and Lucia will be okay. It's just going to take some time. They're going to be so happy to see you, especially Lucia. She's been blaming herself this whole time and thinks it's her fault you had to run."

Michelle fought back tears at the mention of Jesse's name. She had endless tears to cry for him, but she was trying hard to keep herself together for the moment.

"Your dad brought home some other people they managed to save along the way. One of them died last night, but Frank and Junior are here. They were trapped in their fire truck when your dad and Jesse saved them," Anna said. "And your dad found another woman yesterday. Her name's Maggie. She's been helping him search all this time. Emily helped me the whole time I was out there looking for you. They're good people."

"So you all have been driving around looking for me all this time?" Camille was amazed. Not surprised because she knew how much they loved her, but amazed that they had been searching for so long when they had no idea where to look. "How? I mean, where did you go?" She couldn't imagine how they would have found her.

"We drove around neighborhood after neighborhood, mostly to the east. I never realized there were about a million streets around here until I tried to drive down every one of them," Anna said, shaking her head.

Before she could say more, Max came in the front door, followed by Maggie. Max rushed over to Camille and picked her up in a giant bear hug. "Look at you," Max said. "I've missed your face." His tears fell freely, and Camille shed a few more. She'd never felt so loved or safe in her entire life. She had missed her family so much that it hurt, and it was hard to believe that she found her way back to them. She never wanted to leave their side again.

"Are you okay? Are you hurt? Have you had anything to eat or drink?" Max asked one question after another before she could answer.

"I'm okay, Dad," Camille said. "Michelle already fed me muffins. I'm just tired and sore. It feels so good to sit down again."

"Sore? Did you get hurt?" Max asked.

"She drove a car into a telephone pole and twisted her knee at some point. We haven't gotten into any of the details yet," Anna said. She looked at Max with the most peaceful expression on her face. Her family was whole again. Max mouthed *"I love you"* to Anna, then shifted his focus back to his daughter.

The commotion from Max and Maggie coming in and everyone talking woke the kids, Frank and Junior. Coming down the hallway, Damon was the first to see Camille and ran toward her. Wordlessly he hugged her tightly and breathed a sigh of relief. When he'd heard the noise, he'd been afraid that something was wrong.

"I've missed you, sis," Damon said. A little more quietly, he added, "I love you." She whispered back to him, and they just sat there for a moment, feeling happy.

Joey and Lucia were a little louder with their greeting. Joey high-fived Camille and said, "I knew you'd make it back here. Holy fuck, I just knew it." He caught his mom's glare and said a quick sorry for his language.

Lucia walked up to Camille and hesitated. She loved her with all of her heart, and she was scared to death that Camille would never forgive her for freezing up when the horde came. "I'm so sorry, Camille," Lucia started outright crying before she could even begin to try to stop herself. "It was all my fault that you had to run. I froze up when I was in the tree, and you needed my help."

Camille stared at her best friend for a moment, confused by Lucia's words. "It wasn't your fault, not at all," Camille said. "The horde saw me, Lucia. If you had jumped down, they would have seen you too, and we both would have had to run." She closed the gap between them and hugged Lucia hard. They cried on each other's shoulders for a moment until Lucia's tears of guilt and fear became tears of relief.

"I'm so sorry about your dad," Camille said quietly. She knew that nothing she said would help with her friend's grief but needed to say it anyway. "I love you, and I will always love you. You know that, right?"

Lucia nodded and said, "I love you, too."

At that moment, Frank and Junior stepped in from the living room doorway. Both of their faces were lit up with joy at seeing the family being reunited. They had waited for a pause before coming in because they didn't want to interrupt the happy reunion.

"It's gotten a little noisy with everyone talking and the front door being opened and closed, so we're going to head out to do a perimeter check while you guys catch up," Frank said.

JAIME HERNANDEZ

"Camille, this is Frank," Max pointed to the tall, dark man that was built like an ox. "And this is Junior. They're good guys." Camille said a quick hello to both of them. As they headed out the door, Max realized he hadn't introduced Maggie.

"This is Maggie. She's been helping me search for you ever since I found her early yesterday," Max said.

"Hi Camille," Maggie said. She had salt and pepper hair, crow's feet, and smile lines on her face. She gave the impression of being a happy person. She grinned at Camille feeling true joy that she was home safe.

"Hi Maggie," Camille said. "It's nice to meet you."

"Well, let's everyone get settled down here so we can catch up," Michelle said.

"I want to check your injuries to make sure you're okay, and we all want to know what happened and how you made it back home," Anna said.

"I'm fine Mom. There are some pain pills and a knee brace in my backpack," Camille said. "If you could just grab those, that's all I need."

Anna wrapped the brace around her daughter's knee, gave her two of the mild pain pills, and they all settled in to hear Camille's story.

Chapter Twenty-Three

Day 5

Everyone was shocked to learn just how far away from home Camille had ended up when she told them about Bradford, Elizabeth, and the mansion on Lake Road. With all of the zigzagging she'd had to do, she had probably run at least five miles when she took off running from the horde.

"Holy shit," Max said. "We never looked that far north." He shook his head, feeling guilty that he hadn't thought to check the mansions along the lake.

"Even if you had, it's a big area Dad," Camille said. "To use one of your old people's expressions, it was like looking for a needle in a haystack," she said with a grin, trying to lighten the mood. She didn't want her parents to feel guilty about anything.

Anna was beating herself up, too, for not going all the way to the lake. It had just seemed too far away. It wasn't just getting to the lake but going as far to the east as Camille had run. She'd never even tried to search that area. "Motherfucker," Anna mumbled to herself.

"Anna, stop," Max said. "It's like our lovely daughter just said; it was like looking for a needle in a haystack. All that matters now is that she made it home."

"I was lucky to find such a nice couple," Camille said. "They were my last hope, and they took me in. They kind of felt like grandparents; the way they made sure I was okay and had everything that I needed. And then they let me take one of their SUVs."

"About that, you ran into a telephone pole?" Anna asked.

"It was really hard to drive, especially around all of the cars. Whenever there were a lot of zombies, it got pretty scary. I scraped against other cars a few times, hit the gas and the brakes too hard," Camille said. "I was only a mile from home and nearly out of gas when a zombie appeared right in front of me. It was so dark out that I didn't see it until it was too late. I tried to swerve around it, but I hit a telephone pole instead."

"That must have been terrifying," Anna said. She worried that her daughter would be traumatized and full of nightmares.

"It was, but I'm okay Mom," Camille said. "After I wrecked the car, that's when things got pretty scary. A pickup came weaving down the street, and I heard a bunch of guys yelling and laughing, so I jumped into a ditch to hide. They were drunk and acting like dumbasses. They fired their guns into the air, set a house on fire, and even left one of their friends to suffer and die when he got bit by a zombie. They drew in dozens of zombies before they left, so it was a little scary trying to run away in the dark."

"You poor thing," Anna said. She was shocked to hear about the idiots in the truck. "I'm so sorry, Camille."

Max pulled Camille closer and kissed her forehead. "You did the right thing hiding in the ditch. That's one of the things we were worried about. We were driving strange vehicles, so even if we drove right past you, we didn't know whether you would show yourself or not."

"I just went with my gut, Dad," Camille said. "At the mansion, my gut said to trust Bradford, so I ran inside. With the guys in the truck, I knew I had to hide."

"We haven't all had a chance to talk about things we've seen yet," Max started. "But I ran across an evil man yesterday. I stopped at a gas station, and this gray pickup came speeding down the road toward me and pulled in right next to me." Max hesitated with Camille and Lucia listening, but he decided that everyone should know what was out there. "He was a sociopath and a rapist. He was looking for women and had already found some. He won't be going after anyone else." Max said with finality that the others understood for what it was.

"Holy shit," Emily said and shivered. "When we were stuck on the roof of a bar, a gray pickup went speeding past us. We tried to flag him down, but he didn't see us."

Max looked at Anna, and the color drained from his face. If Bill had seen his wife and Emily, they might both be dead instead of him.

"Well, thank god he didn't see us, but we were armed and ready for anything," Anna said, then changed the subject. "Emily and I cleaned out a pharmacy last night…"

"Yeah, I saw the bags," Max said with a laugh. "It looked like one of your usual shopping trips."

Everyone laughed at that because of the way Anna shopped. It was lucky that she did, though, because they were well stocked up on pretty much everything.

"Oh hush," Anna playfully swatted at Max. "Anyway, the whole store had been ransacked. There were bullet holes all over the place, and it looked like the place had been trashed just for the hell of it."

"I ran into a guy at a pharmacy. I was trying to get medications that I thought you would want. This guy had broken in to get high on pain meds and ended up getting bitten by the pharmacist. He was almost gone when I got there, so I stayed with him then put him down," Max said.

"We've gotta be careful out there. Not everyone we come across is going to be a good guy."

"We've been lucky so far, that's for sure," Anna said, shaking her head. She was still processing what Camille had said about the drunken guys and the evil man Max had run into. They'd had some very close calls.

"Now that everyone's here, we don't need to be going back out for a while, do we?" Michelle asked.

"We can take a little break to rest up. Everyone needs some real sleep," Max said. "But we're going to have to figure out a way to get gas. I'm not sure how yet, but I'm going to talk to Frank and Junior about it to see if they have any ideas. In the meantime, we can hit neighbor garages around here for gas cans. It's a start, at least."

"Won't the power go out soon?" Damon asked.

"Yeah, I'm not sure how much longer we'll have it. Maybe a day or two at the most," Max said. "If we're only hiding from zombies and not from people, we can use the grill by the pool to cook and heat food. There are so many trees that the smoke may dissipate enough that it won't even matter if people are around."

"It's going to get extremely hot in the house," Joey said. "With everything boarded up, we won't get any kind of breeze in here."

"We'll have to figure out something," Max said. "My biggest concern is gas and water. We need to keep all of the vehicles fueled up and ideally have extra in the gas cans. I'm not sure how long the water will keep running either."

"When the water treatment plant goes down with the electricity, there should still be water for a little while. We can purify it with bleach. During my shopping extravaganza," Anna paused to laugh. "I grabbed a couple of bottles. Those will go a long way."

"Well, everyone should shower as often as they want to before we lose the water. I haven't had one in days," Max said.

"Yeah, we noticed," Camille laughed and held her nose.

"I'm going to go ahead and hit the shower, then get some sleep," Max said. "Can you ladies please get Maggie set up? She hasn't slept in a while either."

"I've got her covered," Anna said. "Anyone else needing sleep, now's a good time to do it. The sun's about to come up, and we're going to have a lot to do today. I want to make sure everyone is well-rested."

"The medication must have kicked in; I can hardly keep my eyes open," Camille said with a yawn. "Goodnight everyone," She hugged her mom and dad then headed to her room with Lucia.

Before long, everyone was lying down except for Michelle. Frank and Junior had come back in from their perimeter check and took over the living room. It was a little bit of a tight squeeze, but they had managed to find a place for everyone.

She went back to baking in the kitchen. It seemed like a silly thing to do, but there was nothing that needed to be taken care of at the moment, at least nothing she could do on her own. With Anna's bottomless pantry, Michelle was able to whip up several more batches of cookies and desserts before anyone in the house started to stir. When she started to hear people moving around mid-morning, she cooked a big breakfast. There were a lot of people to feed, but Michelle was in her element and made more than enough for everyone. She'd just about finished up all of the remaining fresh food in the fridge and started on the freezer. She was going to make sure that everyone ate well until they were forced to live on canned and dried goods.

Chapter Twenty-Four

Day 5

Everyone was in a good mood over breakfast. Camille's homecoming had considerably lifted everyone's spirits. Getting some solid sleep had helped to energize and invigorate. There was a lot of laughter which didn't come as easily as it had only six days ago, so it was good to hear. Even though her heart was aching, Michelle felt happy seeing everyone together and enjoying themselves. As they were finishing up, Max announced plans for the day.

"There are some things we need to get ahead of while we still can," Max said. "Gas and water are at the top of that list. Junior here used to work at a gas station and knows how to get the pumps working as long as we still have power, so that's going to be our first priority."

"I've got some ideas for when the power goes out, too, but they're messy and dangerous. We need to get as much as we can now. These trucks and SUVs aren't too good on gas," Junior said. "Frank and I are going to head out in a few minutes to get started."

"All this bottled water we've been grabbing isn't going to go that far with our group. We need trucks full of water. I want to hit a Costco and take every last bottle they've got," Max said. "That will keep us going for a little while."

"Joey and I can go hit all of the neighbor's garages for gas cans since you guys are going to be out," Damon said.

"Absolutely not," Anna said.

"Like hell you will," Michelle said simultaneously.

"Mom, we can't just all sit at home when there's stuff that needs to be done," Damon said.

"He's right," Max said as both Michelle and Anna fixed him with angry glares. He held his hand up as he continued. "There's too much to do. The boys have proven themselves to be more than capable. I'd rather have them checking garages up and down our street than have them driving anywhere."

"So what, all of us women are just supposed to stay the hell home?" Anna seethed because she was pissed about Damon going out.

"Of course not," Max said. "I was going to suggest that you, Emily, Maggie, and I hit Costco. It's too dangerous for just two people. Plus, we can carry a lot more water that way."

"Do you think four people are enough for Costco?" Maggie asked. "There could be hundreds of zombies inside. Hundreds outside, too."

"The water isn't going anywhere," Emily said. "Maybe we should all go together for the gas. Anna and I had a rough time at a gas station. I think you need more than two people if you want to get the work done while someone else keeps watch."

"I agree," Anna said. "We had a very close call when it was just the two of us. I think I'd feel a lot better about it if the four of us were to go with Frank and Junior. Get as much gas as we can before the power goes out, then we can start clearing all of the water we can find out of the stores."

Max considered it for a moment. "Okay, we'll all go together for the gas. You're right, and there's safety in numbers," Max said.

"What about us?" Camille asked about herself and Lucia.

"You two, along with Michelle, can keep up the perimeter checks. You handle anything that needs to be taken care of here while we're all out," Max said.

"I don't want the kids out doing that by themselves," Michelle said adamantly. "You heard what happened to the boys the other night." She shot an evil look at Frank and Junior because she just couldn't help herself. They both quickly looked away, not wanting her to unload on them again with her mama bear temper.

"Michelle, I understand your concern. I really do. I don't want my kids or my wife out there. We've all learned how to fight and kill the dead. The kids know what they're doing, and things are only going to get worse as time goes on," Max said. "Everyone will eventually have to be able to do a little bit of everything. It's the only way we're going to survive this. I feel better about the girls staying at the house right now instead of going out there where we know bad people are lurking around. They can handle a few zombies."

The kids were all excited about their jobs, while both mothers swore under their breath. Not entirely under their breath, as Michelle said, "Motherfucker," just loud enough for everyone to hear. Anna and Michelle understood what was necessary, but they weren't happy about it. They grudgingly admitted that Max was right.

"If anything happens to one of the, Max," Michelle started.

"I know, Michelle. Everyone will play it smart and not take any foolish chances," Max said.

"We should be heading out now," Frank said. He wanted to get started as soon as possible. They could lose power at any time and would miss their chance to get gas the easy way.

"We wanted to try to get the neighbor's truck across the street and take that to the gas station," Junior said. "If we're all going, I think we should try for more of the neighbor vehicles. It's safer to keep the SUV and the new truck here if we have to leave your house for good at some point. Just like we've been leaving the Wright's vehicles stocked and in their garage in case of an emergency. We've got a big group of people here, and that way, we know we'll be able to fit everyone and our supplies."

"It can't hurt to have a few extra trucks. That's a good idea, Junior," Max said. "Well, this changes things a bit. Boys, you can do your thing. Girls, you take care of the house with Michelle. Everyone else, let's grab what we need and see about getting some of the neighbor's trucks."

Michelle restocked everyone's backpacks with bottled water and a two-day supply of food. "Just because there are two days of food in those packs doesn't mean you stay out there for two days," she said. "Get the trucks, get the gas, and get back here safely."

She packed two lighter backpacks for Joey and Damon. "I expect you to check back in here at least every two hours," Michelle said. "Don't make me come looking for you, or I'll kick both your asses," she warned. They both nodded and shared a quick grin knowing that Michelle's temper was simmering just under the surface. Joey and Damon hurried out the door before anyone could change their mind about letting the boys go house to house. They were both eager to be out there doing something.

"Be careful out there," Anna called after them.

Max left one of the radios on the counter while everyone got their weapons ready. He wanted one at the house and one with them, so Michelle could reach them if there were any problems. He was hoping to find more while they were out because he didn't like having any part of the group separated without a way for everyone to communicate. They grabbed their bags and headed out the door.

The six of them quietly made their way toward the brick wall at the front of the yard. Joey and Damon were already out of sight. Max figured they had probably hopped fences to start at the house next door to the Wright's place. There was a large red pickup across the street two houses down. The house looked normal as if it were just an average day.

"Let's try for that one first," Frank said in a low tone as he pointed at the red truck. Max unlocked the gate since there was no reason for all of them to climb over the fence or wall. He closed it behind him but didn't lock it to make it more accessible when they returned. Zombies weren't capable of opening it.

They inched toward the street, where nine zombies were shambling around together. They weren't interested in anything in particular around them; they just walked in a pack. Nine zombies up against the six of them were no problem, even with the zombies grouped together. Frank was so lethal that he would probably take out at least two before the rest of them finished with their first. His height and build gave him a great advantage.

"Frank, Junior, Anna, go left. Maggie, Emily, and I will go right," Max whispered the instructions.

The zombies turned toward them when they were just a few feet away. Max went for a big guy on the right. The man had been through a horrible attack leaving one side of his face ripped open to expose his snapping jaw. His cheek hung down near his neck, held by a few thin strips of flesh. Max plunged his knife through its eye, splattering milky, bloody putrid fluid, and the man dropped to the ground. To his left, Anna thrust her knife through the ear of a half-naked middle-aged man with a huge beer gut. To his right, Maggie and Emily had already dropped their zombies. He was impressed when he saw how proficient and fast they were. Frank and Junior were finishing off the last two on the left, having already taken out the first three on their side.

They made their way across the street while keeping an eye out for more zombies. There weren't any in sight. They took a closer look at the truck and the front of the house. The truck was only a few years old and looked to be in good condition.

"The husband usually rides his motorcycle to work, and the wife takes her car," Anna spoke quietly. "The house should be empty."

Junior tried to open the front door, but it was locked, so Emily looked around the planters next to the door to check if there was a hidden key. "Found it," Emily said with a grin when she pulled the key from under the second planter.

"Emily, unlock it. Frank and I will go in first," Max said. "The rest of you follow. It should be empty, but I don't want to take anything for granted."

As soon as the door was unlocked, Frank led the way inside. "Wait for a second," he said and held his hand up. Max was immediately on high alert, thinking that a zombie must have been right inside the door. Frank turned around with the keys for the truck in his hand and a smile on his face. "The key was on a table just inside the door. I hope they're all this easy," he said. Everyone breathed a sigh of relief.

"Let's try for the white truck two doors down. It would be nice to have at least two vehicles, maybe three if we can," Junior said. "I don't want to start any of them until we're ready to go, or we'll start drawing in some of the dead."

They walked to the next house, which bore signs that zombies had been through it. The front door was halfway open and blood-streaked the railing and the door frame. They stopped to listen for any noise coming from within but heard nothing, so Max and Frank entered first. They cleared the living room, and then the rest of the group came in. Just beyond the living room was the dining room, which led to the kitchen at the back of the house. There was a raspy moan coming from the rear of the house, and they heard the telltale sound of feet shuffling across the floor as the zombie was alerted to their presence.

"I've got this," Frank said. Max followed out of caution, but Frank took the zombie down with a quick thrust of his knife. As he wiped his blade on the fallen zombie's shirt, he said, "You know, I think I prefer a hammer or an ax. One quick hit and not so much of the squelching noises and fluids coming from their eyes and shit."

Max stifled a laugh as Frank sheathed his knife and pulled out his ax. While everyone else was grateful for the knives, Frank was such a tall, muscular man that it was easier for him to crush a skull with a tool. He towered over most of the living and the dead and had the weight to back up his swing.

Anna and Emily entered the kitchen after clearing the rest of the house to make sure it was free from zombies.

After a glance at the dead body on the floor, Anna said, "Why don't you guys take the kitchen? We'll check the living room and dining room."

Max looked for a key rack in the kitchen then joined Frank in checking the kitchen counter and drawers. Junior and Maggie checked the dining room while Anna and Emily looked around the living room. After just a couple of minutes of searching, Emily softly called out, "Found them!"

"What do you think?" Junior asked. "Should we try for one more?"

"It can't hurt," Maggie said. "I noticed a blue pickup across the street about two houses down."

They all went back outside and watched for zombies as they crossed the street. In the front yard of the house with the blue truck, a lone zombie lurched toward them. Frank brought his ax down on its head in one hard swing, and the zombie was down. He shared a quick grin with Max. The front door of the house was unlocked and appeared to be empty. After a ten-minute search, no keys were found.

"Well, it was worth a try," Anna said. "Why don't we get the other two trucks before we go any further? There's no point in walking much more when we can drive those two until we find a third. I'm sure we'll have plenty to choose from well before we get near the first couple of gas stations."

Everyone was agreeable, so they split up to ride in the red and white trucks. Max, Anna, and Maggie took the white truck while Junior, Frank, and Emily took the red one. Max had only driven about half a block when he saw a newer silver pickup in a driveway. There were three zombies on the sidewalk, so Frank and Junior went to kill the zombies while everyone else went directly to the house's front door. It looked clear, and the front door was unlocked, so they went inside. Two minutes later, they came out with keys. Anna and Emily took the silver truck while everyone else piled back into the first two. A moment later, they were on their way to the first gas station.

Chapter Twenty-Five

Day 5

With Max leading the way, they drove to the nearest set of gas stations. The intersection held a pharmacy, a small shopping plaza, and two gas stations. About a dozen zombies were lingering around in the middle of the street, but most of the area was clear. They pulled all three trucks into the first gas station and pulled up alongside the pumps. Max, Anna, and Emily went with Junior to clear the inside of the building so he could turn the pumps on while Frank and Maggie stood watch outside. The dead were still slow as hell, so they had a good five minutes before the stragglers in the street would reach them. When they did, they would take them out together.

The gas station's door was ajar, which was a good sign because any zombies inside would have been able to make their way out at any time. Max went in first with the others following, and they quickly cleared the aisles. Their luck was holding without a zombie in sight. Junior went to turn the pumps on and got them started without a problem. Max, Anna, and Emily went looking for fuel cans in a large area full of basic car supplies. They found ten gas cans and grabbed some oil, antifreeze, fix-a-flat, and windshield washer fluid. An involuntary shiver ran down Emily's spine as she thought of her last attempt to grab gas cans. She shook it off and headed back outside with the others.

"Why don't you fill up the trucks while the guys and I start taking out those zombies?" Max suggested to Anna, Emily, and Maggie. "If we can keep their numbers down, we should be able to hit the other gas station when we're done here."

Anna didn't like being told what to do but understood that her husband was trying to make feasible plans on the go. The women agreed, and each went to fill up one of the three trucks. They were amazed that Junior could get the pumps running and were determined to get as much gas as they could before the power went out.

The zombies in the street had reached the edge of the parking lot, and a few others were approaching from other areas. The group wasn't making much noise, but it was enough to attract the dead in the quiet of the day. Frank went to work with his ax, cleaving skull after skull. Junior dashed around and between the zombies with deadly thrusts of his knife. Max went to the other end of the parking lot past the gas pumps to make sure none of the dead came in through a blind spot and was glad he did. Half a dozen zombies had been slowly making their way around the corner of the building toward the front. They were separated enough that he was able to take them all out himself. When he finished, he looked back toward the pumps to see that all of the trucks were full and the women were filling the gas cans. Plans never seemed to work out, but this time everything was going smoothly, and it felt good. It was hard to always stay on high alert with adrenaline rushes and crashes, so he was relieved to feel less pressure than usual.

Frank and Junior continued to kill the occasional shambler coming from the street while Max kept watch on his side. A couple of minutes later, all of the gas cans were full and ready to go. The gas station across the street was deserted, and they'd already attracted most of the nearby dead. So, it looked like getting gas there was going to be a lot easier. Frank, Max, and Junior headed over to the trucks and lugged all of the heavy gas cans into the truck beds.

"Go ahead and drive across the street," Max said to Emily, Anna and Maggie. "We'll kill the few stragglers on the sidewalk and meet you there in a minute." There were only four zombies currently in sight, so it only took a moment for the guys to kill them. They all met at the gas station and prepared to clear it.

The glass doors of the gas station were smeared with dried blood. Max sighed when he realized this one wasn't going to be as easy as the first. The parking lot and street were clear of the dead. They didn't have to worry so much about that this time.

"Emily, Maggie, you want to keep watch?" Max asked. He had a feeling they were going to need more muscle inside the gas station, so he wanted Frank and Junior with him. Anna would not want to stay outside when only two people were needed, so he planned on her going in.

Junior held the door open while Frank went inside with Max and Anna close on his heels. It was a bloodbath. Blood stained the floor, the counters, and all of the displays within sight. They could hear raspy moans and shuffling feet moving around the tiny aisles of the little store. Max took the first zombie out as it stumbled out from behind the register. It wore a store uniform and had a multitude of bites over most of its upper body. Max thrust his knife into its ear, and it fell to the ground. Frank nearly took the heads off of two of the dead as he swung his ax. Anna killed two child-sized zombies without a second thought. She'd seen so many of the dead when the horde came through, and not much bothered her anymore. Junior stepped ahead to the next aisle and found a crawler wearing a store uniform. He plunged his knife through its ear then wiped it off on the dead guy's shirt. Max had thought that was all of them, but they heard scratching and light thumping noises coming from the rear of the store.

"Let's clear out whatever's moving around back there while Junior gets the pumps going," Frank told Max. "Anna, watch Junior's back."

Frank and Max found half a dozen zombies in the storage room. The door was lightweight and could be pushed open from either side. The dead had heard them making noise and were making their way out the door as the guys approached. "Fucking A," Max said as he stabbed the first through the eye. The sickening squelch of the burst eyeball smelled putrid as a bloody, milky fluid ran out. "Why the hell are there so many in here?"

"It's strange, that's for sure," Frank replied as he cracked skulls with his ax. "Maybe the store was crowded when the shit hit the fan. You remember how fast they all turned and attacked each other."

"Yeah," Max said. "Still didn't expect to find so many in here." He killed another, making a point to thrust his knife through the dead woman's ear instead of her eye. He didn't think he'd ever get used to the smell and sound of a bursting eyeball.

The dead were coming out of the storeroom, moving at an achingly slow pace; otherwise, the guys wouldn't have been talking so much while they killed them. The setup made it almost too easy, but Max knew better than most not to take any situation for granted. That's when mistakes were made, and zombies would get lucky.

When all the zombies were finally dead and Junior had turned the pumps on, Anna went back outside to see if

212

Emily and Maggie needed any help. Max and Frank only found three gas cans on the shelf, so they went back to the storage room to see if there were any more.

"Well, would you look at that," Frank said with a little laugh. There were two dozen gas cans sitting among other supplies on the back wall. They weren't heavy, but they were awkward to carry, so it took them a few trips to bring all of them out to the pumps.

"Wow, that's a hell of a lot," Anna said with a smile. "We'll have two of the truck beds full with all of those."

"We'll probably only be able to make one more stop before we take these back to the house," Maggie said.

"Frank, keep watch, would you?" Max asked. "The rest of us can fill these up, and we can get out of here before more zombies make their way over." As Max filled some of the gas cans, he looked at the sky to the east. The fire he'd accidentally set seemed to be burning itself out. There was far less smoke than there had been the day before, and the smell wasn't nearly as strong as it had been. He was relieved that it wasn't going to spread any further.

The intersection around the gas station was still nearly free of the dead. As two zombies got a little closer to the parking lot, Frank was quick to take them down. He kept looking around in every direction to make sure none could take them by surprise. Nearly ten minutes later, all of the gas cans were full and loaded into the truck beds.

"There's a gas station at the next main intersection," Emily said. "Do you want to head there or go for a smaller one?" The next intersection was a busier one with a lot of shops and restaurants.

"Let's try the path of least resistance for now," Max answered. "If there are many zombies in the area, we can head for a different one."

213

Everyone got into their trucks and followed Max and Maggie down what used to be a busy street. There were many scattered, abandoned, and wrecked cars filling up the roadway, so Max started weaving around them. The closer they got to the intersection, the more zombies he saw. "Fuck," he mumbled. There were too many to risk it, so he slowed to cut down another street while watching his rearview mirror to make sure the others safely followed him.

"No worries, Max," Maggie said as she sensed his tension. "There are plenty of places to choose from."

Max nodded and lit a cigarette. At the end of the street at the next intersection, there was a small, older gas station, so he planned to try that one next. About halfway there, several dozen zombies shuffled around in the middle of the street. They had been wandering aimlessly but saw the trucks coming and shifted their focus to the vehicles.

"Motherfucker," Max said in frustration. He slowed and took the next right down a little side street. The others followed closely behind him. They were about to enter a maze of small housing developments, and he didn't want to get caught up in any of those. He slowed to a crawl at each stop sign looking for a street he could cut down that would lead them back to the main road. At the sixth stop, he finally found what he was looking for and turned left. A minute later, they were back on the main road and a few blocks from the next gas station.

"The street looks pretty clear," Maggie said with surprise. There were many businesses in the area, so she had expected to find more cars and zombies than they were seeing.

"Let's hope our luck holds," Max said. As he eyed the gas station coming up on his right, he saw only a few of the dead in the parking lot. The opposite corners appeared to be completely free of zombies, so he pulled into the gas station and right up alongside a pump. The others drove in behind him and parked at other pumps.

"Good call back there," Frank said as he and Junior got out of their truck. "I was afraid we were going to get lost in that development."

"There's a lot of twists and turns in there," Max said. "So it took me a minute to find the street I wanted."

"I don't know why the hell we're always running into random crowds of zombies like that," Anna started. "Nothing and then dozens of them." She had been getting irritated with the detours as her hatred for the dead grew.

"There generally doesn't seem to be much rhyme or reason," Emily said. "They just pop up everywhere."

Anna walked closer to Max. "Don't think I didn't see you were smoking back there," she admonished.

"Oh shit!" Max thought to himself. Just as he was about to apologize, she surprised him with a sly grin. "It's okay, baby. Enjoy them while you can." She figured cigarettes would be hard to come by soon, and if they helped Max's nerves, she was okay with it.

Max looked at Anna dumbfounded. "Seriously?" he asked tentatively. He hadn't been thinking, or he wouldn't have lit one when he did. Anna nodded and said, "Just don't come complaining to me when you can't find them anymore."

"Well, now that you've got that settled," Frank started. "Let's get moving here."

Fifteen minutes later, they had as much gas as they could carry, and they headed back home.

Chapter Twenty-Six

Day 5

Damon and Joey were excited to get out and go looking for gas in neighbor garages. As soon as they had gotten the go-ahead, they'd hurried out the door before anyone could change their mind. They'd hopped fences into the Wright's yard and then the next yard beyond it. They crept and stayed alert of their surroundings, but they also felt like kids again running around and sneaking into places.

"The people who lived here are dead," Damon said. "It's the family Camille killed before she ran off from the horde." They were crouched by the fence, looking around the yard and the front of the house. Everything looked clear, so they moved to the garage. At the side door of the garage, Joey tried the handle and found it unlocked.

"Ready?" Joey asked, and Damon nodded. He opened the door to find the garage free of the dead. Enough sunlight shone through the windows of the garage door that they had good visibility. A quick look around turned up two full gas cans by the lawnmower. "Awesome," Joey said.

"Hey, these people are dead and gone," Damon started. "Why don't we check out the house? We might find some good supplies inside." He nodded toward the door that led to the attached house.

"Cool man, let's do it," Joey said with a grin.

They opened the door to the mudroom and stood silently for a moment to make sure they couldn't hear any zombies moving around inside. They fully expected the place to be empty but knew better than to act on assumptions. Greeted by nothing but silence, they made their way inside.

"Let's clear the place first just to be safe," Joey said. "Then we can take our time looking through things." Together they quickly checked every room in the house then made their way back to the kitchen off the mudroom. They started opening kitchen cabinets and drawers, finding knives, matches, batteries, a can opener, and a couple of flashlights. Damon opened the pantry, and his face lit up. There was a whole shelf full of nothing but junk food. "Hey, look what I found," he said to Joey.

"Yes! I'm going to grab some bags from the mudroom," Joey said with a grin. They filled three large recycled bags with nothing but junk food then noticed a container on the top shelf of the pantry. Damon pulled it down and opened it. "It's full of candy!" he said gleefully.

They bagged up all of the bottled water and canned foods, then gathered all of the bags by the mudroom. They wanted to check the master bedroom for weapons. The room and the attached master bathroom were a mess, with a lot of dried blood on just about everything. They guessed that this is where the family had attacked each other because there were only small blood smears throughout the rest of the house.

"This place is nasty," Damon said as he carefully opened a drawer on a nightstand. There wasn't anything useful there. "Anything on your side?" he asked Joey.

Joey's face turned beet red. "Um, some adult toys or some shit," Joey said, then quickly closed the drawer. They both burst out laughing. "Glad you took that side," Damon said. "I sure as hell don't want to touch that shit."

"Let's check the closet," Joey said. 'Whoa, check this out." He pulled an expensive shotgun down from a custom-made rack in the closet.

"That is sweet," Damon said excitedly. "There's gotta be some shells in here." He looked through the closet and found six boxes on the top shelf. A look through the rest of the closet didn't reveal a gun cabinet or any other weapons, but they were both thrilled about the shotgun.

"My mom's going to kill us for searching inside, but wait until everyone sees what we found," Joey grinned. His mom couldn't get too mad, or maybe she could, but it wasn't like she could ground him.

"Let's take everything outside. It's going to take a couple of trips to get all of this back to my house," Damon said. Joey carried the shotgun and bin full of candy while Damon grabbed all of the bags of junk food and the supplies they'd found in the kitchen cabinets and drawers.

"Do you think we should bring the gas cans back first to soften the blow?" Joey asked while thinking of his mom's temper.

"We can make two trips and leave everything outside by the enclosed front porch," Damon said. "We'll go inside to check in quick, then head back out to find more. We don't want to take the gas inside the house anyway."

They were ready to carry their newly found supplies outside, stopped to take a look out the side door of the garage, and saw three zombies slowly shuffling their way. "I've got this," Joey said as he quietly dropped his bags. There was no reason for Joey to go up against three on one, so Damon set his bags down and followed him.

A twenty-something man in jeans and a t-shirt led the three, his teeth gnashing loudly in the otherwise quiet of the day. Dried blood ringed his mouth and splattered his shirt. Joey couldn't even tell where the man was bitten because of all the dried blood from others. He quickly darted to its side and kicked the back of his knee, causing the dead man to stumble and fall to the ground. Joey thrust his knife through its ear then jumped back to his feet, ready for the next one. Damon had gone after the second zombie that looked like she'd been a soccer mom before her abdomen had been viciously torn open. As she moved, bits of what little of her entrails remained slipped out and hit the ground with a splat. Damon quickly overtook her and plunged his knife through her ear. Joey was face to face with the last zombie, an unremarkable middle-aged woman dressed in cargo shorts and a tank top. She had a small bite mark ringed with purple on her left forearm but otherwise appeared free of blood or injury. One small bite was enough, as she reached for Joey in search of her first meal. He grabbed her by her long hair and stabbed his knife through her ear.

They looked around to make sure they hadn't drawn the attention of any more zombies. There weren't any within sight, so they started grabbing supplies and carried them over to the fence. It only took two trips to carry everything, but it would take a little longer to climb up and carry them over into the Wright's yard and then on to Damon's house. Working together quietly, about a half-hour later, they had everything just outside the enclosed front porch.

"We'd better go check in with your mom before we head back out," Damon started. "She said every two hours, and it's been almost three."

"Fuck," Joey said. "We're gonna hear about that." He shook his head and hoped for the best.

Michelle must have been watching for them because she opened the door before they could. "Get inside," she said in a loud whisper. When they closed the door behind them, she got louder. "What did I tell you about checking in? Do you have any fucking idea how worried I was?"

"Sorry, Mom," Joey said quietly.

"Yeah, sorry," Damon echoed Joey. "We didn't mean to worry you."

As Michelle's expression softened, Joey said, "We found gas, a very nice shotgun, and some other supplies. It's all stuff we need." She pulled both boys in for a hug then ushered them to the kitchen.

"Sit down and have a sandwich. You need something to eat before you go out there again," Michelle said. Damon and Joey both looked at each other with surprised expressions. They couldn't believe they had gotten off so easy for being late, and on top of that, she was going to let them head back out. They both quickly wolfed down their food, eager to search more garages and houses.

"We'll try to check back in two hours, but you know how it is out there Mom," Joey said. "We're being careful, and there are hardly any zombies around."

"We promise not to be gone for too long," Damon chimed in.

"You boys be careful out there and don't make me come looking for you," Michelle admonished as they headed back out the front door.

"Wow, that went better than I thought it would," Joey said quietly.

"Yeah, I thought your mom was going to go off on us for sure," Damon said.

"Let's keep heading the same way and hit the house next door to the one we just cleaned out," Joey said.

220

"Sounds good to me," Damon said with a grin. Excited to be out on their own again, they planned to scavenge as many supplies as they could. They hopped fences until they were two doors down from the Wright's house. It was a large home that seemed promising. As they crouched on the ground beside the fence, they tried to get a look at the front door. They saw dark splotches on the light-colored door, which was ajar and could only mean one thing.

"The door's open, so it might be empty," Joey whispered. "Want to check out the garage first?"

The garage was attached to the house the same as most of the homes in the area. They figured they could check the garage for gas cans then see if the place looked empty. As they silently crept around the side of the garage, they were surprised to hear the raspy moans of the dead because there weren't any in sight. They double-checked the area around them and found it clear.

"There can't be that many zombies in the house," Damon said in a low voice. "Where are they coming from?"

Joey shifted to look at the privacy fence that started at the rear of the house. "Shit, I think they're in the backyard," he whispered. "That sounds like a hell of a lot of zombies."

"Well, the fence seems to be holding, and they can't see us," Damon said. "Let's check the garage quickly and get out of here."

They moved silently into the garage and found one large gas can in a corner. The door from the garage to the house stood open. "Want to go take a look?" Joey mouthed. Damon nodded, so they carefully slipped through the door which opened into the kitchen.

"Keep low, so they don't see us through the windows," Damon breathed. There didn't seem to be any noise coming from inside the house, but they did a quick walk-through anyway, to be sure. While they were at it, they decided to check the master bedroom for guns. It seemed to be the place that most people kept their weapons.

"You can look in the nightstands this time," Joey said with a sly grin. He didn't want to find any more adult surprises. "I'll check the closet." Damon shook his head and checked both nightstands. He didn't find anything useful but some prescription medications. Not knowing what they were, he pocketed both to give to his mom later. Joey found another shotgun in one of the bedroom closets. It wasn't anything fancy, but he knew eventually, they would need all the firepower they could get.

They quietly left the bedroom and took a peek out the dining room window into the backyard. It was nearly half full of the dead.

"I don't think we should try to find anything else in this place," Damon said. "Way too many fucking zombies out there. If we make any noise trying to go through stuff in the kitchen, we'll be screwed."

"We should probably grab the gas can and head back home. When all of the adults come back, we're going to have to take out all of those zombies," Joey said. "There's way too many of them, and they're too close to home."

"Yeah, if they break through the fences, we're done," Damon agreed.

They carefully made their way back through the garage and grabbed the lone gas can then darted for the fence to head home.

Chapter Twenty-Seven

Day 5

Just as Joey and Damon hopped the fence back into their yard, they heard the sound of vehicles on the street. They listened for a moment then saw Max opening the gate. After all three trucks came through, Junior hopped out to close the gate behind them. He carefully guided everyone to park off to the side of the driveway between the trees so that none of the vehicles would be blocking one another in. The adults all quietly made their way toward the front door.

"Look what we found," Damon said softly with pride. "Gas, guns, supplies, a shitload of junk food, and a huge tub of candy."

"Language," Anna gently admonished him.

"But Mom, look," Damon whispered. "It really is a shitload." He couldn't help but wear a huge grin on his face. Anna shook her head and stifled a laugh.

"Check out this gun," Joey pointed out the expensive model they'd found two doors down.

"Nice," Max said as he picked it up. "I've always wanted one of these."

"Let's get everything and everyone inside," Anna said. "Then we can catch up some more."

Everyone grabbed a bag or weapon from the boys' small stockpile then slid through the bars across both doors and into the house.

Michelle was eagerly awaiting everyone's return. Camille and Lucia had just finished a perimeter check, and now that everyone was home, she felt a calm come over her. She hated every minute that anyone was out there exposed to danger. She'd been cooking, and the countertops were nearly overflowing with a dinner that smelled amazing.

"Um, before everyone starts eating, we've got something to tell you," Joey said. His expression serious, he continued, "Three houses down the backyard is full of zombies. Too many to count."

"Two houses past the Wright's place. We got a gas can from the garage and one of the shotguns from a bedroom," Damon started. "Oh shit, and these prescriptions, too." He handed the medications to his mom. She grabbed the bottles then glared at him for his language. He looked down for a second, then continued, "There's way too many of them to leave them be. If they all start pushing up against a fence, I think there are enough of them to bring one down."

"Well fuck," Max said. "I guess we'll have to reheat dinner later. Thanks for cooking, Michelle." Her face fell when she realized that no sooner had she relaxed because everyone came home that they were all going to go out again.

"Sounds like we could use everyone," Frank said. "If we want to do this quietly, we're going to need a lot of hands." He didn't speak for Junior, but generally, if Max and Frank were going, it went without saying that Junior was too.

"I'm game," Emily said as she patted her knife. Anna and Maggie nodded in agreement. Joey and Damon were practically going to explode in excitement at the chance to help the whole group by killing some zombies. Camille and Lucia weren't quite as excited, but they were determined to do their part. Lucia was secretly terrified, but her resolve was firm.

"Damn it," Michelle said. "Motherfucking hell. Seriously? The kids need to go?"

"We need everyone, Mom," Joey said. "You know there's strength in numbers."

"The kids aren't kids anymore, Michelle," Max said gently. "They know what they're doing. If we don't take out those zombies, we could lose our safety here."

"I know," Michelle said in frustration. "Doesn't mean I'm fucking happy about it. If the kids are going, then I want everyone carrying a gun. I know we can't use them, but if we get jammed up out there, I'd rather make some noise than lose someone," she said with finality in her tone.

With that settled, everyone who hadn't already geared up grabbed what they needed from the weapons on the counter. It would be dark in a couple of hours, so they had no time to waste.

"Are we hopping fences, or are we walking down the street?" Junior asked. It didn't matter to him one way or another, but he wanted to know what the plan was.

"The street was clear when we came in," Anna said. "If it still is, I say we take the path of least resistance. Save our energy for the zombies." Climbing up one tree over a fence was no big deal, but going over a few of them would be hard for Michelle and Maggie at the very least. Michelle was petite, and Maggie had quite a few years on all of them.

"Let's just go out the gate and see what we see," Max said. "If it's mostly clear, then we'll cut across the front yards. Let's get moving."

They all walked down the driveway to the gate. Max took a quick look and saw a couple of zombies tottering in the street by the edge of the driveway. He pointed and nodded at Frank. He would quickly take down the two while everyone made their way out. Before everyone was through the gate, Frank had split the skulls of both zombies. There weren't any others within sight, so they cut across to the Wright's front yard and crossed until they were down to the fourth house. Before they reached the front yard, they could hear the raspy moans of the dead behind the home.

"Frank and Junior, on me," Max said. "We should quickly take out the few that are close to the gate, or else we'll all get jammed up before we even get started. Then everyone but Camille and Lucia follows behind us. Spread out and watch each other's backs. This yard covers nearly a whole acre, so we've got a lot of ground to cover. Lucia and Camille, you close the gate behind us and stay near the rear of the house. Kill anything that comes your way and watch to make sure no more get into the yard," Max finished quietly. He had wanted to make a quick game plan that would protect everyone as well as possible and felt that was about the best they could do. The girls were certainly capable, but he knew Lucia had only killed a handful of zombies herself, so he didn't want her in the thick of everything.

Frank, Junior, and Max eased into the yard first, with Frank swinging his ax and Max and Junior thrusting their knives. Everyone else followed after they cleared the area just inside the gate. The guys moved deeper into the yard, with Frank taking out zombies left and right. For each one they killed, Frank took down two. They watched each other's backs as more than fifty zombies slowly closed in

226

on them. They couldn't even see how many there were in the rear half of the yard.

"Spread out!" Max yelled. "Everyone spread out, or they're going to box us in." He felt a twinge of fear at the sheer number of zombies shuffling through the yard. It was much more than he had expected.

"Anyone need help, make sure you yell out," Frank hollered. "If you get cornered, use your gun!" His height and build gave him an advantage, but he didn't like what he was seeing. The dead were everywhere. Raspy moans, reaching arms and shuffling feet surrounded them. Zombies stepped out from behind trees and seemed to come from everywhere. He wasn't sure they were going to be able to pull this off.

Anna came running up toward Max and plunged her knife through the ear of a zombie that had been only steps away from him. They exchanged a quick look then continued killing the dead. They had all learned that kicking and shoving them away would buy time when there were too many of them. They moved nonstop, stabbing, kicking, and pushing the zombies in every direction. Max barely had time to take in Anna's movements as he killed one zombie after another, but he was glad to see her plowing through the dead like they were nothing.

Junior, Frank, Max, and Anna found themselves in the dangerous position of being cut off from everyone else. With zombies coming from everywhere, they'd gradually pushed deeper into the yard with dozens of the dead between them and the others. The zombies were relentless, but they were slow as fuck. Adrenaline ran high as they kept killing and killing. Junior wound around two of the dead to plunge his knife into the eye of a tall thin woman who almost got the jump on Frank.

Emily, Maggie, and Michelle wound up together in the same area as the zombies closed in on them. They thrashed out and killed them one by one. When too many zombies bunched up together, the women spread out so the zombies would follow. As long as they could keep them from getting too close together, they thought they could handle them. Michelle plunged her knife deep into the eye of the zombie in front of her then felt a hand grasp her shoulder. Before she could stop herself, she screamed in fear and disgust. As she tried to turn away from the grabby zombie, Emily was suddenly there, thrusting her knife through its ear.

Damon and Joey finished off most of the zombies closest to the house, leaving about half a dozen spread out for their sisters to handle. Hearing Michelle scream, both boys darted toward the women. By the time they got there, Michelle was back to killing the dead with a vengeance. She hadn't realized it before, but she needed this. She had so much pent-up anger and grief over losing Jesse that each kill brought her immense satisfaction. The thought briefly crossed her mind that she understood why Joey had been so adamant about going out there that night they found out he'd lost his dad. She shifted her focus back to the dead in front of her, careful not to let any distraction allow her to make a mistake.

Maggie cried out suddenly as a zombie grasped her arm with both of its hands. As it leaned forward to take a bite, Damon jumped on its back to pull it away and plunged his knife through its ear. The zombie dropped to the ground, but its grip held tight, causing Maggie to fall with it. It took every ounce of strength Damon had in him, but he managed to pry the fingers loose from their death grip on her arm and helped her back to her feet.

"Damon, behind you!" Maggie yelled. He turned around just in time to avoid the gnashing teeth that were about to tear into his shoulder. "Motherfucker!" Damon yelled as he furiously stabbed the zombie in the eye. The rancid, milky fluid that spurted out didn't even phase him. "Keep moving," he called to Maggie. He had lost sight of Joey but found himself paired up with Maggie, so he moved on to the next zombie. He hoped that Joey had met up with one of the others because no one was supposed to be on their own. Maggie and Damon moved together, killing the dead, and he found himself surprised at how capable she was. She looked like a grandma to him, so it was crazy that she was out there killing zombies like everyone else.

Camille and Lucia had been left with half a dozen zombies to kill when the boys had taken off. Camille was used to stabbing them and didn't think much of it, but it was still pretty new to Lucia. To her credit, Lucia didn't tremble in fear or hesitate. She went straight for the closest zombie and kicked the back of its knee, causing it to fall to the ground. She stabbed her knife through its ear, then got up and headed for the next one. The second one wasn't so tall, so she grabbed it by the hair and plunged her knife through its eye. She gagged at the sight and smell of the burst eyeball but moved onto the next. A few feet away, Camille killed the three that had been nearest to her. With that, their part of the yard was completely clear of the dead. They could hear the others yelling and struggling to kill zombies deeper into the yard and contemplated what to do. Max had told them to hold their position, but their families were in the middle of it and were in danger.

229

"I'm going to go. I'll pair up with the first person I see," Camille said hurriedly. "You stay here. We need someone to keep watch here, Lucia. I have no doubt you can kill any zombie you come across, but someone needs to stay here," she finished. Lucia nodded, knowing that her best friend trusted her, and Camille took off toward the others.

Max, Frank, Junior, and Anna were in the rear quarter of the yard with the back of the fence in sight. Still running purely on adrenaline, they put all of their focus into killing the last two dozen zombies. They spread out and kept moving so that the dead would do the same.

In the rear third of the yard, Emily, Michelle, and Joey took out the last few stragglers that came out from behind trees. About ten yards behind them, Camille had caught up to Damon and Maggie. She helped kill the last half dozen in the middle of the yard.

Everyone kept looking around in every direction to make sure they hadn't missed any. Gradually they all came together near the middle of the yard.

"There's nothing left behind us," Max said tiredly. "Let's work our way back toward the house to make sure there aren't any strays left."

They walked toward the rear of the house with Frank and Emily taking out two zombies along the way. Lucia kept a close watch on the gate to make sure no zombies came from the street, attracted by all of the yelling and noise they had made killing the dead. Three zombies were moving achingly slow from the front yard toward the gate, but otherwise, the front was clear. Lucia looked back to see everyone coming from the backyard up to the house. A slight noise to her right grabbed her attention, and she saw a crawler on the ground. She quickly bent down and killed it. A moment later, everyone was back to join her near the gate. To her relief, nobody was injured. They were covered with blood and gore, but everyone was whole. They had all fought together and survived. She couldn't help but smile.

Chapter Twenty-Eight

Day 5

Back at the house, everyone was exhausted. Anna refused to let anyone covered in filth sit on the chairs or couches, so they all took quick turns in both showers. They were able to find clothes that fit well enough for everyone but Frank. Max laughed at him wearing a pair of his sweatpants that were skintight and only came down to the top of his calves. Anna threw away most of the detritus-covered clothing, but she put Frank's clothes in the washer so that he would have a pair of pants to wear that actually fit him.

"Hell, man," Max laughed. "Sorry, I can't help it. You look like you're wearing my wife's capris."

Frank tried to shoot Max an evil glare but burst out laughing himself. "Just be happy I'm not sitting on your couch buck naked," Frank teased.

"No naked asses on my furniture," Anna called from the kitchen. "You'll have your clothes soon enough."

"Yo, you look like a pendejo," Junior laughed. "I think it suits you, boss."

Before long, everyone had showered and settled in to eat the dinner Michelle had prepared earlier. Their zombie clear-out had taken several hours, and it was late in the evening by the time they ate. They had all worked up quite an appetite. Michelle was in her element handing out second and third helpings and then pushing dessert on everyone. She had baked so much that morning that there were enough sweets to last a few days.

With appetites finally satiated, talk began about plans for the next day. "I think we should try to get more gas before the power goes out," Max said. "It's going to be a hell of a lot harder to get once that happens."

"You want to unload the gas cans from the trucks and drive those out again?" Frank asked.

"Seems like a good idea to me," Junior started. "No need to risk trying for new vehicles when we have so many here at the house now."

"After we get gas, I think we should look for some generators," Anna said. "At least a portable one. It's going to be hot as hell in here when the power goes out."

"As long as it runs quietly, I think it's a good idea," Max agreed.

"We can get a lot of good supplies when we're shopping for the generator," Frank said. "Solar panels would be a smart move. The sun hits the roof of your house perfectly since the pool area doesn't have any trees."

"So we make a gas run or two, then the next priority is a generator and solar panels and whatever else we need to go with it," Max said.

"Don't forget a stop to get Frank some damn pants," Junior said with a grin. Frank just shook his head, knowing he wasn't going to live this down anytime soon.

"That will pretty much take the whole day, won't it?" Emily asked. They didn't want to make any of their runs in the dark.

"I would think so," Maggie chimed in. "We might not even get that much done. Although, one can hope."

"Same plan as today?" Michelle asked. "You guys go out while the girls and I are here and the boys go scavenging? Or are we all going?"

233

"I think for gas, we should stick to the same plan," Anna said. "But we may all need to go for the other stuff. Hitting a big store isn't going to be easy."

"We need to hit a few of them," Max said. "Sporting goods, Lowe's, and eventually Costco. Those are closer to us than any of the others. I'd rather not venture out any farther than we have to at this point."

"Isn't there a small place off Dover?" Maggie asked. "Farm Surplus or Tractor Supply or something, but they have generators and a lot of camping and survival gear, probably radios too. It's not that small, but it's better than the big box stores."

"I forgot about that place," Max said. "Nice call, Maggie. After the gas run, I think that should be our next stop. They'll even have clothes for you, Frank." Max grinned.

Damon, Joey, Camille, and Lucia sat and quietly followed the conversation. Damon and Joey shared a quick smile and a quiet high five when they realized they would get to go back out to scavenge more neighbor houses. Camille didn't like being left at the house, but she understood that someone had to keep an eye on things there. Everyone had to work in pairs, so it made sense to leave her, Lucia, and Michelle at home. Michelle would cook, and knowing her, she would wash every dirty towel and piece of clothing in the house while she still could. The girls would keep watch and do occasional perimeter checks.

"Seems like we've got a good enough plan for tomorrow," Anna said. "We should all try to get some sleep."

"I'll take first watch," Emily offered. "I'll wake someone to take over in a couple of hours." With their setup, no one had to stand watch, but someone needed to check the view, now and then, just to make sure nothing got into the yard.

"Thanks, Emily," Max said. "Feel free to wake me up first." Everyone said their goodnights and headed for beds or couches to get some sleep. They had a big day ahead of them in the morning.

About two hours later, Emily was bored with staying in the house, so she went outside for some fresh air to help keep her awake. As soon as she left the enclosed front porch, she heard the telltale sound of zombies shuffling around. She couldn't see anything in the yard and didn't think there had been a breach in the fence, so she went for a quiet walk out front toward the wall. Peeking through the small openings on either side of the gate, she noticed that the zombie population was getting pretty heavy on their street. All of the noise they had made earlier must have gradually drawn them to the area. From what she could see, there were at least two dozen out there, maybe more. They were unfocused and stumbling around aimlessly, not interested in any particular house or yard. She thought it might be safe to leave them be as long as their numbers didn't grow too much but thought it was best to go ahead and wake Max to see what he wanted to do.

She went back inside and went to Max and Anna's bedroom door for a moment to listen and make sure she wasn't going to interrupt anything. Hearing nothing, she pushed the door open and softly called out Max's name.

"Huh? What?" Max mumbled as he woke up. "I'm awake. Give me a second." Emily stepped out and went to the kitchen. Max came in a moment later.

"Sorry, I was going to let you sleep longer," Emily started. "But there's quite a few dead in the street out front. At least two dozen or so that I could see. They're just shuffling around like usual, but I figured you'd want to know about it."

"Fuck," Max shook his head. "We did make a hell of a lot of noise killing those zombies earlier. Mind heading back out with me so I can take a closer look?"

"Not at all," Emily said. "Let's do it."

They quietly made their way to the wall near the front of the yard. Max looked through the openings around the gate but couldn't see far enough in either direction to know what he was dealing with.

"I'm going to pop up to get a better look," Max mouthed to Emily. It was a risky move, but the wall sat back far enough from the road that as long as he didn't make any noise, the zombies were unlikely to notice him in the dark. He boosted himself up and carefully climbed up the wall, crouching on top of it. There were at least a hundred zombies wandering around his street. He silently watched them for several minutes and saw that they were shuffling eastward down the street. They moved so fucking slow that it was hardly noticeable until he actually settled in to watch them instead of just taking a quick peek at them. As long as nothing distracted the dead, they'd keep moving on the path they were on and wouldn't be a problem.

Just as Max was about to climb back down, he heard the sound of rapid gunfire. It was so loud that he couldn't tell how many guns were being fired, but it had to be at least half a dozen. They sounded like they were coming from someplace nearby. The noise sounded so close that his reflexes told him to duck, but whoever was shooting was probably a street or two over. It was too close for his comfort. The zombies in the street slowly turned their heads to the south, so the backs of their heads faced Max as they clumsily turned their bodies and stumbled toward yards and houses across the street. After a minute or two of silence, Max heard the distinct sound of shotguns. The zombies were entirely focused on the noise and slowly continued their pursuit of a potential meal. Max nearly jumped out of his skin when he heard Frank and Junior softly call up to him.

"Fucking A, man," Max whispered. "You scared the crap out of me."

"The gunfire woke us up, so we came out to see what was going on," Frank said quietly. Junior and Emily stood beside him.

"Hey, you smell that?" Junior asked. Max wasn't sure what he was talking about, so he sniffed the air, but Frank responded before Max could say anything.

"Fire, probably a house," Frank said. He was about to pull himself up on top of the wall when Emily stopped him.

"Hey, give me a boost, would you?" Emily whispered. She wanted to see what was going on for herself.

In less than a minute, all four of them were crouched down on top of the wall. About one block over, presumably where the guns were fired, flames crept up into the night air. Someone had set a house on fire. The faint sound of distant voices and car doors slamming came from the same area. As the vehicles pulled away, it sounded like a few shotguns were randomly fired. Nothing about the situation made sense. The way the guns had been fired made Max think of the drunken guys Camille had seen and hidden from. His gut told him that it wasn't people in a fight for their lives but a bunch of idiots pulling stupid shit.

"What do the houses look like on the other side of that block?" Frank asked Max. "Heavily treed yards, big lots, small?"

"They're decent-sized lots. Brick houses," Max thought about it as he mentally pictured the exact section of the street. "Not many trees, chain link fencing, no wooden privacy fences."

"Well, that's good news," Junior started quietly. "The fire will probably burn itself out once the house is gone. It shouldn't spread to anything else."

Max breathed a huge sigh of relief. The thought of leaving the safety of their home because of a bunch of dumbasses had him worried. If the fire had been anywhere on his street, they would have been screwed.

The guys lit cigarettes, and Emily declined. They all sat perched on top of the wall for a good two hours or so. They couldn't see the house from their vantage point, but they could see the flames dancing in the air. All of the zombies had shambled out of sight. They were probably at the burning house, drawn by the noise and the fire. The flames died down, but thick smoke still billowed through the air.

"We're good," Frank said. "It may take another hour or two before it's just the smoldering remains, but it's not going anywhere."

"I think we ought to start keeping watch outside," Max said. "We were fine doing it in the house up until now, but I don't want to take any chances after seeing this."

"I'd say that's a good idea," Junior said. "Do it in pairs like we do everything else."

They continued whispering for a few more minutes before climbing down and heading for the house. They were all disturbed by what had happened, but they needed to get some rest before the sun came up. Emily said she'd wake Michelle and Maggie to take the next watch and would fill them in on what had happened before she went back to sleep herself. Max went back to bed but felt restless, not falling asleep until he'd been lying there for a good half hour.

Chapter Twenty-Nine

Day 6

By the time Max woke up the next morning, everyone else was already up and about. It was just after dawn, but the smell of bacon cooking in the kitchen helped pull everyone from their beds. Michelle had started cooking breakfast at the end of her and Maggie's watch and had sent Joey and Damon out for the next shift.

"Morning, baby," Anna greeted Max with a kiss and handed him a cup of coffee. Everyone else was standing around the kitchen and the living room, eagerly awaiting the breakfast that Michelle was just finishing up.

"How's the house fire looking?" Max asked.

"From what we could see, there's still smoke, but I think the fire's about out," Maggie answered.

"It's probably just smoldering ashes by now," Frank added. Max looked at him and started laughing.

"I thought my wife washed your clothes," Max managed between laughs. Frank was still wearing the skintight short sweatpants from last night.

"Hey, no making fun of my outfit. It's kind of grown on me," Frank deadpanned, then said, "Jeez, give me a minute, bro, I just woke up. I was about to get my clothes out of the dryer."

"Food's ready," Michelle said. She made up two heaping plates to take outside for the boys then everyone else helped themselves. As they all sat down and got comfortable with their waffles, eggs, hash browns, and bacon, the lights suddenly went out.

"Damn it," Max said in frustration. "There goes today's plan." There was no point in rushing to get more gas with the power finally out. They would be able to get it, but it would be hard as hell to do. Without power, getting to the gas pumps was no longer their number one priority.

"It was bound to happen," Emily said. "I was kind of surprised that we didn't lose power sooner." She was right, but no one felt like responding.

The electricity failing put a damper on everyone's mood, and they ate their breakfast mostly in silence. Anna lit a few of her decorative jar candles so they could see well enough to eat. With all of the windows boarded up, it was very dark inside the house. Max went to the rear patio windows and exposed the holes that Damon had made at the top of the boards. The little bit of light that found its way inside made a difference, and Anna had no shortage of candles, but it was going to get hot and uncomfortable pretty fast in the heat of the summer.

"Camille, Lucia, go relieve your brothers so we can start hashing out a new plan for today," Max said. While waiting for the boys to come inside, Max thought about what their next move should be. A few minutes later, the boys came in with their empty plates and sat down to join the others.

"I guess we hit the tractor place today," Max said to murmurs of agreement. They hoped to find at least one portable generator, solar panel kits, and some other valuable supplies when they went there. If no one else had hit the store yet, they might find everything they needed and not have to hit a big box store. They were still going to have to go to Costco at some point to get water and food supplies, but at this point, that was their second priority.

"How do you want to do this?" Junior asked. "Same as we did with the gas stations, or should we have everyone go?"

"Do we feel comfortable leaving the house unattended?" Anna asked in response. "After that fire last night, I'm not sure what we should do."

"If we leave people at the house and those dumbasses come around, there's not a hell of a lot they can do to protect the house. They might just have to hide," Frank said.

"Not necessarily," Max said. "We have more than enough guns and ammo to hold off anyone that tries to get in here."

"We're talking about people, not the dead," Frank went on. "If we leave anyone here, they have to be prepared to shoot people. That's not going to come easy for everyone," he finished solemnly.

"I can do it," Damon spoke up with his expression stoic.

"Me too," Joey said quietly but firmly. They had both learned that they were willing to do anything to protect their family and believed they could shoot a living person if it were an 'us versus them' situation.

Anna put her hand over her mouth and gasped. She didn't want her son to be placed in such a position. It killed her that he volunteered to do it, but she recognized that he had pretty much grown up over the last week.

"No," Michelle said. "I don't want you in that kind of fucking danger."

"Everything's dangerous Mom," Joey said. "I'd rather go out to help get supplies and kill zombies, but if someone needs to handle business here, I can do it."

"The odds of anyone coming around here are small," Damon said. "We'll probably be bored off our asses, but if anything needs doing, we can do it."

Max exchanged a glance with Anna then with Michelle. Both women were unhappy but were resigned to the inevitable. Whoever stayed behind needed to be a good shot, but they needed muscle for the supply run. Leaving Joey and Damon to protect their home made the most sense, and it didn't hurt that it seemed unlikely that anyone would try to get into the house.

"Okay, boys, you cover things here while the rest of us go out," Max said. "The radio is on the counter, so use it if you need to."

Everyone got their gear together, and Frank came out of the laundry room, having changed into his uniform pants. They each wore a backpack with water, a small amount of food, extra weapons, and ammo. Everyone had a gun and a knife on their belt, except Frank. He preferred his ax. He had a gun but would use his ax before a knife every time.

"Are we taking the three trucks again?" Anna asked.

"Seems to be our best option," Max said. "We can easily fit three people in each one, and the truck beds give us a lot of room to put supplies."

"Damon, Joey, go unload all of the gas cans," Michelle instructed. "Put a couple in the SUV and Max's big truck, so they're there if we need to leave in a hurry at some point. Leave the rest out."

"Send the girls back in," Anna told them. "They need to get ready to head out with us."

The boys went outside to clean out the trucks while everyone else finished getting ready.

Camille and Lucia came inside, surprised to learn of the day's plans. They'd figured that they would be left at home with Michelle again. Camille was eager to get out and made sure her supplies were ready to go. Lucia was nervous as hell. She was trying her hardest at doing better and being a valuable part of their group, but she still had less experience than everyone else. Killing some of the zombies in the neighbor's yard the evening before had helped her confidence grow a little.

Camille noticed the look on her best friend's face. "You can do this Lucia," she said softly. "You've already done it. It's okay to be afraid, but you saw for yourself how your instinct just kind of kicks in and takes over when it has to."

"Thanks," Lucia said. "To be honest, I'm terrified, but I know I won't freeze up again."

"Let's get moving," Max said. Everyone went outside and split up between the three trucks. They'd grown accustomed to working in specific pairs. Max was with Maggie, Anna with Emily, and Frank with Junior. Camille, Michelle, and Lucia each climbed into one of the trucks with the others. Damon and Joey waved as they pulled out of the driveway then went inside to get weapons ready just in case they had to protect the house.

The tractor place was nearly five miles away. A quick, easy trip under normal circumstances but with their new normal, it could take them half a day or more to get there. The drive started well enough, with their street clear of the dead. It seemed that all of the zombies had been drawn to the house fire a block away. They made it to the intersection where they had gotten gas the day before, and they dodged around a dozen or so zombies in the street. Another half dozen were lingering around the door of one of the gas stations. There were the same wrecked and abandoned cars to traverse, but they were used to them. They'd driven through this area many times, searching for Camille.

With Max leading the way, they slowed at the next big intersection. There were zombies everywhere. The streets, gas stations, and pharmacies that sat on each corner were full of them. Max looked toward the pharmacy. It held the greatest concentration of the dead. He saw that all of the windows around the door had been bashed out. He knew there had to be other people out there surviving and was glad to see evidence of other living people. There were far too many zombies to maneuver around, so he put his truck in reverse, and the others did the same behind him. He backed up to the first side street and took a right turn. It was more of a secondary road and would take him to the next street he had been planning on. Most of the north/south roads were only two lanes, and this one was no different. He slowly drove forward, hoping he wasn't forced to take another detour, at least not until he got them to a broader street. Turning off this one into the smaller housing developments could add hours to their drive.

Up ahead, there was a two-car crash where one car had rear-ended the other. The accident was confined to the right lane, so he carefully veered to his left to go around it while keeping his speed down in case any zombies were to walk out from around the other side of the crash. He breathed a sigh of relief when he passed by without any dead in sight. A little further down the road, eight zombies were tottering around in the middle of the street. Not wanting to risk damaging the truck nor wanting to take a detour, he slowed to a stop and got out of the truck.

Before he could walk back to Frank and Junior, they were both already out of their truck. Their view of the zombies was obstructed while they were in the vehicle. When they saw Max in the street, their first instinct was to make sure they had his back.

"There's eight of them in the road up there," Max started. "I figured it'd be easier just to get out and kill them so we don't damage the trucks."

"Good call," Frank said as Junior nodded. Seconds later, Anna and Emily were at their side.

"There's no reason for the three of you to take on eight by yourselves," Anna said. "No unnecessary risk, remember?"

The five of them approached the dead, who now had turned their focus on the new, potential living meals. The zombies had barely taken two steps by the time their skulls were getting caved in or their brains slashed through with a knife. They were all dead on the ground within thirty seconds.

"Now for the fun part," Junior said. "Moving the bodies."

Frank was strong enough to pull the first one out of the way by himself. Anna and Emily dragged another while Max and Junior grabbed a third. The other five had fallen to the left, so there was no need to move them when there was plenty of room to drive around them on the right side. Six days in, the bodies started to smell something awful, but they wore heavy-duty gloves, which kept the smell off their hands.

"Alright, let's get back on the road," Max said. He got back into his truck and lit a cigarette.

"I would have helped, you know," Maggie said, a little annoyed.

"I know. I trust you, or you wouldn't be riding with me," Max said with a bit of a smile. "I saw you in action last night when we cleared that yard." She thought she was being overlooked because of her age but realized it was foolish thinking after hearing Max declare his trust in her. She smiled back and settled in for the ride.

They were able to make it to the next main street as planned and headed east in the general direction of the tractor place. The street was one of the few four-lane streets in the area that gave them a lot of room to maneuver. Max was focusing on what was in front of him when Maggie pointed out smoke about half a mile ahead. As they got closer, they found another single house set on fire. Max slowed to a stop to get a better look. There were at least two dozen charred zombies shuffling around the yard in front of the house, their blackened skin flaking away with each step. The houses around on either side looked normal and separated enough that the fire wasn't likely to spread, but Max was disturbed by the fire. The cars in the driveway were full of bullet holes, and the windows had been shot out. It looked like people were out setting fires for no reason.

"Fucking dumbasses," Max said in frustration. "There's no need for this shit. There's gotta be forty thousand houses in this suburb alone. Plenty of places to find supplies. But if these motherfuckers keep setting fires, we could end up with a real problem on our hands." He was fuming at the idiocy of it all.

"There's nothing we can do about it right now. Let's just stay focused on the plan," Maggie said gently. Something about her voice seemed to have a calming effect on Max.

He returned his focus to the road ahead and weaved around all of the static cars. About three blocks down, a cluster of about two dozen zombies shambled around the left two lanes of the street for no apparent reason. As they drove past in their three trucks, every last zombie turned first its head and then its body toward the vehicles. They were out of sight before any of the dead could take more than a step in their direction.

"Strange how they do that," Max said. "Grouping together in random spots for no apparent reason."

"Maybe they attacked someone there, and once the person turned, they all just stood around because nothing else caught their attention," Maggie said morbidly. "I think some of them have probably stayed in one spot for days."

"We'll probably never know," Max said as he thought about it some more.

They continued on their route without much difficulty as they wound their way around cars and occasional zombies. They had one more big left turn to go, and then it was a straight shot to the tractor place. The quiet of the day was suddenly interrupted by the sound of gunfire. It was so close that Max thought they were under attack.

"Holy shit!" Max yelled. "Are they shooting at us?"

Chapter Thirty

Day 6

Max reflexively ducked as he heard a cacophony of gunshots ring out. He popped his head back up and looked in every direction, trying to figure out where it was coming from. A glance at Maggie showed that she was doing the same thing. He checked his mirrors to make sure the others were okay driving behind him. Frank was gesturing wildly to the left, so Max looked again to his left but didn't see anyone. The noise was deafening and made all the more terrifying because he didn't know where it was coming from. Another look in his rearview, and he saw Frank turning down a long, tree-lined driveway. Anna followed him in her truck, so Max reversed and made the turn. Fearing the worst, that one of them had been shot, Max jumped out of his truck the second he put it into park. Frank was holding his hand up for everyone to be quiet.

When everyone hurried to crowd around Frank, Max breathed a sigh of relief. No one was injured. He grabbed Anna's hand and pulled Camille in close. Anna was shaking with rage, thinking of how her family had just been in mortal jeopardy at the hands of a bunch of assholes.

"I saw them," Frank said quietly. "They're about two houses down on a side street off to the right. It looked like a dozen or so guys firing shotguns up into the air and maybe at the house. A few pickups were in the street and on the lawn. That's about all I was able to see."

"We figured we'd better pull over somewhere out of sight before they get back on the road," Junior said. "I don't think they saw us, and they couldn't have heard us over all of that gunfire. We should stay here until they're gone, hermano."

Max just shook his head. His adrenaline was running high, and his anger nearly matched it. "Good thinking. We'll stay put until they're well on their way."

"What the hell is wrong with these people?" Anna seethed. Looting was one thing because everyone needed supplies. Shooting things up and setting fires was something else, and she wasn't having it. Max watched as her temper boiled and was about to say something when Michelle spoke up.

"Those fuckers try anything, and I'm shooting every last damn one of them in the head," Michelle fumed. She held Lucia close, overcome with emotion.

Emily and Maggie listened in but didn't say much. They were as upset as everyone else but didn't voice their anger. Instead, they both stared in the direction of the side street where the guys were still firing weapons and making a shitload of noise.

"They're going to draw in a lot of the dead," Frank said. "It could help us since we're headed in the opposite direction."

"Or it could fuck us if all of the dead in the neighborhood head that way. We could find dozens or even hundreds of zombies coming down the street," Max said.

"You smell that?" Junior asked. The hint of smoke was in the air. "I don't see flames yet, but I think they just set the house on fire."

Max's shoulders slumped as he looked toward where the house sat, just out of sight from their position. They stood around watching and waiting for a few minutes before the smoke grew thicker and flames were visible in the air. The sound of multiple car doors slamming shut signaled that the group was getting ready to leave, so everyone hunched down to make themselves less visible. Even if the assholes drove right past them, they wouldn't see them unless they knew where to look.

Seconds later, three brand new pickups and an SUV came tearing down the main street. There were guys in the beds of all three trucks, so there had to be at least two dozen men altogether. They sped right past the group and turned south onto the next main road.

"Looks like they hit up a dealership," Junior commented offhand.

"At least they're headed south," Max said. "We're not heading south in any way for any reason. Everything we need is to the north."

"Seems like they're moving around a lot," Frank said worriedly. "Avon, Bay, Westlake… no rhyme or reason to their madness."

"South is good," Emily chimed in. "It means we know they're out of the way for now. We can get back to our plans."

"Well, they're gone now, and they're far enough away that they won't hear us on the road," Anna said. "Let's get going."

They got back into their trucks and resumed their route. Handfuls of zombies were popping up everywhere, no doubt in response to all of the noise the idiots had made, but they were able to make their left turn at the next intersection. From there, it was a straight shot, barring any detours. The two-lane road was mainly lined with small businesses and shops. It didn't turn residential until about half a mile past the tractor place. None of them had driven down Dover since the whole thing started nearly a week ago, so they weren't sure what to expect. There were small pockets of zombies, but otherwise, the area seemed almost deserted. Only a handful of wrecked or abandoned cars filled the street. It was almost like the area had been empty when the zombies had first started.

"There are quite a few assisted and independent living places around here, just behind a lot of these storefronts. That's a lot of immobile people," Maggie told Max. "Maybe that's why we aren't seeing much here. Those places are probably full of zombies that can't get around."

Max passed a small bakery, a neighborhood coffee shop, a dentist's office, a candy store, a barbershop, a handful of boutiques, and two of the four bars that stood in the tiny suburb. It was eerie seeing the area abandoned and looking like an old ghost town. The place had always had a small-town feel about it, and the storefronts were designed to accentuate that motif. He wondered if maybe the dead who had been here had followed the horde out a few days ago. The area had the fewest number of zombies of any place he'd seen so far.

"Well, whatever it is, it can only work to our advantage," Max said. "This supply run could end up being a lot easier than we expected."

He drove across a set of railroad tracks then made a sharp right turn into the parking lot of "Tractor, Farm & Outdoor Supplies." He chuckled to himself upon reading the sign. No wonder none of them could remember the name of the place. It was a little odd and didn't accurately describe the type of store it actually was. The place definitely didn't sell tractors.

The others pulled in behind him, and they all parked close to the side door, which was actually the main entrance to the building.

"This is pretty creepy," Anna said with a shiver as she looked around. "Where are all of the zombies?"

"There's definitely something strange about it," Michelle said. "Isn't there a big church down the road? About a mile or so before the lake, I think. Maybe everyone went there when it started."

"If they did, I sure as hell hope they stay there," Max said. "Let's get going and do what we came here to do."

With no zombies anywhere within sight, they decided to all go inside the store together. If it needed clearing, it was safer to do it with numbers. Frank opened the door, and Junior listened for a moment. Not hearing a sound, he called out, "Here zombie, zombie, come on boys, good zombie, zombie, come here," to see if anything started moving inside the store.

Camille and Lucille had to stifle their giggles at hearing Junior calling out to the zombies. Everyone else wore a smirk or a smile, which lightened the mood. "I think we're all clear," Junior said with a shit-eating grin. Fighting laughter, they all made their way inside the store, which appeared clean and empty. There were no streaks of blood, no sounds of shuffling footsteps or raspy voices, and no foul smells. Knowing better than to take anything for granted, they still took the time to clear the store aisle by aisle then checked the office, restrooms, and the large storage and receiving room at the back. The place was empty.

"Let's start shopping," Max said with a grin. "We'll rotate one person on the main door just to be safe. Camille, you've got first watch."

The men headed over to the generators first and found a pretty good selection. While a generator was going to be very useful, it was also going to be noisy. They took some time to compare several portables and one stationary. Any generator that was going to be of much use was going to be heavy. Between the guys, they could manage well enough with what was available. The store had huge flat pallet-like carts to load large items, so they started filling a few. They took several smaller portables and two of the largest on the shelf. Most used gas, but they chose two that were propane operated after noticing the giant cage of propane bottles outside. If they were settling in for the long haul, it made sense to stock up on both gas and propane.

"Let's get these loaded up and then break into the propane. We'll take them all," Max said. Between the generators and the propane, they had enough supplies to fill two of the truck beds. "Is it clear out there, Camille?" Max asked.

"I haven't seen a single zombie," she answered. "I can keep watch outside while you guys load everything. Let everyone else keep shopping."

"Thanks, baby girl," Max said to his daughter.

While the men did their thing, Michelle, Anna, Emily, Maggie, and Lucia searched the store for other items on their list. "Lucia, here's everyone's sizes. Gather up some clothes, shoes, and gloves for everyone," Michelle said as she handed her a piece of paper. "Get extras of everything for Frank," Michelle added, smiling as she thought of how he had fit into Max's sweatpants.

Michelle tore the remaining list in half, keeping one for her and Anna and giving the other to Emily and Maggie. "Okay, we're looking for water purifier tablets, prepackaged food, water bottles, and a cooking stove for starters," Michelle told Anna. Anna grabbed every single bottle of water purifying tablets and every single prepackaged and freeze-dried food on the shelves. Michelle looked through the water bottles and grabbed a case of twenty-four, awkwardly setting it onto her pallet cart. There was only one cooking stove on the shelf, so she added it to her growing pile.

Emily and Maggie went off with their list. They quickly found heavy-duty flashlights, batteries, emergency blankets, and ponchos. "Oh, look," Emily started. "Stormproof matches! They're not on the list, but we might need these later."

"Take all of them," Maggie said. "Those could be invaluable if we have to relocate."

Anna and Michelle started looking at tents. "I honestly have no fucking clue what to get here," Michelle said.

"Me either," Anna laughed. "Let's just grab enough to sleep at least twelve people. If it's not what the guys want, they can switch them out. I'm guessing tents that sleep two to four people?"

"That's probably about right. Hell, we have to grab sleeping bags, too," Michelle said. "Do we get them for summer and fall temperatures, or do we want the ones rated for the cold?"

"Let's grab lightweight and extreme cold. If we have to leave the house, we're only going to be able to take so many supplies with us, and that's two dozen sleeping bags right there," Anna said. She was starting to realize that their list was unrealistically long but figured they should keep on shopping until they ran out of room in the trucks.

"Ooh, binoculars," Michelle exclaimed. "Grab several of those." Anna added them to one of their pallet carts.

At the other end of the store, Emily and Maggie were looking at radios. "I don't know the first thing about them," Emily said. Maggie shook her head; she was feeling lost just looking at them. "Maybe Frank and Junior should pick through them."

"Sounds good," Maggie said. "Anything else?"

"All-weather backpacks," Emily answered. "Probably over by the tents." They went looking and found a small selection of heavy-duty packs. After looking through them for a moment, they added a dozen to their pallet.

The men came back inside after all of their heavy lifting was done. They'd filled one truck and more than half of the second one. Looking at all of the supplies the women had found, they weren't sure they could fit much more.

"You start loading all of this stuff up. Pack it as tightly as you can, and you can fill the backseat of the white truck. It has the biggest extended cab," Max said. "We've gotta check out the solar stuff."

"And the radios," Emily added. "We had no idea what to grab."

Frank and Junior went over to the small selection of radios and knew exactly what they needed. Unsure of what batteries the women had grabbed, they went ahead and cleared the rest of the batteries from the shelf. Max started looking for solar panels but didn't find any. It didn't appear that the store carried them, so they would have to work on that another day at a different place.

Lucia suddenly appeared at the door with her pallet full of clothes, gloves, and boots. They took up a lot more space than expected but could be rolled up and jammed into any open spaces in the trucks. The boots all fit in half of the backseat of the red truck. Looking at the silver truck, she figured that she, Camille, and her mom could easily fit in the backseat together so they could put more supplies in the red truck.

Seeing that they could squeeze a few more things in, Max added zip ties and some rope. With that, they were fully loaded. He couldn't believe that they'd found most of what they had been looking for in one trip.

"We're done here," Max said, and everyone loaded into the trucks. It had taken them several hours to get to the store, partly because of the idiots with the guns, and they'd spent well over two hours shopping. Everyone was tired, hungry, and eager to get back on the road. During their entire shopping trip, not a single zombie had shown up. Max was relieved but also unnerved. It just didn't make any sense.

Chapter Thirty-One

Day 6

His curiosity piqued, Max decided to head north down Dover rather than go back the way they came. He planned to head west at the first light, which hung over a mini intersection. He'd grabbed a pair of binoculars to keep with him when they'd loaded all of the supplies at the tractor place, and as they crested a slight incline in the road, he looked ahead with the binoculars.

"Holy shit," he said. There was a decent-sized automotive shop and used car sales lot up ahead with a chain-link fence surrounding not only the building but the entire lot. Presumably, it was to deter would-be thieves from stealing cars. The entire lot was packed full of zombies who seemed to be standing around, not focused on anything. "What in the name of fuck?" he said aloud as he stared. His eyes were drawn to the front gate of the lot, which was secured with a heavy chain. Someone was rounding up zombies, but the how and why didn't make any sense. Why wouldn't they just kill the dead rather than gathering them all together like that? He couldn't understand why the zombies hadn't knocked the fence down yet, and then he realized it was probably because nothing had captured their attention. Somehow, they were lured into the confines of the fence, and then their captors must have left. Max cringed when he thought of what was probably used to lure the dead. Only a living meal would have held their focus long enough for someone to chain up the gate and leave them there. They made no effort to push through the fence, and unless something else grabbed their attention, they would probably shuffle around the parking lot indefinitely. That could all change quickly if they saw or heard Max and the others in the trucks. The sheer number of confined bodies could take down the fence in seconds, unleashing a mini-horde into the town.

"We've gotta get out of here before we draw any attention to ourselves," Max told Maggie. He handed her the binoculars so she could get a better view just before he turned left to head west and away from the town. He glanced at Maggie and saw that she was shaking.

"I can't think of a good reason that anyone would be gathering the dead like that," Maggie said with a hint of fear in her voice. "I just don't know what to make of it, and that scares the hell out of me."

"I don't know how they're going about it either," Max said. "It would take a lot of work to try to capture them and close them in like that. Why take that kind of risk?" He lit a cigarette and drove in silence for a few minutes as he and Maggie were both left alone in their thoughts. He wondered where the rest of the town went and if more zombies were rounded up in the area. There were more than 100,000 homes and countless businesses to scavenge in the local suburbs. Max vowed to avoid returning to that town. Everything about it felt wrong.

He drove along carefully and had to slow to edge his way around another car accident that took up more than half of the road. With all of the supplies they had in the back of the trucks, they couldn't afford to hit anything. He managed to weave around the accident then dodged a few zombies in the road that had been behind the wrecked cars. By the time the zombies moved enough to block the road, all three trucks were past them.

The drive home was going faster than the trip out there due to all of the zombies that were trapped. The further they got from Dover, the more of the dead they came across. Max sighed in frustration as he was forced to make more detours the closer they got to home. As he slowly navigated a nearly blocked-off intersection, he noticed the beverage store on the corner had been shot up. The glass doors of the store had been shattered, and the walls were full of bullet holes. Max hoped that it was the same group of dumbasses that were already causing trouble and not a whole other group.

Since the shit hit the fan, he and his family had been focused solely on reuniting and surviving. He could only imagine that there had to be others like them hiding out in their own homes or local businesses. He'd found Maggie that way, and Camille had found refuge with the kind couple in the mansion on the lake. On the other end of the spectrum, there were the idiots shooting things up and setting fires. Or people like Bill. He shook his head at the thought of the sociopathic rapist from the gas station a couple of days ago. With most of the population dead, he desperately hoped that more of the good than the bad had survived.

Max kept checking his rearview mirror to make sure the others were following him without a problem. They passed a few more shot-up buildings and houses before reaching the next turnoff toward his home. He was a little worried about what he saw because there were no dead on the ground. It wasn't self-defense and collateral damage; it was simply destruction, apparently for the fun of it. One house in his neighborhood had already been burned down.

He hoped that nothing else would happen. The fires and things they had seen were spread out over a few suburbs, so he hoped the odds were in their favor. He sure as hell wasn't about to give up the safety of his home because of a bunch of assholes.

About half a block before his last turn, a handful of zombies blocked the two-lane road. Max slowed to a stop to kill the dead and clear the road. Eager to make herself useful, Maggie was out of the truck before Max had put it in park. Seeing her in the road ahead, Frank and Junior rushed out of their truck, thinking something big was going on. Before everyone else could join them, Max held up a hand, letting them know to stay put. Four on six was an easy matchup, especially with the zombies staggered across the two-lane street.

"Geez, I thought we had a problem up here," Junior said as he eyed the dead. "Maggie went flying out of the truck so fast I wasn't sure what we were going to find."

"Just making myself useful," Maggie called back as she took out the nearest zombie.

Frank quickly halved the skulls of two of the dead with his ax. Max and Junior took down the remaining three.

"No more of that," Max said pointedly to Maggie. "You've already proven yourself. We do everything in pairs and don't take any unnecessary risks." He returned her unexpected glare. "You jumping out ahead of everyone like it's some kind of damn race is a good way to make a mistake and get yourself killed."

Frank and Junior stayed silent as they watched the brief exchange. "Sorry," Maggie relented. "I was just freaked out about the zombie trap we saw back there. I wasn't thinking."

Together they grabbed three of the bodies and moved them to the side of the road to clear the right lane.

"Zombie trap?" Frank asked. Max nodded. "I'll fill you in when we get back to the house. Everyone's tired," Max said. "We need to get home and get settled in."

They got back in their trucks and made the last turn toward home. Their street was clear of zombies, so Max hopped out to open the gate, and everyone pulled down the driveway. He locked the gate behind them then parked alongside the others.

Everyone headed into the house, leaving most of the supplies out in the trucks. Once they had a chance to eat, catch up and do whatever else needed doing, they'd start organizing the supplies they'd gathered.

Damon and Joey greeted them at the door. They both breathed a sigh of relief when they saw that everyone had made it home safely.

"How have things been here?" Max asked the boys.

"Quiet," Damon said. "It was so quiet that we raided four garages across the street for gas cans. We didn't go inside the houses this time because we wanted to make sure we could keep an eye on things here while we were doing it."

"We've got six more full cans," Joey said with a grin. "We brought back two empties just in case you wanted them."

"I'm proud of you boys. Thanks for handling things here while we were gone," Max said. "We got most of the supplies we were looking for. Solar panels will have to wait for another day."

"Everybody grab something to eat," Michelle called from the kitchen. "The power is out, but the food in the fridge is still cool. There are plenty of leftovers from yesterday so let's enjoy them while we still can."

Once everyone had a plate of food, Max started telling them about the fenced-in zombies off Dover. "It was pretty fucking creepy, to be honest," he said. "I can't figure out why someone would gather them up like that."

"Sounds like they're not all that secure either," Frank said. "We were wondering why you had stopped. Without binoculars, we had no idea what you were looking at."

"I say we stay away from Dover," Anna spoke up. "There's plenty of other places we can get supplies. Hell, just think about the number of houses around here, not even counting all of the stores."

"Sounds good to me," Emily said. Like everyone else, she felt a bit weirded out about the whole thing.

"We've gotta figure out a plan for right now. We've gathered supplies that we need here, and we've gotten a lot of stuff that we'll need if we have to leave here at some point," Max said. "We should unload all three trucks then redistribute everything between all of the vehicles and the house."

"Should we assume that if we leave here, we're going to do it in a hurry?" Frank asked. "Or should we only pack up the supplies we'll need on the road and leave those in the trucks?"

Max thought about it for a moment. There were no easy answers when they were trying to prepare for anything and everything. "All of the camping type gear, emergency blankets, things like that, we should split between the Wright's cars, the SUV, and my new truck," Max said. "Then put about half of everything else out there and the other half in the house. We'll keep the three pickups mostly empty so that we can use them for supply runs."

"If something happens to one of the trucks on a supply run, we'll always have at least four vehicles here stocked and ready to go," Junior said. "Sounds like a good plan to me."

"Four cars seem like a lot for just eleven people," Michelle said. "A lot of gas, too."

"Yeah, but we can carry more supplies that way," Anna said. "If we are forced to leave at some point, I want to have as much stuff with us as we possibly can. I don't want to be on the road wishing that we'd brought more and having to make any risky stops."

"Hell, I'd really like to stop at that industrial place off of 83 and get plows for the rest of the trucks and the SUV. Something that can help protect the front of our vehicles," Max said.

"Junior and I know how to install them. We did a few of them with some of our buddies last winter," Frank said. "It'll make some noise, but as long as you can keep the zombies off of us, we can get the job done."

"Okay, so what's our priority?" Maggie asked. "We're talking about a lot of plans here, and we need to make a run for water, too."

"Well, before we can do anything else, we've gotta unload the trucks," Max started. "As long as we're unloading, we might as well organize as we go. We can send the boys over to the Wright's with any supplies we want to put in their car and truck."

"Hell, it's barely noon," Frank said. "When everything is done, we can head out for water. We've still got nine hours of daylight."

"Camille, Lucia, you're on cleanup duty. Damon and Joey, do a perimeter check," Anna said. "By the time you're done, we'll have plenty of stuff ready for you to move."

"Let's get to it," Max said.

Chapter Thirty-Two

Day 6

Forty-five minutes later, they had everything unloaded and semi-organized on the ground near the trucks. They had enough propane to cook for months and enough gas to drive the cars and run the generators minimally for a few days. Gas was going to be a priority after they stocked up on water. They planned to get the generators set up in the morning since they were going to make a Costco run and because they didn't want to do that heavy lifting in the heat of the afternoon.

"The boys can sort through everything like we talked about," Max said as the last of the supplies were unloaded. "We've gotta head out soon if we want to make the water run today. I don't want to be out there in the dark if we can help it."

"I've got the new radios set up on channel ten with extra batteries for each one," Frank said. "We leave a radio with the boys, and we take one for each truck."

"Sounds good to me," Junior said. He wanted them to be able to communicate with each other from the trucks. After seeing the assholes shooting up that house and setting it on fire, he wanted to make sure they could talk if they needed to without having to pull over.

"I don't want the girls on this run," Michelle said suddenly. "We're hitting a big fucking box store. Who knows how many zombies will be in there? It's too much."

"I agree. All of the kids stay at the house," Anna said. They all bristled at being called kids. "Knock it off. You know what I mean."

JAIME HERNANDEZ

"We could use more numbers at the store. There's safety in numbers," Frank started. When Michelle's deathly glare fixed upon him, he stopped. She was a little scary, and he didn't want to get into it with her when it came to the kids.

Max looked at Anna. "How about we leave the girls and bring the boys?" he asked. "We could use the muscle."

"Really? What happened to leaving the boys at the house to keep any eye on things?" Anna asked with a hint of anger in her voice. "The girls aren't up for that if something happens." She couldn't help but be fiercely protective of her kids. "They've done enough for today. It'll take them hours to organize the stuff from the tractor place."

"The kids are staying here, end of conversation," Michelle said in her don't fuck with me tone of voice.

Max relented because he knew he wouldn't win the argument. He couldn't blame Anna and Michelle for being protective over the kids. Hell, he was protective over them, but life was different now. As time went on, he figured both moms would adjust to their new normal. Michelle was already trying to learn how to live without Jesse. He couldn't blame her for wanting to make sure her kids stayed safe.

"Alright, sounds like a plan," Max said. Joey and Damon had expected to sit out this trip. They were going to organize the supplies and keep an eye on things. Camille and Lucia didn't mind sitting home. They would have gone, but the morning trip had been a lot for them. They would make themselves useful while all of the adults were gone.

267

Everyone grabbed their restocked backpacks with water, weapons, and ammo. Frank handed out radios to Max and Maggie, Anna, Michelle, and Emily, two for the kids to err on the side of caution and one for himself and Junior. Michelle and Anna fussed over the kids for a moment then everyone loaded up into the trucks. Damon ran ahead to check the street to make sure it was clear of zombies, then opened the gate so everyone could pull out. He locked the gate behind them.

As usual, Max led the way. He felt responsible for everyone in the group and thought it was up to him to lead them and keep them safe. He would have liked to have Anna ride with him, but everyone had gotten used to working in their regular pairs. He was happy to see that she had bonded with Emily because Anna was slow to trust and rarely let a new person into her circle. Michelle was her best friend and was like a sister, but she had to let herself check out at times with her grief over Jesse, and Max didn't blame her. His heart was heavy with the loss, but he had to push it aside and compartmentalize things so that he could function.

They slowly drove west toward the Costco, about three miles away. If it wasn't looted yet, there would be enough water to fill the three trucks, which would leave them well stocked for a while. Max ran his hand through his dark beard as he thought about what they might find once they got there. If it were overrun with zombies, they'd have no choice but to make a plan B.

"Max, are you seeing this?" Maggie asked as she pointed at a convenience store to their right. The building was shot up. Quite a few zombies were wandering about the parking lot, but there were no visible bodies on the ground.

"Shit, I hope it's that same group of idiots that we saw out there this morning," Max said. "I'd hate to think of even more of them out there being reckless."

"If it's the same group, they sure do move around a lot," Maggie said.

As they approached the next intersection, a blue minivan went speeding down the cross street. Before Max could say anything, he heard Frank's voice coming through the radio. "What do you make of that?" Frank asked.

"Hopefully, it's more good people out here surviving and getting supplies. We might have been too far away for the driver to notice us," Max replied.

"A minivan driving around on its own makes me think the same thing," Frank said. "Doesn't fit the pattern of those idiots."

Max agreed and set the radio down. Up ahead, there was a large, long since deserted car accident involving at least half a dozen cars. There were no curbs on the side of the road, so he was able to carefully steer to the right while staying on the shoulder and watched his rearview to make sure the others did the same. They didn't see many zombies shuffling around until they came upon a church to their left. The old brick building with a bell tower occupied one large corner of the intersection. The heavy ornate doors to the church hung open with zombies inside that were visible from the street. The church lawn was full of several dozen of the dead stumbling around. Max sighed, thinking of how many people had probably rushed to churches back on day one. He guessed that most of them were probably full of zombies.

As they drove through the intersection, he almost missed the store on the opposite corner. It looked to have been fortified. The doors and windows were covered with sheets of plywood, and the place looked deserted. A week ago, it had been a thriving store, so someone had to be holed up in there. No one was surrounded or asking for help, so he wasn't going to stop and approach. That could be an excellent way to get himself shot, even by good people. It gave him hope to see evidence of others surviving. On this short trip, seeing first the minivan and now the store felt like a good sign.

His radio chirped again, only this time it was Anna. "Did you see that store?" she asked.

"Yeah, and I'm hoping there's a family in there safely getting by," Max said. "I don't want to stop and draw in zombies or maybe find that we're not welcome."

"Me either. I was just happy to see it," Anna said and put her radio down. She knew there had to be pockets of people spread out in the suburbs. They weren't the only ones to survive. She felt good seeing that someone was presumably safe inside that store.

Max was surprised that they hadn't been forced to take any detours yet. They weren't on the biggest main street, but the road used to see a good amount of traffic. It was nice to drive for a change without having to zigzag all over the place to avoid zombies. They were only about a mile away and were making good time. It wasn't long before they could see the big sign in the distance. Maggie grabbed the binoculars to see what the parking lot looked like then gave Max the details. "There aren't that many cars, and I can only see about a dozen or so zombies. It might not be too bad," Maggie said as her optimism grew. Max smiled in response. Somehow or another, the day was turning out to be a good one. They needed it to keep everyone's spirits up.

Max slowed as they neared the parking lot to make sure there weren't any unseen surprises. There were three zombies on the side of the store and two in the street, leaving them with about twenty to kill before they tried to go inside. Max picked up the radio and called out to Frank. "Can you take care of the two in the street? Then meet us by the front door, and we'll take out the rest of them together," Max said. "On it," Frank replied.

Frank, being a beast of a man, was able to kill both before the others had pulled up to the store, and he parked alongside them just as they all stopped by the front door. "Let's spread out in pairs and get this done. Shouldn't be too hard," he said. He and Junior went straight for a group of four that were clustered together. Max and Maggie killed the three on the side of the building. Anna, Emily, and Michelle went further out into the parking lot to start taking out stragglers. As a group, they finished the last few that had hovered near the front door of the building.

"Does everyone have their radios?" Max asked and got nods and murmurs in response. "Okay, until we know what we're dealing with inside, let's stay together. If it's completely overrun, then we head back out and find a plan B." They all knew from previous experience that the huge entrance inside the store and the entire front end with the cash registers were wide open. They hoped to get a good feel for what was inside as soon as they went in. The automatic sliding doors were stuck in the open position. This made it much easier for them to get inside and boded well for what they might find. If the store had been full of the dead at one point, a lot of them might have made their way out the open doors.

As they walked in, they were relieved to find that the large skylights all over the store allowed the sun to shine brightly inside. They had flashlights but probably wouldn't be working in darkness. A lone zombie with horrific bite wounds slowly shuffled toward the group. The store vest he wore indicated he had been working when everything went to hell. His bottom jaw was exposed entirely from all of the skin and tissue being ripped clean from the bottom of his face. A large chunk was missing from the side of his neck, and bite marks covered his shoulder and hands. His teeth gnashed as he lurched forward in anticipation of a fresh meal. Frank casually stepped up and shattered its skull with his ax. They all stood quietly for a couple of minutes to see if any others would make their way toward them, but none of the dead appeared.

"Alright, this place is huge. I say we start down this first aisle along the wall and make our way to the opposite end," Max said. "We'll be able to see down all of the aisles in this half of the store." Everyone nodded in agreement as Max led the way.

They could hear the sounds of raspy moans and shuffling footsteps, but they hadn't seen any of the dead yet. When they got to the third aisle, they saw two zombies down at the far end, slowly making their way toward them. With Junior at his side, Max motioned for everyone else to stay where they were. The two of them quickly took out both zombies then rejoined everyone else. With moans still echoing around the store and unable to pinpoint their locations in the large space, they continued with their plan. They passed three more aisles before the noise got louder. Confident that there were dead down the next aisle, Max paused at the end and took a quick peek. Six zombies were stumbling forward, only

272

about ten feet away. "I've got six up close," Max said quietly to the others.

Frank, Junior, and Maggie stepped forward first, so the four of them focused on the six zombies while Anna, Michelle, and Emily kept watch. They didn't want to get too bunched up in the aisle. Maggie reached for an emaciated middle-aged woman that had several bites of flesh missing from her arm. As she grabbed the woman, it stumbled forward and clutched Maggie's shoulders with both hands, and its teeth came dangerously close to grazing her face. Maggie managed to plunge her knife deep into its eye, and it dropped to the floor. Max was face to face with an enormous man, even bigger than Frank. "Shit," he swore. He should have let Frank have this one. He kicked one of its knees which caused it to lose its balance. As soon as it was down, Max thrust his knife through its ear. Junior twisted and turned, taking down two of them before Max had even gotten a good look at them. Frank caved in the skulls of the last two on the left with relative ease.

They went back to the end of the aisle then continued their search. They made it past the water aisle and to the tire section before things took a turn. There were at least two dozen zombies in the tire and automotive area. Max hadn't accounted for the tire shop attached to the corner of the store and the wide-open garage doors. "Everyone spread out," Max instructed the others. "Michelle, keep watch in the middle, so nothing sneaks up on us from behind." The long aisle that ran down the middle of the store, effectively splitting the place in two, had been free of the dead from what they'd seen so far, but they hadn't cleared the other half of the store yet. Michelle stood with her back to the others, trusting that they would protect her as she made sure no surprises came from the other side.

Junior dashed through the crowd as he thrust his knife. He was fast and wiry, so he killed the zombies in his path as he made his way to the big doors leading to the tire shop. When he reached the automatic door, it took every ounce of strength he had in him to force it closed. With the power out, the door was stuck in the open position, and he needed to make sure that no more of the dead came in through the door.

"Junior, watch your back!" Emily yelled suddenly. Junior turned just in time to fight off a zombie that had been less than a foot away. He plunged his knife through its ear as adrenaline coursed through his veins. He had been seconds away from being bitten, and without Emily's warning, he would have been a dead man. He tried to shake it off and got back to killing the other zombies.

Anna cringed as a dead hand grazed her hair and shoulder, thankful that she had chopped her hair off or else she would have found herself entangled in its hand. She angrily thrust her knife through the dead man's eye and turned to face the next one.

Frank's ax got stuck in a zombie skull. He pulled on it a couple of times, but it wouldn't budge. He quickly grabbed the knife from his belt and took out the closest two zombies. Then he turned back to his ax and let it fall to the floor with the dead body. He leaned down, and with one foot on the zombie's chest, he used both hands to rip his ax free from its head. He refocused his attention on a zombie walking toward him.

Emily grabbed a young child by its hair and forced her knife through its ear, then turned to its sibling and did the same. Her area was briefly clear, so she looked to see who might need help.

Maggie stayed pretty close to Michelle to be sure none of the dead could sneak up on her from behind. She killed several zombies as one after another shuffled toward her. She looked around and saw that they were finished. Everyone looked a bit winded, but all of the zombies were dead on the floor.

"I've got half a dozen coming this way," Michelle said with her back to the others. Maggie and Max were closest, so they helped her take them out.

"Holy shit," Max said as he wiped the sweat from his forehead. "I had forgotten all about the tire place."

"We all did," Frank said. They all looked around to make sure everyone was okay and ready to go because they still had to clear the other half of the store. Everyone took a moment to gulp down some water and get prepared for whatever was coming next.

Chapter Thirty-Three

Day 6

"Michelle, do you mind staying in the middle again?" Max asked. "Just in case any of them moved around and got into the side we already cleared."

"I'm on it," Michelle replied.

The store was enormous, and clearing it out was taking a lot more time than they had expected. Because of its size, the areas they had previously cleared could end up with another stray zombie or two. They moved to clear the other half of the store but did it from the long, wide middle aisle. The first few aisles were empty, but then they started finding small pockets of the dead just as they had on the other side of the store. If the dead weren't slow as hell, they probably would have all made it to the group by then since they had made a lot of noise killing the zombies around the tire area. It was a painstakingly slow process, but they finally cleared that side of the store and met back up with Michelle.

"What about the restrooms, breakrooms, things like that?" Frank asked. He wasn't sure if they should clear every inch of the place or not, since the water was on the far end that was fully cleared.

"Fuck, better safe than sorry," Max said. "What about the storage room and loading docks?"

"I think we should make sure those doors are sealed off," Anna said. "No need to go back there and clear them. If the loading dock doors are open, we could attract a hell of a lot of attention from any dead that might be out back behind the store."

"Agreed," Emily said. "Let's get this done." She was running on pure adrenaline and didn't want exhaustion to take over before they finished.

"Hell, there's a bakery section, customer service, lots of places for a stray zombie or two," Junior said. "Let's stick together, make sure every last area gets cleared, then do what we came here to do."

They were nearest to the bakery, so they went there first and found a zombie caught up in some boxes in the back. Junior killed it then they moved on to the storeroom that ran the width of the rear of the store. Max leaned in toward the door to see if he could hear anything on the other side. "There's something back there, but I can't tell how many," he said. Max looked around at the closest shelves hoping to find something heavy to block the door. "That big ladder ought to do it," he pointed to the ladder that reached the top of the highest shelves. "Let's push it in front of the doors and lock the wheels. The dead won't be able to push it away, and if they try, we'll hear them."

Frank and Junior pushed the ladder in place and turned the wheel locks. It was heavy and wasn't going anywhere. To their left was a doorway leading to the public restrooms and the employee breakroom. Maggie put her ear to the door but couldn't hear anything. "I can't tell if it's empty or not. If any zombies are back there, they must not be anywhere near the door," she said. They lined up to clear the area. Maggie opened the door while Frank, Max, and Junior walked through.

"I hear something in the bathroom," Frank said. He looked and saw that the door had to be pushed to be opened. "Never mind, they'd have to pull the door open from the inside, and we all know they aren't capable of that." A quick look at the breakroom showed the same. There was no need to clear out the rooms if the zombies were trapped inside of them. They left the hallway and went back inside the store. Together they headed for the customer service area to make sure there were no surprises waiting for them. Two zombies were moaning and reaching their arms out over the chest-high counter, but they couldn't seem to find the door. Frank made quick work of both of them with his ax.

They walked past the registers and found a crawler moving at a snail's pace. Emily was closest, so she bent down and thrust her knife through its ear. As they neared the front door to grab pallet carts to carry water, they realized that the front door was still stuck open. It was possible that a few zombies might have entered the store while they were clearing it out. "Damn it," Max said. "We should have had someone keep watch at the door." He looked out to the parking lot and saw only a handful of zombies in the distance, and they didn't appear to be interested in the store.

"Okay, Maggie and Michelle, you two keep watch up here while we get the water," Max started. "That way, nothing gets in here without us knowing about it. Keep an eye on your backs in case any of them already came in. If a lot of them start coming toward the door, call one of us on the radio." Of the seven of them, he wanted the five with the most muscle to get the heavy cases of water. Maggie and Michelle were both tough and very capable when it came to killing zombies but probably had the least physical strength of anyone in the group. "Everyone else, grab a cart. We'll pile them high then unload them into the trucks."

278

With that, everyone else grabbed a pallet cart and made their way toward the water aisle near the rear of the store. Halfway there, Max stopped, and the others stopped behind him. There was a lone zombie in the aisle to his left. To be that far into the store already, it must have gotten in shortly after they started clearing the first half of the place. The zombie was a mess. It was a young blonde woman nearly naked from the waist down with strings of flesh hanging in the little spot where the shoulder meets the neck. Another chunk had been torn from the thin flesh around her collarbone, exposing bright white bones. Dried blood ringed her mouth and stained her chin. Her long hair was matted with bits of grass and dirt as if she'd taken a tumble on somebody's lawn. Max grabbed her by the hair and stabbed his knife through her ear. He looked back to everyone else and said, "Let's go."

The rest of the way to the water aisle was still clear from earlier. Once there, Max decided not to take any unnecessary risks. "We need someone watching our backs here. It's going to be noisy grabbing the water," Max said. He turned to Anna. "Want to be our lookout? Then we can just focus on loading up and not worry about watching our backs."

"Sure," Anna said. She didn't mind keeping watch, and someone had to do it. She stood a few feet away from the others so she could easily watch both ends of the long aisle.

They could hear a faint thumping sound from another part of the store. Max motioned for everyone to stop again so they could listen for it. The thumping sound was joined by more thumping. "Shit, I think it's coming from the storeroom. They heard us moving around or at least heard you guys push the ladder in front of the door," Anna said.

279

"Are you sure that ladder is going to hold?" Emily asked nervously as the noises multiplied and grew louder. "It sounds like a lot of zombies back there."

"Fuck. Anna, watch our backs on this end," Max said. "Emily, watch from the middle aisle. If they manage to break through the door, you'll see them. We'll still have plenty of time to get out of here if there's too many to kill."

There was more water than they could hope to fit inside the three trucks. Max, Frank, and Junior began loading case after case onto the large carts. They grabbed a bunch of gallon-sized containers knowing that they would be easier to use for things like cleaning up. They stacked enough drinking water to last quite a while. Anna kept watching her end of the aisle while the men finished with the water.

"They're through the door," Emily called out from her place in the center aisle. "The ladder didn't hold."

"How many are there?" Frank asked as he brought up his ax.

"I can't tell for sure, but I think there's less than it sounded like," Emily answered.

"We should see if we can take them out," Junior suggested. "That way, we know it's safe to come back here, and it'll be easier to clear the store next time."

"Alright, let's do this," Max said. "But if there's too many of them, we'll just grab the water and go."

As the five of them headed toward the storeroom doors, Anna quickly called Michelle on the radio to let her and Maggie know what was going on. As they got closer to the doors, they saw half a dozen zombies slowly shuffling out. All of them were dead on the ground in less than a minute. In front of the doors was a large open area before the start of any of the aisles. They all looked around but didn't find any zombies other than the ones they had already killed. The zombies thumping on the door had echoed loudly through the store, making it sound like there were a lot more than there was.

Max bent down to look at the ladder. He was deeply troubled that the dead had managed to push the doors open when the ladder had been blocking them. Looking at the wheels, he noticed that the wheel locks were broken. They hadn't realized it earlier because they appeared to have locked, but the wheels had still moved freely. The zombies had just enough momentum, pushing up against the doors, to slide the ladder about a foot to the side. That was all the space they'd needed to get through. "The wheel locks are broken," Max told the others.

"We might as well at least take a look in the storeroom," Frank said. "If there were more, they probably would have come out with the others."

"Yeah, it'd be good to know for next time," Junior said. "If it's bad, we'll lock up the doors with a chain and leave them."

"Anna, Emily, keep on the lookout while we head back," Max said. "Make sure no surprises sneak up on us from this end."

Max, Frank, and Junior started into the huge room at the back of the store. There were ample skylights, giving them good visibility, and by the darkness at the rear of the room, they could tell that all of the loading dock doors were closed. No stray zombies would be making their way inside that way. As they made their way further into the enormous room and past pallets stacked high with all sorts of bulk goods, they heard the telltale sound of zombies shuffling around. They slowly and carefully covered the room in a grid pattern while staying together. They found the first zombie in a store uniform tangled up in plastic from a partially unwrapped pallet. Its eyes locked on the three of them as it struggled to break free to indulge in a meal. Frank quickly took it down with his ax. The second zombie was just around the next corner, his raspy moan and shuffling feet giving them advance warning and making it another easy kill. The storeroom was very organized, and it didn't take long for them to make their way through it. They'd only found six zombies in the whole place.

"People must have cleared out of here fast when it all started," Junior said. "I was expecting a hell of a lot more than that."

"Me too," Frank said. "I'm glad we've got it cleared. It's going to be pretty safe next time we come here for supplies."

"If we can seal off the front of the store, we'll be in great shape," Max said. "Let's double-check everything on our way back to make sure we didn't miss any." They headed back through the storeroom, making sure they looked everywhere. The place was so clean and neatly laid out that there weren't many places a zombie could hide. Confident that the large storeroom was completely clear, they went back to the double doors where Anna and Emily were keeping watch. "We're all good. There were only half a dozen left back there," Max told them.

"Well, let's get back to the water," Frank said. "I'm not even sure we can fit this much into the trucks. I think we ought to take all of this out there, then see if there's any room for more. And we know we can make another run back here to get more later on." They all moved back to the water aisle, where their carts were sitting piled high, ready to go.

Just then, the radio clicked, and they heard Michelle's voice. "We've got about a dozen or so getting close to the trucks and another half a dozen a little further back," she said.

"On our way," Max replied. They pushed the cumbersome carts toward the front of the store while Anna continued to watch their backs. They saw the dead getting closer to the entrance, but none had made it near the door yet.

"Let's take care of these now before they get any closer," Frank said. Anna kept an eye on the store behind them while everyone else approached the dead. They naturally fanned out to help keep the zombies spread out. Michelle was tiny, but she was lethal. She took one down before anyone else even had a chance to try. To her right, Maggie killed a thin teenager, and he dropped to the ground. Frank started heavily swinging his ax and took out three in quick succession. Junior jumped into the middle of the group of zombies, thrusting his knife until the three closest to him were down. Emily and Max had each taken out two while Michelle finished off the last one. The half dozen or so that had been further away in the parking lot were slowly shuffling toward them and had just started to enter their kill zone. They all went to work, and within thirty seconds, the zombies were on the ground dead. Max was about to speak when suddenly Maggie let out a blood-curdling scream.

Chapter Thirty-Four

Day 6

Max's blood ran cold when he heard Maggie's scream. Everyone turned toward her as quickly as they could. Two dead hands locked around her calf from behind, and a zombie's teeth were starting to clamp down on her leg, almost as if in slow motion. As the teeth came close, all she could think to do was to throw herself forward to buy herself a few precious seconds. She landed hard on her hands and knees then tried to kick the zombie in the head with her free leg. It was a damn crawler that had come out of nowhere and grabbed her from behind. Michelle was the closest to her. She grabbed the zombie by the back of its hair, pulled it backward, and thrust her knife through its ear. With it dead and no longer a danger, she tried to pry its hands loose from Maggie's leg but couldn't get them to budge. Frank towered over her even when bent over and used his great strength to pull the fingers free.

Everyone was scared. Max, Frank, and Junior's minds flashed back to when Jesse was bitten, and Max had desperately searched his arm to see if the teeth had broken the skin. Anna gasped and covered her mouth with her hand. Emily shook her head in denial then turned to focus on the parking lot. Someone had to keep watch while they checked on Maggie. Michelle sat close to Maggie on the ground in an attempt to calm her as Max came over to examine her leg. He grimaced when he saw that two teeth were caught in her jeans.

"Deep breaths, Maggie," Michelle said as she wrapped her arm around her shoulder.

Max knocked the teeth off then gently pushed her pant leg up, holding his breath as he prepared himself for what he was going to find there. There was a half-circle red mark but no blood. He examined it more closely and noticed there were no teeth marks, no imprints of any kind. He ran his fingers over the smooth, unbroken skin and breathed a sigh of relief. When Maggie threw herself forward, she had saved her own life. The zombie had missed its chance to bite down on her with only a second or two to spare.

"You're okay, Maggie," Max said with a smile. "There's no bite. Your skin is just a little red; I'm not even sure it's going to bruise." Maggie collapsed entirely into Michelle's arms as her tears of relief flowed. She'd thought she was done. Everyone knew that even the tiniest break of the skin was a death sentence. She couldn't believe that she was okay. Her hands were scraped, and her knees took a hard hit, but she was okay. She pulled herself together as Michelle and Max helped her to her feet. She hugged Michelle again and tried to express how grateful she was. "Thank you," was all that she managed to say. Michelle gave her another squeeze then let her go.

The range of emotions from fear, not knowing, and then finding out Maggie was okay caused everyone to take pause for a moment. Relief flooded through every last one of them. Max grabbed some water, and everyone took a break for a few minutes. They kept a close watch on both the parking lot and the store's entrance, but they all relaxed for a moment. They had come so close to losing one of their own, but the quick actions and reactions of everyone working together had started to become second

285

nature and helped to ensure their survival. Max lit a cigarette and offered the pack to Junior and Frank. There were no more zombies in the parking lot or on the street, and as far as they knew, there weren't any in the store. It felt good to take a few minutes after the scare.

Max eyed the parking lot more closely and noticed an oversized black truck at the far end of the lot that he didn't remember seeing earlier. He hadn't exactly counted cars or anything when they got there, so he dismissed it when he saw no movement around it. The street remained free of zombies, and the parking lot was quiet. Across the street, there was a free-standing restaurant in front of a pond with several empty parcels of land around it. A slight movement caught his eye when he just happened to look in that direction. A half dozen or so zombies were slowly shuffling out from behind the restaurant. It would take them a while to get to the street and even longer to get to the store, so they probably wouldn't be an issue. He mentioned them to the others to err on the side of caution.

"There's at least half a dozen coming from behind the restaurant across the street," Max said. "We'll probably be out of here before they become a problem, but I wanted to make sure everyone saw them." There was no such thing as being too careful.

"Let's start getting this water loaded up," Junior said. "We can relax when we get back home." It was getting late, and they wanted to get back to the house before the sun went down.

They started bringing all of the carts of water out to the trucks. Emily and Anna watched everyone's backs inside the store while Michelle and Maggie kept an eye on the parking lot. Loading the water would make some noise, and they were bound to draw in a few of the dead. It took a while, but Max, Frank, and Junior managed to fit most of the water in the beds of the three pickups. They filled the rear seats of two of the trucks with the rest. It was a tight fit, but they got it all in. There were two cases left, and those could be stuck in the backseat with Michelle in the third truck.

They hadn't even begun to go through the store for other supplies. With water being such a huge priority, they planned to make more runs in the future for other supplies they needed.

Exhausted from all of the heavy lifting, they all stood around for a minute to catch their breath. "You know," Frank started, "we need to find a way to close the front door. So the next time we come back, we'll know the store is still clear."

"Either that or block it off. The zombies always go for the path of least resistance," Junior said. "If there's no one inside to attract them, they're not going to try to get through any kind of barricade."

"What if we make a big line of carts?" Anna asked. "They're heavy when you have a bunch of them. We push those in place, and the dead aren't going to get inside."

"That's a great idea," Max said. There were two cart corrals nearby that he pointed out. "We take those two rows, put them together, and push them in front of the doors."

The long rows of carts were heavy and difficult to steer, so they broke them down into a few smaller groups. Max, Frank, and Junior each pushed a bunch in front of the doors and made one long row of them when they were done.

"Probably more than we needed," Junior said. "But it'll definitely keep the dead out."

The group of zombies from the restaurant had grown to about two dozen, and they were halfway through the parking lot heading toward the trucks. "We're ready to go," Max said. "Let's just leave them. No need to take unnecessary risks."

They got in their trucks and turned out of the parking lot before the zombies could pose a threat. A handful came up from the rear side of the store, but they were too slow and still too far away to be an issue. Max turned onto the main road with the others following him. The trucks were weighted down with all the water they had loaded, so Max was careful about hitting holes or driving off shoulders. They made it a mile before they had to take a slight detour. About two dozen zombies were shambling in the road, and it wasn't worth the risk to stop and take them all out. Max cautiously turned down a side street that he knew would bring them back out on the other side of the dead. The little street had quite a few shot-up cars. There were so many bullet holes that it was impossible not to notice the destruction. He looked to his right at the nearby houses and found that two of them had been shot up as well. Shaking his head in frustration, Max picked up the radio. "You guys seeing these cars and houses?" he asked.

"Yeah, those cars would have been hard to miss. It just doesn't make any sense," Junior replied.

Anna's voice came over the radio. "This shit is starting to freak me out. Do you still think they're just destroying property, or do you think they're killing people?" she asked.

"I'm not sure, but I don't like what I'm seeing," Max answered. "Let's just get home."

Max continued around the block until they were back on the main street, and the zombies they'd detoured to avoid were well behind them. He concentrated on the road in front of him because there were quite a few static cars and little pockets of zombies to weave around. By the time they got around them, they were only about a mile from home. Max was on high alert as they got closer to the house, making sure there weren't any zombies on his street. "Keep an eye out, Maggie, so I don't miss anything," Max said.

"It's empty," Maggie responded. "Maybe they all followed us out when we left earlier. Could be the zombies we passed coming home are all from the neighborhood."

"Well, other than the neighbor yard and that big group last night, we haven't had too much activity since the horde came through here," Max said. Reminders from the horde were all over the street. Dried blood stained nearly black, tattered remnants of clothing, occasional odd shoes, intestines and bodily organs that were drying out in the summer sun, and even random limbs still lay in and around the road.

Max picked up the radio and called Damon at the house. "We're almost home. If there aren't any zombies around the house, we should be there in about two minutes. Is everything good there?"

"All clear, Dad," Damon said. "No problems. I'll go open the gate for you."

Max slowed as he neared their house when he saw three zombies on a sidewalk. A closer look into the front yard revealed several more. It was the same house they'd cleared together the day before that had the backyard full of zombies. He wondered if something was drawing them there.

He called the others over the radio. "Quick stop. Three zombies on the sidewalk and maybe half a dozen in the front yard," he said. Frank and Anna responded, and they all pulled over. Everyone got out because they weren't sure if there were more coming. They needed numbers if they ran into more of the dead. Frank and Junior quickly destroyed the three zombies on the sidewalk. They all entered the front yard together but spread out so they could safely kill the zombies there. Anna, Emily, and Michelle went to the left, Frank and Junior stayed in the middle, and Max and Maggie went to the right. It wasn't too hard taking out the first six zombies, but then they saw another dozen a bit further back. *Where the hell are they all coming from?* Max wondered. He focused on the few closest to him and started killing. A few of them were too close together, and as Max stabbed one through the eye, another grabbed his arm. He swung around fast and plunged his knife through its ear before its face got anywhere near his arm. Maggie took out the third one that was nearest to her. Their area was clear, so they looked toward the others to make sure everyone was okay. They were all finishing off zombies of their own, and then it was quiet again.

"I'm going to check the gate. I can't figure out why they're attracted to this yard," Max said quietly to the others. He approached the gate and found it was still secure from how they had left it. He walked back over to the others. "Maybe we should check inside the house. What do you guys think?" Max asked.

"The door is closed, and the window isn't broken. I'd say it's a fluke," Frank offered.

"Yeah, they weren't in the backyard this time, and the gate was secure," Junior said. "Maybe the boys were out here while we were gone and made a little noise. If the zombies didn't see them, they would just linger around the last area that had their attention."

Max thought about it for a moment. Everything Frank and Junior said made sense. It had to be a fluke that the zombies were there because there was no other way to explain it. "Alright, let's get back in the trucks. I want to make another quick pass to make sure none showed up on the street while we were busy."

They slowly reversed down the street about a dozen houses and didn't see any of the dead. They drove back toward Max's house and beyond to make sure things looked clear that way. Everything looked good, so when they reached the house again, Max pulled into the driveway with the others close behind him. Damon was there waiting and opened the gate to let them through, then closed and locked it behind them.

Chapter Thirty-Five

Day 6

Everyone got out of the trucks feeling tired, hungry, and ready to get inside. It was nearly dark outside, and it had been a very long day. Walking into the house, they smelled freshly cooked food that took all of them by surprise. Camille and Lucia stood grinning in the kitchen with counters heaped full of steaks, burgers, baked potatoes, and grilled vegetables. With the power out, everyone was momentarily surprised. Anna and Max hugged their kids and said hello while Michelle did the same with hers.

"How did you guys pull this off?" Anna asked. She looked around at the many lit candles that allowed them to see well enough and noticed the patio door. One of the boards was taken down, but two of the iron bars still covered the doorway, and the sliding glass door was in place.

"We grilled out back by the pool," Joey said with a big smile. "The door is still secure with the bars over it and the boards on the other side."

"We can put the board back up if you want," Damon said. "We had all this food thawing in the freezer since the power went out, and we figured we could cook it on the grill instead of letting it go to waste."

They could all see that the kids were very proud of themselves, and everyone was hungry after the work they'd been doing all day. "Looks good," Max said as he grabbed a plate. Everyone else followed his lead and piled their plates with some of everything. They got comfortable and ate, savoring every bite until they were full. No one knew when they would have a real meal again. There weren't any more steaks or burgers anywhere in their near future. They had plenty of canned and dried goods, but perishables wouldn't last another day.

With dirty dishes from eleven people piled in the sink, Camille and Lucia started cleaning up. They knew the water wasn't going to last much longer, so everyone took turns taking cold showers. No one minded the cold too much because the house was uncomfortably warm without AC and no open windows to create a breeze.

Max stepped into the living room to talk to Frank and Junior. "We're going to have to figure out something to make the temperature in here tolerable. It's going to be an oven in here all summer," Max said.

"The generator can't run the AC. It's just too much," Junior responded. "I'll think on it and see if I can't come up with something."

"Knowing Damon and Joey, I wouldn't be surprised if they figure out a solution," Frank said with a laugh. "Those boys are damn near incredible with their ingenuity."

Max grinned as he took pride in the boys. They were doing better than a lot of grown men would be in the same situation. They were creative, determined, and damn near fearless.

It was fully dark outside, so there wasn't much to do. Michelle went into the kitchen to see if there was any more food that was salvageable from the freezer. It was full of thawed vegetables, melted ice cream, and liquid popsicles. She dug around and found a large package of chicken hidden under the soupy mess. It was thawed but still cool to the touch, so it was definitely safe to eat. "Hey

Joey," She called. "Is the grill still hot?" She held out the package of chicken.

"It might be warm but not hot enough to cook that," Joey said. "Damon and I can get it fired up again."

"Hey, we need to go grab what's left in the Wright's freezer," Damon said. "There might still be some stuff in there that we can throw on the grill."

"I'll get the grill going while you boys check next door," Max said with enthusiasm. "I thought we just ate our last home-cooked meal. I'll cook up whatever you boys can find."

Damon and Joey checked the flap on the board by the window near the front door to make sure the yard looked clear, then happily headed out to get more food. They silently made their way across to the fence and climbed up and over into the Wright's yard. Once inside, they went straight to the farm-style kitchen at the rear of the house and used their flashlights to check the freezer.

"There's still a lot in here," Joey said with a grin as he pulled out packages of steak, ground beef and pork chops. Everything was thawed out. Damon went to the mudroom off the kitchen to grab a couple of bags to carry the meat in, eager to bring it back home to grill.

Back at the house, Max, Frank, and Junior cracked open semi-warm beers from the fridge in the garage as they stood around the grill out back by the pool. "Tomorrow, we're going to have to go looking for solar panels," Max said. "The generators are going to help, but they're going to burn through gas pretty fast, and I honestly don't know how much noise they're going to make. We're probably going to have to use them minimally. The solar panels should help out quite a bit."

"That's going to mean hitting another big box store," Frank said. "Are we bringing everyone or leaving the kids home again?"

"Michelle and Anna are going to want them at home," Junior replied. "They're going to give you a hell of a hard time if you want to bring them."

Max ran his fingers through his beard as he thought about it. They could really use Damon and Joey for extra muscle. Lucia and Camille could stay at the house to keep an eye on things. Then he thought of Anna and Michelle. He knew they would both be against it, but he figured it couldn't hurt to discuss it. The kids knew how to defend themselves, and they wanted to help out. If they left them at home, the boys would probably go out on their own anyway to scavenge more neighbor homes. They couldn't stand being stuck in the house while everyone else was out doing important things. "I'll run it by the momma bears. Hopefully, they'll go along with at least bringing the boys and leaving the girls at home."

"Good luck with that, mano," Junior said with a laugh. "Anna and Michelle are pretty scary when it comes to the kids." The guys shared a good laugh and enjoyed their beers while standing around the grill. It almost felt like an ordinary evening grilling out back by the pool.

Inside, Anna, Michelle, Emily, and Maggie were relaxing on the couches in the living room. They were all tired from spending the entire day on supply runs. Anna had enough candles spread around that they could see well enough. The house was stuffy, and the candles weren't helping, but it wasn't too bad. Daytime was going to be much worse.

"I don't know how we're going to handle it in here all summer," Anna said. "It's going to be hot as hell and everyone is going to be miserable."

"We'll figure it out. Hey, maybe we could use the generator to keep the pool up and running," Michelle said with a laugh. "Jump in to cool off anytime."

"That would be amazing," Emily laughed as she wiped the sweat from her forehead. "I think the guys might have other ideas."

"I'm just picturing us all lounging around the pool in the middle of the damn zombie apocalypse," Maggie laughed. "Laying on our floats and sunbathing." She laughed harder, and the others joined in.

"Ah, one can dream," Anna said as the laughter died down. "No more bikinis for us." She would miss all of the family time they had spent in the pool over the years with the kids and the cookouts with Jesse and Michelle. She felt a pain in her heart thinking of Jesse and glanced at Michelle. She worried about how her best friend was holding up because she couldn't imagine what it would have been like if Max hadn't survived. It seemed like Michelle was doing her best to keep busy, but Anna knew she was probably shedding many tears whenever she was alone. It was nice to see her laughing about the pool.

Camille and Lucia were out doing a perimeter check. Anna and Michelle had become much more comfortable allowing them to do it because they'd proven themselves to be quick thinkers and quite good at killing zombies. They would rather keep them safely inside the house at all times but knew that was unreasonable and unrealistic.

Joey and Damon came through the front door, interrupting everyone's thoughts. "Look what we found,"

Damon said excitedly as he started pulling packages of meat out of the bags.

"Wow, you did good, kiddo," Anna said.

"Let me have it so I can season it up, and then you can take it to the guys out back so they can throw it on the grill," Michelle said. Any excuse to do anything in the kitchen made her happy and distracted her mind from other thoughts.

As she was getting the meat ready, Camille and Lucia came in from their perimeter check. "Everything looks good," Lucia said.

"It smells amazing out there," Camille added. "The whole time we were walking around, all we could think about was the smell coming from the grill."

"It made me hungry again," Lucia said with a laugh. She noticed the meat Michelle was seasoning and piling onto a tray, and her eyes got big. "Oh, that looks so good! I didn't think we were going to have any more real food." Her smile shone brightly.

"We'll go ahead and take it outside," Camille said as Michelle finished up. The girls both took the trays out back so Max and the guys could cook it and then came back inside to hang out with everyone else.

Out back, Max, Frank, and Junior were having fun standing around the grill talking and having a few beers. It felt like a typical night.

"Maybe tomorrow morning we can start bringing all of the water inside," Junior started.

"Let's not worry about it right now. This is the first good night we've had since this whole thing started," Max said. "Let's just take it easy and enjoy tonight, and tomorrow we can worry about everything else." The night air smelled of great food, and the smoke rose in the dark

297

sky. For the first time since the world went to hell, they were able to enjoy the moment without fear of what tomorrow might bring.

Epilogue

"I said they're having a fucking party!" A man's voice came over the radio.

There was silence on the other end, and then a gravelly voice replied, "How many of them did you say there were again?"

"The boys counted seven of them out picking up supplies, and I saw four kids back at the house," the man continued. "There were three pickup trucks filled up."

"They did two different supply runs, and both times they filled up the trucks," A third voice said over the radio. "They probably have enough supplies to hole up in there for quite a while."

"They're grilling out back like it's a damned cookout. The fucking smell is making me hungry, damn it!" The first man was becoming agitated.

"Calm your ass down, Brad," The gravelly voice said. "Eleven of them can't handle the crew, especially if they ain't expecting us," the voice chuckled. "Let 'em eat and enjoy the moment. It won't last long. We'll be there soon."

Author's Note

Thank you for reading! If you have a moment please leave a review on Amazon. Your reviews help us indie authors more than you may realize. Each and every review helps to generate more exposure for the *Chronicles of the Undead* Series creating more opportunities for other readers to discover and read the books.

Look for Chronicles of the Undead Book 3 this winter!

About the Author

Jaime Hernandez is a lover of all things horror, animals, zoos, tattoos, reading and writing. Born and raised in Ohio, she met her Texan husband online in a FB group, married him, and moved to Dallas. She has two amazing daughters and four crazy dogs. She's a proud stay-at-home mom and author. In her past life she was the owner of a pet sitting business, but her true passion has always been writing. She's a huge fan of the zombie apocalypse genre in both books and on the big screen.

To keep up with all the latest news about upcoming books, interact with the author and other fans, have a chance to win some amazing swag and possibly have a character named after you in a future book, please join the Jaime Hernandez Fan Club and follow the Jaime Hernandez Author page on Facebook.

Books By Jaime Hernandez

Chronicles of the Undead Book 1: Urban Gridlock

Chronicles of the Undead Book 2: Suburban Jungle

The Zombie Road Fan Fiction Collection (Anthology)

Made in the USA
Monee, IL
24 June 2021

72221840R00174